BINDING FATE

THE FATES ALIGN DUOLOGY
BOOK ONE

ALYSSA ROSE

ALYSSA ROSE BOOKS

First edition April 2018

Cover Design by Artscandare Book Cover Design

Edited by: Ashley Olivier

Proofread: Roxana Coumans

ISBN 979-8-9893613-0-4 (ebook)

ISBN 979-8-9893613-1-1 (paperback)

ISBN 979-8-9893613-2-8 (hardcover)

Second edition, 2023

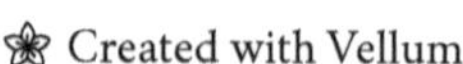 Created with Vellum

ALSO BY ALYSSA ROSE

The Fates Align Duology:

Binding Fate

Enchanted Fate (releases August 6, 2024)

Coming Soon!

The DarkFlower Jungle Saga (Serialized Novellas):

Lost and Lonely

Dark and Defiant

Found and Fated

For
Pam and Frank who always encouraged and supported me, Liz with your
endless advice, and Mary who fell in love with my characters and motivated me
to keep telling their story.

CONTENTS

THE BEGINNING

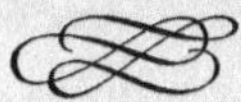

One cold dreary night, a wild wind blew as Alzerion stood peering out the arched window, squinting. He studied that storm-grey expanse, like ink spilled across the sky. Only a few pockets of light were able to escape. The clouds kept shifting—moving—roaming. They loomed above the palace beckoning the townspeople to come. He looked down at his fists, clenched. Would she be coming in this muck? He took a slow breath, steadying himself. The king did say she was invited. Could she face him? His cinnamon-red eyes stared out, again. It had been a few years since he saw his mother. No, since she left him here to *better himself.* That was what she called it. He shook his head. Fighting back the pricking he felt in his eyes. *Breathe Alzerion. Focus on tonight's event.*

It's not the night for this, he thought. The townspeople will have to walk in this storm. He knew that the people of Bachusa were some of the most loyal, and that they would come. In his mind he was thinking, calculating, was there another way? No, there were no options. The event was too important. He personally helped the queen plan each detail, down to the guest list. It had to be tonight. His lips curled up in a thin, sly smirk. Nobody would miss this. This would be seen as the event of the year.

Alzerion turned his head enough to see the maids and servants rushing around, speaking with the king and queen. He knew they wanted today to go perfectly. He hoped it would, too, for Aironell. Alzerion glanced down at the light pink basinet. He smiled at the little princess, as he rubbed his fingers against the white lace trimming of the basinet. This event was for her. To show off Bachusa's bright new hope! She laid there so tiny. Snoozing. *Please let today go well*, he pleaded. No hiccups or altercations. He knew what was being said in town.

The wind howled. He focused his attention back out the window. He watched as the wind picked up. In the distance the townspeople looked like tiny specks. They were still trudging toward the palace. Alzerion glanced down as lightening stabbed the sky followed by a loud boom. He quickly turned, *phew*, the princess was still asleep. Blissfully unaware. He licked his lips and then from the window he looked back down at the palace. The palace stood majestic even in the storm. It was an enormous gray structure with stones that appeared dark and imposing. It was a fortress. A safe haven for the princess. How lucky. Nobody wronged her. To start fresh, would be something.

Alzerion crouched forward looking as if he were hunched a bit. "Don't worry, little one, nobody will. Not if I can help it." He spoke in hushed tones. Forcing himself to release the tension rising in every muscle in his body.

He stood back up and craned his neck up to see the colossal tower that loomed above. He remembered doing some of his tutoring sessions up there, when he was younger. Then he heard a creaking sound. It was the mahogany doors to the entrance. *Finally*. His cinnamon-red eyes surveyed the entrance and watched as the doors opened revealing the family crest; a fleur-de-lis inside a crown. People.

Anything to keep his thoughts at bay. He could sense them, no, feel them festering. Alzerion moved. He grabbed the edge of the basinet and slid it as he strolled away from the window toward the thrones. He took his position and placed the basinet near him, like instructed.

The Great Hall was perfect for this. It was a huge room with crystal and gold chandeliers, and at the far end of the room, up front against a stone wall with an arched window in the center, were King Francisco and Queen Evalyn's thrones. They were made of old, dark cherry. Alzerion rubbed his hands against the delicate damask design that encircled the fleur-de-lis. Then he patted the red velvet seat cushions. He turned. Watching and waiting as the townspeople funneled in. The room was packed. He smiled and nodded as people locked eyes with him. Nobody dared come that close to him, by the thrones, but he watched as they mingled. Despite the travel, he witnessed pleasant chatter. Nobody looked worse for wear. He kept his distance.

His eyes continued to scan the Great Hall. His face tightened. Eyebrows pulled in as he saw her in the crowd. Part of him wanted to smile—to run and hug her. His lips started to part but then stopped. He bit down on his lower lip, hard. He felt the sharpness poking into his skin. A rush of mixed emotions flooded. Like he was being pelted by a hundred jabs of the thick wooden swords they used for training. She looked the same, yet different. Her cheeks looked fuller but her eyes had a slight hollowness to them. Could it be guilt? He shouldn't hope. At least *he* wasn't here, with her. Her eyes met his. He forced a tight smile. He couldn't do otherwise. He was on display, just as much as the royal family. It may have been the princess that everyone wanted to see, but he, too, had to look the part. Had to seem cheery. He steadied his breathing to block out the memories. *Those horrible fights. Voices that shook his very core. Nights that felt like the dawn would never come.* He ran his fingers through his disheveled hair and continued to smile.

He saw the king and queen meander through the large group as they made their way to their thrones. The king's dark curly hair frothed over his crown. He stood tall compared to people he passed. The queen's silver butterfly clip sparkled ruby red as she strolled forward. Once the king and queen were up front all eyes followed them. *Whew.* He had a brief pause. A short amount of time that he didn't have to pretend.

The king and queen were beaming. The king looked regal in his long black doublet. Elegant gold trimming ran down his sleeves. The queen perhaps was the only one that rivaled him in appearance. From that clip sparkling in her dirty-blonde hair to her deep red velvet gown with flecks of gold. Once it was silent King Francisco turned to Alzerion and nodded.

Alzerion bent over the light pink basinet. He kept that fake smile plastered on his face. Everyone saw her. The princess, who was long awaited, was cradled in his arms. He held her up for a better view. This is what he was here for. *No matter the cost. He already paid the price. Plucked from his home and sent here. Three years of tutors, etiquette classes, and military training.* He gazed down at the princess. She was snuggled in her light pink blanket with red roses embroidered over it.

As Alzerion looked at her little face with those delicate features, the princess opened her sparkly cerulean blue eyes and looked out. Instead of crying, she moved her lips into the cutest curve, while she held a silver rattle. The townspeople smiled, clapped, and cheered for the princess. The king raised his muscular arms, and some of the chatter died down.

Then the king said in his deep voice, "Alzerion will be the Royal Watcher for Princess Aironell." Alzerion bowed his head as the king spoke.

The crowds boomed. The loudness brought back those troubling thoughts. He focused on the room, so he wouldn't wince—wouldn't drop the princess. He looked up to see his mother. He finally gave her a smirk. Her eyes teared up, practically radiated with warmth. A slight mix of regret lingered, though. He knew that she was proud of his accomplishments— knew she loved him, despite sending him away. The king told him so. The king promised they would treat him like one of their own.

He remembered that day. His tutor was sick, so the king filled in. He was in no mood for lessons and the king set him straight. Told him that his mother was not the bad guy. One day he would understand. That was the day the king gave him the necklace. Alzerion held the necklace, now, in his right hand. It was a gift to him from his mother. Alzerion pulled it out of his pocket and held it up. He made sure to maintain a firm grip on the princess with the other hand.

The heart-shaped necklace twirled about as he held it by the chain. It was so radiant that it sparkled in the light. The necklace was called the Lost Hope, and it was his gift to the princess. There was such an applause. There was a lot of oohs and awes as he put it on Aironell. Once this was done, he walked toward the queen and placed Aironell in her arms before stepping off to the side. Then the king and queen moved forward and held Aironell up and out for all to see once more. The applause and pleasant chatter rebounded across the hall.

Alzerion smiled wide. He did love his mother. It would take time to mend, but he vowed he would. After all, it wasn't her. It was *him*. Alzerion vowed he would be better. It was what she wanted. He would be different than those ties that bound him, tight. Like he was being constricted, slowly, day after day. One wrong move and it would all go to crap. He knew what to do. Study. Work hard. Train. Now, he can add, take care of the princess. Someday things would be different, they had to.

Not all were thrilled about the birth of the princess. Outside of the palace someone stood not joining in the festivities. He couldn't believe how the townspeople just welcomed this baby. Did they forget all that Bachusa had been through? He stood at a distance wrapped in his dark black cloak, with a scowl plastered across his mouth. They'd pay—one way or another— the royal family would suffer. For now, that would have to be enough.

THE SEARCH

Inside the safety of the Family Room stood Queen Evalyn and King Francisco. King Francisco patted Queen Evalyn's back as they stood inches from the garnet fleur-de-lis shaped table. He pressed his leg against it as he continued listening to his wife.

"What are we going to do?" Evalyn asked as she broke away and paced, her cerulean blue eyes regarding the room as her fingers twisted around one another like a pretzel stick.

She spied her comfort spot, and slowly paced toward the bay window. She pushed the blush-colored curtains to the side and fiddled with the deep blue oval necklace around the square neckline of her dress. Then she peered out the chiseled bay window.

"What are we going to do about what, dearest?" replied Francisco. The scraping of his boots against the floorboards, mingled in her thoughts.

Evalyn smoothed her dress as she sat on the plush seat-bench of the bay window. Her gaze shifted between her husband and staring off in the distance.

"What are we going to do about Aironell? It's getting too risky to have her out and about in the town, with all these attempts on her life. It has been tough since her birth," she mustered. Nails dug into the twisted grooves of the design at the base of the window. The queen, occasionally, glanced over at her husband.

King Francisco's head bowed as he walked closer to his wife. Click. Clack. Each step brought him nearer. He sat on the ruby red armchair closest to the window and gazed at her.

"My love, then we will keep her inside until it is safe." He sounded so firm, so sure of his words. She gazed at him, for a moment. He thrust his shoulders back and puffed out his muscled chest.

"How will we know when it is safe?" Queen Evalyn probed as she turned slightly to her husband. "How do you not feel angry or worried? We have done so much for Bachusa. We have enhanced its overall peace and beauty, we staved off invaders, we meet with our people and interact with them; which is more than has *ever* happened before we took the throne," she reminded as she counted out each benefit with her slender fingers.

Francisco kept strong eye contact and nodded.

"Darling, I know what we have done. I assure you our people are most appreciative," Francisco commented as he stood and moved next to Evalyn by that window. He grabbed her hands and wrapped his fingers in hers.

"I just don't understand how we got here, to the moment our own people have forsaken us?" She rocked, slightly. Back and forth as she continued searching out toward the town.

This time Francisco placed his hand under her chin and gave a faint smile. He pressed his lips to her forehead. "Evalyn, I know it's hard to be hopeful but we must. The people haven't abandoned us, just a small group of unhappy people. We cannot condemn all of the town."

Evalyn took a deep breath and nodded.

"If we must, then we will keep Aironell in the palace, where she is safe, until we are sure she is no longer threatened and we—"

There was a knock at the studded door.

"Enter," boomed King Francisco as he stood up and moved briskly to his ruby-red armchair nearest the door and sat. Queen Evalyn fixed the bottom of her dress as she gracefully moved and stood behind her husband.

"Sire," responded Alzerion who entered and scanned the room with his warm cinnamon-red eyes. He quickly patted at his disheveled hair, to no avail.

"What can we do for you, Alzerion? We were just discussing matters regarding Aironell."

The queen stepped toward Alzerion and patted his shoulder. She raised an eyebrow, "Alzerion, you seem a bit out of sorts."

"I'm sorry your majesties. I ran here in quite a hurry."

"Alzerion, just breathe. What could have been so important that you ran here?" Francisco chided.

"I'm sorry. I hate bothering you both. I know you're busy, but I'm at a loss; in all senses of the word."

"Alzerion, what does that mean?" Evalyn probed.

"It means, well, um, uh-" he tried to find the words.

"Relax," Evalyn instructed. "I'm sure it can't be as serious as you think."

"It's Aironell. She's … missing!" he blurted out.

The queen couldn't believe her ears. It couldn't be real. She shook her head and focused on Alzerion. He looked away from them.

"You were supposed to be watching her!" The king's clenched fist pounded on the nearest table. "That is your job. We have to find her!" The king stood. "What were you doing that you lost her?"

With head hung low he replied, "I promise I only turned away not even five minutes, Your Majesty. I was signing the papers for the Royal Army. The ones saying that we would acquire the new weapons that you requested."

"Francisco, just have him go find her. Our little girl is probably scared to pieces." The queen was soft-spoken. She strode closer to her husband, and adjusted the gold amulet with the family's seal.

Francisco gazed into her glassy eyes, rubbed her shoulder, and nodded.

"Alzerion, tell the soldiers to go look for Aironell. Don't you dare return unless you have her! Do you understand?" the king commanded as he pointed his jeweled finger at Alzerion.

"Yes, sir!" Alzerion responded as he shifted his legs together.

Then Alzerion left and with clenched fists, he thrust open the door and left at a fast-paced stride.

Meanwhile, the queen placed her hands on Francisco's broad shoulders and turned him toward her. She hugged him, tight, while rubbing at the nape of his neck.

Then she whispered, "He will find her, Francisco. You know that better than anyone." The queen paused, held a breath for a few seconds until she steadied her voice and leaned back. Then with such an evenness to her voice she said, "He has to."

"I know but, he- he has to learn," he sighed.

"He will." She reached to clasp his hand. "Remember, he is fourteen. He does have a great deal of responsibility and work. He took his eyes off her for five minutes to tend to his other job. Don't forget all the hard work he does with the army. All that training to become the Commander-in-Chief of the Royal Army; which isn't far off for him."

"Do you think I was too hard on him?" asked King Francisco with a downcast glance.

"I think you could have handled it better," she replied, smooth and creamy. Then she gingerly rubbed his hand to her cheek as she continued, "You didn't have to be so cross with the boy. Until he learns, we should give him all the support and confidence that he will need to succeed. I know it's difficult. I had to compose myself so as not to panic."

"All right, when he comes back, I will apologize. However, I want him to realize the severity of this situation."

Queen Evalyn nodded. Arm-in-arm she led them to the bay window. Each sat on the plush cushion and peered out, lost in their thoughts.

Alzerion gathered the soldiers. He ordered them to change into their dark gray slacks, black boots, and chocolate-brown leather jerkin with a gray long sleeve shirt underneath. Then they clasped on their leather scabbards and swords around the waist. They needed to be ready for anything. Soon after that, they left the barracks and set out to find Aironell. As he was walking, he looked back at the palace and peered into the large bay window at the king and queen. He could see them clinging to one another, frowning. The queen fiddled with her necklace as the king looked out with wrinkled eyebrows.

The soldiers moved on. They searched the far Grimlands. It was a place where questionable people would tend to hide. It was a large expanse, but it was dark, cold, desolate, and grim. Alzerion looked high and low, but Aironell was nowhere to be found. They checked each cliff, mountain, and even cavern that they could think of.

Then he had soldiers go to Abandoned Alley and see if she was there. That particular alley branched off from town square. Alzerion searched Town Square and then waited there for the soldiers to return. Soon enough, they came back with heavy eyes and heads that hung low. Again, they kept moving. After searching for nearly three hours, the soldiers met up at Prairie Flats. It was a vast land with no mountains, no ditches, and no nothing. It was nearly flat, except for the occasional boulder. He waited there for everyone to return, even as the wind began to pick up.

Alzerion sat on the grass, like a pretzel, in disbelief. *I'm one of the best trackers in Bachusa. Why can't I seem to find one little girl? How could I have let Aironell slip through my fingers?* He sat frowning and biting at his lower lip while focusing on where they've searched and what they could do next. He finally knew what it felt like to fail— he hated it.

Most of all, how could he go back to the palace and tell the king and queen their daughter was gone? It did not make any sense. He just sat on the grass with his legs curled into his stomach and thought. There was something he was missing because there was no way she could have just disappeared. Bachusa, he knew, was quite enormous, so she had to still be here, somewhere.

Then a tall burly man stood before him. "Alzerion, can we talk?"

"Of course, Quairken. What's on your mind?" Alzerion asked as he stood up.

Quairken placed an arm around Alzerion and ushered them away from the group and continued, "I didn't want to be overheard by the others. Let's take a stroll about."

Alzerion nodded as they slowed their pace as they spoke.

"What is on your mind, Quairken?" Alzerion asked as he grabbed a handful of the tall purple prairie clovers.

"I'm concerned about what we should do next, sir. The others seem exhausted from the search and it's getting late."

"What are you suggesting?" Alzerion asked with raised eyebrows while he gazed at his fingers twisting the clovers in his hands.

"Maybe we should head back to the palace, sir," responded Quairken. "We're having no luck, and I think we will lose morale soon." Quairken's voice never wavered.

Alzerion twisted the last of the clover into a tight knot as he bit the inside of his cheek. Then he glanced at Quairken. Unsure as to what they should do, he turned away and looked beyond. He just gazed out in the distance at the slender purple clover fields. It was mostly flat all except for the few bushes that managed to grow in the field. Then he felt a pat on his shoulder and Alzerion took a breath in and exhaled.

"Quairken, I hope you know how much I appreciate you."

"I know, sir."

Alzerion turned around to face him. "Do you really think it best that we head back? I don't know what to do if we go back without the princess."

"Alzerion, you always figure something out," Quairken reassured while propping the back of his legs against a boulder that was hidden by the clovers.

"Alright," Alzerion nodded and started back toward the soldiers. Alzerion observed the men. Each had this downcast look. Some draped their arms over their head, with labored breaths. Many had taken to sitting in the field of clovers and the lucky ones sat on smooth stones. As he approached he watched them stand swiftly.

"You all can head back," boomed Alzerion with legs spread out in a wide stance. "Go back to the palace. You all worked very hard, and I thank you very much. I'm sure the king and queen will be glad to know how loyal their soldiers are. It's getting late, and I'm sure you would like to wash up and get some rest."

Alzerion heard mumbling and continued, "It's alright. It will be getting dark soon and without daylight we won't be very effective at tracking."

The soldiers nodded, got up, and headed back to the palace, but Alzerion merely sat back down. With right foot tapping at the ground he looked up and saw that Quairken had not left with the others. "Quairken, you should head back too."

"I'm not sure if I should. I'm not trying to disobey an order, but it seems wrong to leave you here."

"I appreciate the gesture, but get," he waved. "I'll be fine. Plus, I'm just not ready to admit defeat yet," he added as his chin dipped toward his chest with a downcast stare.

Quairken nodded, turned, and started the walk to the palace.

"Francisco, why don't you come sit by me?" Evalyn implored. The queen motioned from the couch to her husband who had this vacant expression as he stood watching the door. "You can't just keep standing. We don't know when they will return."

"I know you're right, dearest, but I feel useless," he admitted as he turned around to face his wife. "I just have a bad feeling about this."

With a pained look that narrowed her eyes, Queen Evalyn stood and moved to Francisco; closing the distance between them. "I'm here with you."

She placed her slender hand on his broad shoulder. This time Francisco grabbed her hand, caressed it, and gingerly kissed it. In a swooping motion he entwined their hands together like the threads of a string. Then he escorted Evalyn back to the couch where he sat down next to her.

"I will try to calm," Francisco reassured, "I just—"

He was cut short by the sound of boots trudging in the hall outside the Family Room. A glowing smile escaped his face and with his heart racing, King Francisco stood up and promptly strode to the door and opened it. His demeanor shifted as he met with Quairken.

"Come," King Francisco said with a flare of his hand.

He led Quairken into the room and allowed him to sit in the chair closest to the queen. He positioned himself on the couch next to his wife.

"Quairken, tell us what happened," demanded the king. "Where is Aironell? Where is Alzerion?"

"What I think my husband is trying to say is welcome back from your search. Would you like some tea?" she motioned to the little silver kettle that sat atop a white lace cloth.

"Thank you for the offer, your majesty, but I'm fine," Quairken replied and then took a slow breath. "I will explain."

He told them all the places they searched, such as the Grimlands, Abandoned Alley, and Prairie Flats, but all to no avail. Then he told them how Alzerion sent them all home and how he stayed there. He looked up at the king and queen.

King Francisco pulled out of his own thoughts as he noticed that his wife's expression shifted. He could see this haunted look on her face like a murky white washed over her.

"Thank you for keeping us informed, Quairken," king Francisco replied. "Isabella was looking for you earlier, so you may go."

Quairken stood, bowed his head and left the king and queen.

"Oh, Francisco," the queen sobbed.

Francisco hugged his wife to calm the tide of her emotions, but could only watch as the stream of her tears kept running down her cheeks, like a flood.

"Darling, remember you said to have faith in Alzerion, so that is what we must do," he said while he pulled out a silk handkerchief from his pocket and started dabbing away at her tear-stained cheeks.

"Francisco, I appreciate that," she was able to muster between chocked sobs.

Francisco patted her back and saw Evalyn start to take slow breaths. "Francisco, what if he cannot find Aironell and he could be in danger out there all alone," she said with more control in her voice as she continued to use the handkerchief.

"Alzerion is tough. He will be fine. He wants to find her, so we should try to remain calm and—"

"I know, but still, I'm worried about him."

"Me too," Francisco admitted as he placed his arm around her shoulder. Evalyn let her head lean against his chest and they sat there taking in the comfort of the couch, while they found solace in the other. The king's heartbeat was as steady as the rhythmic patter of rain drops.

Alzerion was still just sitting on the grass, thinking. He was going over again and again the possible places Aironell could be. However, each time, he came to the same conclusion: they already searched there. The wind picked up blowing his cloak, so Alzerion stood up and started walking back. As he stepped his boots scraped the ground like a little child dragging their feet. After about a half-hour walk through Prairie Flats, he was back on the trail and was about to pass by Founders Path when he heard a noise.

It was a faint sound, but it was enough to pique his interest. He looked around but couldn't find the source of the noise. So, he continued. A few more minutes on Founders Path and the noise grew louder. He ran toward the sound and stopped right in front of a rock enclosure that was situated just off the side of the path. Nestled snug in the enclosure was a basket with blankets, and not just any blankets but pretty pink ones with red roses as a decoration. He knelt down beside the enclosure and pulled out the basket. Then he leafed through the blankets and saw her. It was Aironell, all safe in the blankets that he laid her in. A grin spread across his face.

He pulled Aironell out of the basket, laid her in his arms, and wrapped the blanket around her tiny body so that she would not catch cold from the windy evening. He looked into her precious eyes and rested his forehead to hers.

"It'll be all right," he said with such sureness and then gave her a sweet kiss on her cheek.

Alzerion stood up and headed back onto Founders Path, which became Royal Lane the closer they got to the palace. Alzerion had to stop a few times to readjust Aironell. For someone so tiny she sure did make his arm go numb so fast. He did this a few times, each time chattering away with her to keep her calm as he moved her from her comfy position. As he came within sight of the palace, he realized something.

Aironell was never far from the palace. Generally, if someone was kidnapping a person, they would try to get as far away as possible, but they did not. Founders Path was about six minutes from the palace adjacent from Royal Lane; anyone could practically see the palace from that path. *It just did not add up*, he thought. He walked through the big front doors and up the grand staircase. He took a deep breath and opened the doors to the family room. Once he entered, the king and queen stood at once. He could see their tear-stained faces start to brighten. So, he walked toward them and put Aironell in the queen's arms.

"Oh, thank you, Alzerion!" she blurted. Then the queen kissed Aironell and pulled her daughter tightly into her chest. Alzerion could see her beaming from ear to ear.

"Of course. Just doing my duty," he replied while watching the king kneeling down beside the queen. He gently rubbed Aironell's little stockinged foot.

"Alzerion," said the king sternly as he turned his head to face him. "You shouldn't have stayed by yourself. You could have been hurt, and then how would we have explained that to your parents?"

"I'm sorry, Your Majesty, I just couldn't face you and the queen." His tone was steady. "If I didn't have Aironell, I didn't want to return, and the soldiers were getting tired."

"I know," replied the king. "You just had us worried, is all."

"But I thought you were furious with me?"

"Alzerion, I was scared, and I took it out on you," the king replied as he stood. Alzerion watched as the king held out his strong arm toward him. Alzerion stepped closer and then the king embraced him. He was not expecting that but felt he should return the favor and hugged the king. He saw Queen Evalyn nod.

King Francisco then placed his hands on Alzerion's back and gave him a pat as he continued, "I just wanted to show you how serious the situation was. I know you are still young, but you have a great amount of responsibility. I wanted you to realize the importance of multi-tasking. It is the only way you will accomplish all your tasks, including watching my daughter. Please forgive me."

Alzerion took a slow breath in and out to keep his jaw from gaping wide open. He felt this warmth in his heart.

"Of course. I'll do better," Alzerion said with a curt nod. King Francisco gave a slight nod and then accompanied Alzerion to the ruby red armchair that sat near the couch. Alzerion waited until King Francisco sat on the couch, before sitting down.

Alzerion continued to watch the family. The king and queen couldn't stop smiling and cooing at Aironell. She looked like a pea in a pod, all snug and so innocent to all the evil in the world. The atmosphere of the room shifted since he arrived with the princess.

THE STRANGER

Alzerion's foot tapped as he studied the shift in the mood. He stood up, slowly, and moseyed his way to the bay window. He sat on the plush seat and gazed outside. After a few minutes of scanning Gorgeous Garden and seeing the tallest building of the town square in the distance, he began biting his fingernail.

He had this nagging sensation churning in the pit of his stomach, as if he ate something that disagreed with him. Alzerion kept inspecting Bachusa, or at least what he could see, but still he couldn't place that feeling. He knelt on the seat and placed his hands on the window, as if trying to get closer. *It has to mean something,* he thought. He quickly spun his head around when he heard a faint sound behind him. It was the king shaking a little rattle for Aironell. He saw the king and queen look back at him, and he forced a smile, so as not to alarm them.

Maybe my senses are trying to warn me of something...but what? He knew this probably had something to do with his magical abilities. Alzerion was one of those blessed with the gift of magic. When he first realized he possessed the power, he was merely six and had to learn that not everyone in Bachusa possessed it.

He remembered learning about the rules of magic in one of his many lessons. Alzerion smirked. He remembered it like it was yesterday.

He sat in the Royal Library at a mahogany table overlooking a sea of books. Books of all kinds. Some new, some worn, and some so old they looked tattered as if the pages might tear. There was one book, so old the pages felt dried out and crinkled as he turned them. It was a huge dark brown leather-bound book with a fleur-de-lis wearing a crown inside a heart with something speckled all around; only later did he learn that it represented magic. The symbol was decorated all over the book, and the title was The Magical Code, written in gold letters on the cover. He flipped the pages to the beginning.

Magic Fact

1. It exists.

2. It is a gift.

3. It is not had by everyone.

Code of Conduct

1. Never use magic to fight a battle.

2. In conflict, your opponent should be magically equipped. If not, then it would be unfair to use magic.

3. Magic cannot be used to manipulate opinions; it cannot force people to do your bidding; it cannot make someone love you!

Magical Ownership

1. The Royal Family has the gift of magic that flows through their veins.

2. The servants in the palace have the gift of magic. Granted, it is limited.

3. The Ancient Family of Sorcery has the gift of magic that flows through their veins since infancy.

4. No townsperson can utilize the gift of magic.

5. The soldiers in the Royal Army are forbidden to use magic. {For reason, see Code of Conduct # 1}

Rules

1. To gain one's full potential, magic must be taught at a young age.

2. There must be a magical book passed down from the generations, filled with spells.

3. All youth should be taught the benefits and consequences of using magic, such as magical accidents or spells gone awry.

"Alzerion, are you alright?" asked King Francisco as he firmly nudged his shoulder.

Alzerion stared blankly for a moment. He shook his head a bit. "I'm sorry your majesty. I was lost in thought."

"We were getting a bit worried. The queen called your name a few times, and nothing."

"I'm sorry to have troubled you both," he said shifting his gaze between the two of them. "I'm fine. I was just thinking about all those days studying in the library."

"Oh, what brought that about?" Queen Evalyn chimed in as she stood, rocking the princess.

"Do tell," King Francisco winked.

Alzerion peered back out the bay window and his lips parted to reveal the faintest smirk. "I was feeling a bit of nostalgia. Sometimes when I sit here, I can't help but think about things. Bachusa is such a beautiful place."

"That it is," Queen Evalyn nodded.

"Well, it's just that. The majesty of the buildings and the wonder of the gardens, I-I-I can't help but to think of the magic of it all."

"Ah," King Francisco replied, "so that's what made you think of the library. All of those days studying about magic and the town history."

"Exactly," Alzerion chuckled. It must have been enough to reassure them because he watched King Francisco stroll back to the couch.

Alzerion turned his attention back to the scene from the window. This time he made sure to tuck each side of the blush curtains into the metal fleur-de-lis holders, to fully clear his view. *It's too dark outside,* he thought. So, Alzerion quickly turned his head to be sure he was not being watched, satisfied, he looked back out the window and then concentrated his gaze on the dark sky. He thought only of a way to get a clearer image and then waved his hand, and with that there was a flash of lightening that lit up the whole sky. Finally, he knew what the problem was. Outside the palace he saw a man gazing at the palace.

Alzerion knew he only had one chance, so he waved his hand again, and this time lightening flashed and there was this loud boom of thunder. Alzerion attempted to tune out Aironell's cry. He could hear the queen shushing her and he even heard the king say, "There, there."

The man outside tried to blend in with the inky-black night, but with another flash of lightening Alzerion could see the man. He was average height with disheveled pitch-black hair that was graying. Alzerion squinted, but could make out the coldness of his maroon eyes. They sent a shiver down his spine. His stomach felt like it was one giant knot. His gaze was fixated on the man's rough looking face. *Ulbrick.* He hoped to never cross paths, ever again.

"Alzerion," the king called.

"Yes, your majesty," Alzerion replied, barely turning his head around.

"Are you feeling alright?" Francisco asked as his eyebrows narrowed. "You seem a bit preoccupied."

Alzerion gulped, and faced the king. "I'm alright, sir."

"Are you sure," Queen Evalyn chimed in as she held the princess against her chest. "You have this look about you."

"I'm sorry if I'm worrying you. I'm just distracted by the change of weather, that's all." Alzerion shifted his eyes firmly away from the window.

"Alzerion, come have a talk with me in the hallway, please," instructed King Francisco.

Alzerion faced the king but kept glancing from the king to the queen, hoping for her to intervene, but she merely nodded at him. He knew that he had to obey. So Alzerion followed the King into the hallway.

Alzerion stood with his back propped up against the crème-colored damask decorated wall.

"Alzerion," the king said as soon as he stepped into the hall.

"Yes, sir," answered Alzerion straightening his back.

"Is there something wrong? I know you said no before, but it seems like *something* is bothering you."

"No, sir, I'm just a little tired."

The king paused and asked, "Are you certain?"

"Positive," Alzerion said. However, he saw the king raise his eyebrow. He knew that the king had doubts, but he couldn't bring himself to confide in him, not yet.

"Well, if that is the case, you should go to bed then. A decent night's sleep should do you some good."

"Thank you, sir." Alzerion bowed his head. Then he left down the hall. As he turned the corner he looked back and saw the king. His head was bent low as he clutched the door, before entering the Family Room. *He definitely doesn't believe me,* he thought.

"Francisco, is he alright?" Queen Evalyn was now standing rocking Aironell in her arms.

"He said he was just a little tired."

"Well, alright. I do hope that's the only thing that's the matter. I'm going to put Aironell to bed, and then when I come back, you and I should get to bed."

"Of course," replied the king, who moved to the fireplace.

The queen took a few steps toward the door, turned to check on him, and she saw a hollowness in his eyes. She didn't know what was unsettling him, but she couldn't remember a time that he looked more perplexed.

"Francisco, I' m leaving now. Please be in our room and ready for bed. I shouldn't be long."

As she left, she saw him wave his hand in acknowledgement.

Meanwhile, when the queen went into Aironell's room, she put Aironell in a small white nightgown that had tiny sky-blue bows along the neckline. Then she sang Aironell to sleep while rocking, rhythmically, in the rocking chair. The queen had this sweet voice and Aironell never had problems falling asleep when the queen sang to her.

Queen Evalyn slowly ambled to the crib and tucked Aironell into bed. Next, she turned on the mobile, because it had a recording of her singing. Then Queen Evalyn kissed Aironell on the cheek. Aironell looked so peaceful like she did not have a care in the world; there was a sweet little smile across her lips.

With an even bigger grin, the queen turned the lights off, walked out of the room, shut the door, and strolled up through West Wing corridor. She entered her bedroom and looked at her husband. She saw that he changed into his soft red pajamas and was, in fact sitting on the bed. He looked up at her with this forced taut-looking grin. However, the Queen could see right through the façade but thought better than to ask him about it now. It was late, and both of them had quite a trying day. So instead, she went into her bathroom and put on her silky red nightgown. Then she walked to her bed and nestled herself under the blankets. King Francisco clapped his hands, and the lights went out. He rolled over to look at his wife. They kissed and slowly dozed off. And soon they were both encased with the dreams and thoughts of night.

Alzerion walked down West Wing corridor and passed Aironell's room. He was careful not to make a sound. He couldn't believe Ulbrick was so near. *What if he knew where the palace guards were? What if he knew when... no that would be impossible.* He shook his head and tried to convince himself that it was nothing. But as he headed past the East Wing corridor, down the grand staircase, out the big front doors, and into Gorgeous Garden, he knew he did not believe himself. He had to figure out what Ulbrick was doing here, no matter how bad it was.

As Alzerion walked through Gorgeous Garden, he grew pale. He could almost blend in with the pure white roses. He took a few deep breaths in and out. Then he smirked, somewhat, at the many flowers and bushes he passed. He looked at the red roses, picked one up, and put it to his nose for a whiff.

That particular flower was his personal favorite, and it was the scent that Aironell loved best. He could remember the first time he ever put the flowers in her room, like it was on replay in his mind. Her face as it lit up. The scent wafting around the room. Her little giggle and coos as she batted at them.

He sat down on a horseshoe shaped wooden bench and propped his back against the backing of the bench. As he sat he tried to dial down his anxieties in order to think about the events of the evening. *How could it be? Aironell was never far away. What kind of a kidnapper would do that?* He felt this cool sensation on his back, which forced his thoughts back.

"Ugh," he groaned as he felt a wetness on his black and red royal robes. "Could this evening get any worse?"

Alzerion stood up and walked out of Gorgeous Garden, and headed on Founders Path. When he came to the point where he had to turn onto Matters Lane, he saw footprints on the ground, which caught his eye. There was only one set of footprints, that deviated from the path. There was nothing but grass and an unflattering view of the palace. There were no entrances, so why would someone walk here?

He followed the footprints. The feeling of being wet long since escaped his thoughts and was replaced with this heavy barrage of questions. Nevertheless, Alzerion followed the prints. He had to duck under some thorny bushes and watch that he didn't trip over branches and tree trunks. *Whoever they belonged to must be clever,* he thought.

The bushes and branches blended with the darkness. Telling one thing from another was a challenge, as was seeing the footprints. He squinted his eyes but still, it was hopeless. It was so dark that the tiniest bit of light would go unnoticed. He stopped for a moment and thought about a bright reddish orange flame. Within seconds Alzerion could feel a heat from the palm of his hands. As he focused, that warmth emitted heat waves that erupted into a tiny fire in his hands. He watched as it flickered low and grew bright as the tips danced in a controlled manner. Then he swirled his flamed hands above and around each other, until the flames became one medium-sized ball of brightness. Proud of his handiwork, Alzerion nodded and the flame ball led the way lighting the terrain. He saw where the footprints branched off again into a more wooded area.

He kept moving nimbly until finally the prints veered to the left, which was toward the palace; except that they still traversed in the wooded space. *How could I have been so foolish?* He knew where this would lead. The prints finally stopped. He disintegrated the flame ball into a thin smoke cloud that blew in the breeze. He knew exactly where he was. He deftly pushed two overlapping branches and then had complete visibility of the palace and the front entrance. It was an elaborate, clever plan. Anyone could walk through the wooded area to get around the guards. They would have been hidden from view. With a bit of magic, hell, you could evade detection as you entered the palace. *It must have been Ulbrick. Did he try to break into the palace? Should I have mentioned seeing him to the King? Where is he now? I must find him.*

Then he heard a faint hoarse voice behind him. He quickly spun around. The man stood there staring at Alzerion with those dark maroon eyes. Alzerion's own eyes furrowed a bit as he continued looking. He knew better than to trust the softness of his gaze. It was an act. As he continued observing his demeanor, Alzerion noticed the slight bulge of muscle on his arms, despite being past his prime. As they both stood staring, neither one saying a word, Alzerion focused on the sky, and then flashes of light crept across the sky.

Hmm he didn't even stir, Alzerion thought. Instead, Alzerion noticed the light reflect off the man's clothes, revealing that he appeared to be covered in dirt, and his face was a bit rough looking. Still, that was not quite as interesting as the ring on his thumb.

It was handsomely crafted of silver with an ornate pattern across the surface. There was a U insignia with what appeared to be a snake etched over the length of the U, and the snake's eyes were crafted of sapphire diamonds. As if nothing could have been more interesting, Alzerion found something else that caught his attention. He noticed the little bundle tucked away in the man's arms. Alzerion could feel the gentle pulse in his neck speed up, ever so slightly. His gaze was fixed on that bundle. He felt like Ulbrick was taunting him, somehow.

Despite every fiber of his being, screaming, that it was a horrible idea; Alzerion inched toward Ulbrick. Alzerion got within arm's reach and prodded at the bundle. Alzerion shot a quick glance at Ulbrick only to see this confident, cocky, and obnoxious smirk. It made Alzerion's blood boil. He knew that it would be unwise to confront him, physically.

Alzerion felt a tingling sensation creep down his spine.

"What's the matter?" asked Ulbrick. "Doesn't this look familiar to you?" He crooned while moving his right arm under the bottom of the parcel.

Then Alzerion smoothed his hand over the bundle and felt the softest, smoothest fabric. Like some sort of silk, which would only have been afforded by someone of means. He started to grow pale. As if his brain and eyes were finally catching up to each other. He took a few steps back as he scanned the entirety of the scene before him. Alzerion could see that the wad did not look like a package, but rather a baby wrapped up. The smooth silks he felt were light pink. He squinted his eyes and could detect roses embroidered around the edges. Alzerion firmly pressed his hand to the bark of the nearest tree. He did so to ground his thoughts. *It was Aironell. She had been lying there in Ulbrick's arms this whole time.* He shook his head to focus his attention on what he should do.

He continued to look at Aironell beneath the wrapped silks and sensed something was not right. *Is she asleep? Has she been poisoned?* He realized that she hadn't moved or even made the slightest coo. Then he saw her face as Ulbrick must have adjusted a small part of the fabric. *He put her in some kind of a trance to keep her quiet,* Alzerion realized, feeling anger start to rise within. He felt like a barrage of heated bubbles rising up that would overflow at any moment.

"What do you think you're doing?" Alzerion said between gritted teeth.

"I'm just doing what should have been done long ago. I'm tying up some loose ends and getting rid of some trash." He spoke with that same hoarse, raspy voice. The only difference was that he detected a hint of glee behind his words.

"You mean you're kidnapping?" Alzerion asked, still a little taken aback. "You can't do this. The princess is the future of Bachusa."

"Oh, just think of this as a favor I'm doing for you." Each word came out with a hint of charm. He saw through that. Plastered across his lips was a sneer. That was the true man, just as he remembered him.

"How is kidnapping the princess doing me a favor? I don't gain anything from this. I care about the child, and it is my duty to keep her safe and—"

"That's precisely the reason why it would be a favor. You would be able to do what other children your age can. If not for me doing this, you'd be cooped up in the palace tending to the princess's every whim, and just wait until she gets older. When she can walk, talk, and think for herself, you'll hate your job. Suddenly, you won't feel so proud about it then when you have to cater to a spoiled brat."

"You don't know what you're talking about," Alzerion frowned. "She'll never be so terrible. Give her to me now."

"Alzerion… you shouldn't be ordering me to do anything. You should know better. I thought you would understand what I'm trying to accomplish here. Let's be civil."

"I can't let you do whatever you want. I always do my job," Alzerion said with his chest puffed out.

"Alzerion, don't test me. Stay out of my way or I'll have to make you."

"I'm not going anywhere until you give Aironell to me, Ulbrick!" Alzerion planted his feet firmly, in a wide stance.

"Well now," Ulbrick chuckled. "I guess you'll force me to use Aironell to my advantage." Ulbrick's foot began to tap. Alzerion noticed it had an almost rhythmic beat to it. *Oh, have I annoyed him? Maybe I'm doing just enough to keep the princess free from harm.*

"If you don't move, Alzerion, I'll hurt the Princess. Granted my plan calls for her to remain alive, for the time being, until I get what I want. However, I guess I'll just have to improvise and use plan B."

Alzerion probed Ulbrick with his gaze. He did not see an ounce of defeat or backing down. He knew that Ulbrick meant what he said, and he had to deter him, somehow.

"If that's what you think. You have lost it. I'll never let you hurt her!"

"Well, if you help me then the Princess would be fine." Then Ulbrick adjusted his grip on the princess and took a few steps closer to Alzerion. "Alzerion, truly I don't need her, not yet."

He was unsure what Ulbrick's game was. His eyes darted to Ulbrick who moved toward him. Alzerion backed up a bit, placing him closer to the Blue Prince Holly bush.

"Then why are you kidnapping her? She is a little girl. They all have put up with so much." Alzerion pointed up at the palace. "If you don't want her then what is the purpose for all this?" Alzerion glanced around as if maybe the broadleaves of the bushes could evoke some answers.

"I have my reasons. For now, you need to move. If you don't I will have to hurt Aironell and I'll make you help me with my plans."

"I'm not going to give in that easy." He said with legs locked firmly and fists at the ready. "I don't want to fight, but I will do what it takes to keep Aironell safe."

Ulbrick was up to something. He hated the thought of helping him, but he also knew that he couldn't let Ulbrick take Aironell, either. He wouldn't be able to forgive himself nor would the King and Queen. So, he just looked into Ulbrick's maroon eyes with more determination than ever as he stood his ground.

"Fine," said Ulbrick with what looked like a faint hint of playful glee in his eyes.

He plastered that annoying sneer across his face. It reminded Alzerion of someone who thought they won. Alzerion took a breath and ran his hands through his hair. A few moments later he noticed Ulbrick hold up his hand with the ring, and they locked eyes. Ulbrick pushed the sapphire diamond on his ring, and in an instant, Alzerion was bound. He couldn't move a muscle from head to toe. It had all happened so fast, and Alzerion hoped he made the right decision by standing up to Ulbrick.

He tried to escape by using some of his magic, but he could not. Then a thought struck him. *The rope keeps glowing light blue. Damn it! It was spelled to repel the use of magic and keep him bound and trapped. Grr.*

Suddenly there was a rustling in the Blue Prince Holly bushes from behind. He wasn't sure what was going to happen to him, but the noise grew louder. Hell, he couldn't even see as he was stuck with only a front view of Ulbrick.

"Ah, Warren, so glad you could join us," Ulbrick hissed.

Alzerion never heard that name before. He could not hear him. This

Warren must be stealthy. Finally, he heard the crunch of leaves and the crack of small twigs. Then the blackness of boots crept into his view. He scanned Warren and noticed that he was also dressed in all black. *It must be so that they can move about undetected.* He locked eyes on him. He had a young face with grey eyes. *Huh, he does not have that same cold and exacting gaze as Ulbrick.*

Warren moved closer and knelt down over Alzerion, and he noticed that Warren couldn't be more than a couple years older than him. He had hair just as black as the clothes he wore. What really caught Alzerion's attention was his smile.

Why is he smiling? What is so funny to both of them that they should be smiling? Alzerion thought to himself.

None of this seemed funny, to him. Nothing made much sense to him, either. Within seconds, this Warren fellow had wrapped his firm arms around him and flung Alzerion over his right shoulder.

"Well done. Now, follow closely," Ulbrick instructed.

Alzerion saw the palace fade from view as Warren followed Ulbrick back through the woods. He couldn't see but he knew that they were headed through the wooded terrain, only to come out onto Matters Lane. They seemed to be traveling on all the least travelled paths, toward the main town. After what felt like forever of just gazing at dirt paths, trees, and dark skies; Alzerion finally saw cobble stones. They were in town. He tried to glance around but Warren tightened his grip like a python gripping its prey.

The best Alzerion could do was see the sides of him, which allowed him to see the tattered sign that read: Abandoned Alley. Finally, they stopped. He heard Ulbrick's hoarse voice mutter something, and he heard the whoosh of a door opening. As the men walked through the door carrying Alzerion and Aironell, the door closed behind them.

Warren dropped Alzerion on a couch and then tended to the fire. Alzerion watched Ulbrick lay Aironell next to him and then clap his hands. He felt the confines that bound him, release. Then lights came on moments later and filtered throughout the little room. Alzerion twisted his wrists and looked around. There were papers tossed all over the place. Stacks of books of various titles just piled on surfaces. The light was warm and the heat that emanated from the wood stove made it feel somewhat inviting. There were pictures of landscapes on the walls and knitted pillows that adorned the couches. The couch he sat on had this softness to it, like it was worn from years of use. Alzerion couldn't help but grin. He knew he would feel right at home, if not for the lingering uncertainty of Ulbrick and his plans.

"Ulbrick, I want some answers," Alzerion broke the silence.

Warren looked between them and stood at attention by the wood stove, with the fire poker in hand.

Ulbrick gave Warren a wave and then sat down on the couch opposite the one where Alzerion sat. "Alzerion, what do you want to know?"

"What do you want? You don't want the princess, yet you brought her here. Why are we here?"

"All in good time."

"Well, who is that man?" He asked as he pointed at Warren. "What is his role in all of this?"

"I guess I owe you some answers." Alzerion's eyes narrowed as he watched Ulbrick cross his legs and fold his hands. He looked like someone who was calmly sitting to tell a good story.

"Warren, come closer." Alzerion's gaze shifted to Warren who stood inches away from him, still with that poker in hand.

"As you have heard, this is Warren. He will become a friend to you. He'll help you whenever you need it, and he is basically my apprentice."

"Nice to meet you," Warren beamed. "I know you must be scared. But in truth, this place is not so bad. Working with Ulbrick isn't so bad, either."

Alzerion merely stared. *How do I navigate through this?*

"Warren, I don't know you so I hope you don't take offense, but I don't know what things Ulbrick has told you but I have no intention of working with him," Alzerion replied. "I know him. This is not the first time we have crossed paths, and I was hoping to avoid meeting again. Apparently, that was out of the question because here I am sitting in the same room with him."

"Alzerion," snapped Ulbrick, "you're here to help us. We have an important mission, and we've made numerous plans. However, if we have your assistance, things will go much smoother."

"Is this why you brought us here?" asked Alzerion.

"Well," said Warren before Ulbrick could speak. "This is why he kidnapped the princess, to be more exact."

As Warren said those words, Alzerion opened to speak but no words escaped. *What is that supposed to mean?* He glanced over at Aironell, then back up at Ulbrick, and he squeezed his eyes tight. He felt this coldness that gripped the very inner of his being. *How did he not see it sooner?* He started to gasp to catch his breath as he leaned forward a bit. He forced his eyes open and his gaze fell between Ulbrick and Warren. He noticed Warren was bent over laughing.

"What's so funny?" snapped Alzerion who finally gained his words.

"You are," Warren replied. "I'm sorry but I can't help myself. You would laugh too if you could see your face. You look like you could catch a fish with your mouth."

Alzerion crossed his arms over his chest and tapped his foot. As he sat there, he stared at Ulbrick with a glassy, steady look.

"What's the matter?" Ulbrick taunted. "You seem surprised by something."

"I can't believe how stupid I am," Alzerion said as he jolted up. "You kidnapped the princess to get to me, didn't you?" Alzerion fumed as his nostrils flared. Alzerion worked to steady his breathing but found it difficult as every muscle in his body tensed.

"Bravo," said Ulbrick as he leaned back against the cushioned head rest behind him. "Yes, I did. The princess is a baby. Until she's older, she is of no use to me. I knew your job was to watch over her, and I thought you'd probably be doing that most of the day. I took her the first time to see what the king and queen would do." He clapped his hands together. "I was so pleased when they sent you to find her. I knew I was correct. I waited until it got dark out and everyone would be in bed. I took Aironell and I saw you as I passed. You were still awake, and I vowed to wait patiently for you."

"What do you want from me? I can't imagine why you would've gone through all that trouble just to see me."

"Warren and I need help to accomplish our goal," he informed Alzerion. "And we know that you can really make all the difference."

Alzerion realized that he had no choice but to offer his assistance. He was in no position to argue, for if he did, Aironell and he probably would not see the light of day.

"Fine," Alzerion sighed. "Tell me what you're up to then."

Once Alzerion agreed to help them, Warren sat down next to him.

The queen awoke with a shudder. Something was wrong. Half-awake she rubbed at her eyes as she sat up and looked around. King Francisco was still asleep, yet she still felt this dread. So, she pushed the button by her bed that rang for Alzerion, but nobody came. Puzzled. *Maybe he was simply sleeping?* Sleep kept invading her own mind. He could be getting ready for practice with the Royal Army or maybe he went to visit his mother. Either way, she reasoned that Alzerion was busy, and she was just being paranoid, so then she laid back down and fell asleep.

And a mile away from the palace sat Alzerion. He was alone on that couch as Warren and Ulbrick decided to rest. So, he looked down at his robes and saw the little heart with the crown around it blinking red. He knew that the queen was looking for him. He was not worried about Warren. He seemed too nice to do any real damage, but Ulbrick, that was different.

Alzerion knew they needed him, so he was not worried for his life but rather of what they were planning. He looked down at Aironell and a rush of emotions surged. He waved his hand, and Aironell awoke from her trance. He felt safe in doing so, since Ulbrick was fast asleep. He cradled her, and she smiled as sleep crept over her.

Alzerion tried to remain calm. He had this ugly feeling. It was the feeling of pure, unrelenting hatred. He loathed what he now was forced to do in order to help Ulbrick and Warren. So, he bent over and kissed Aironell on her head, and he laid down beside her and realized that she could be in danger.

HIDE-AND-SEEK

The next morning had the queen quite busy. She was readying the palace for the town gathering. She was bopping about finishing the details of the brunch. She wanted everything to run smoothly. There was an assortment of pastries, fruit tarts, scones, and various fine meats. The scents made her mouth water, as she sat at a small table, nearby. She inspected each item the servants brought out and placed on the long table. This was set on the left side of the Great Hall. She felt it would allow for people to eat, and still give the option to move about and mingle. Just as the queen was about to eat her raspberry pastry, a servant stood before her.

"Your Majesty," bowed a slender maid. "I— um, h-have some news."

"What is it?" The queen probed as her eyes narrowed. "We are very busy today. What can I do for you, Isabella?"

Isabella strolled closer. "It's Alzerion," she whispered.

Queen Evalyn noticed that Isabella was acting a bit off, so she motioned for her to come even closer. Now Isabella stood so close that she could have touched the queen's arm.

"Isabella, what about Alzerion?" Queen Evalyn felt this shiver prick the back of her ear. Like the tiny hairs were standing on edge.

Isabella let out a long exhale. "He's not here."

Queen Evalyn shifted her eyes around. She saw her husband was deep in conversation across the room. Nobody was around her except for Isabella. "He has to be here." She noticed that her hands started to tremble.

"I'm sorry your majesty, he's not. Before the gathering I thought you mentioned he may have gone to visit his parents?"

"I did, but he should be back by now." She explained while forcing her hands to press firmly on her arms. Anything to control them from trembling.

"I thought he would be back by now. In truth it has been quite some time. Also, he never misses an opportunity to wake Aironell. He loves seeing her little eyes open and sparkle. Anyway, is Aironell still asleep?" The queen focused her thoughts and took a couple slow breaths.

"I'm not sure, Your Majesty. I haven't been in her room yet."

"Well, when you do, make sure to wake her up. Please get her dressed and ready, and when you're done, bring her downstairs to me."

"Yes, ma'am."

Isabella curtsied and as she walked away the queen stared out lost in thought. *How is he not back yet?* She shook her head and stood up. She paced the length of the table and forced a smile, as a couple of townsfolk passed by and bowed. Queen Evalyn gave them a nod and took a stroll around to the front of the room, as she avoided stopping. She didn't want to be interrupted, not now. She feared that she wouldn't be able to hide her emotions.

She felt a rolling sensation in her stomach, like it was tied up in a neat little bow. One that twisted and wrenched. Her face scrunched a bit as she let her hand gloss over her belly. She turned away from the stone walls and headed to her throne. She gave gentle nods as she passed by townspeople, on her way. The queen pulled the bottom of her dress, taut, as she slowly sat herself down. She could feel the hardness of the wood against her arm. In this moment she was grateful for it. She felt her body sink right in. People were smiling, chatting, and some were even singing the anthem of Bachusa.

The queen picked at the ends of her long braid as she continued to scan the room. There was the king. He nodded at Sir Harris, a lesser noble, and she watched as the king turned. In that moment he met her gaze. She took a few gulps to moisten her throat, as the king meandered across the room toward her.

He put his hand on her chin, lifted her head up, and smiled sweetly. "Dearest, what's the matter?"

She could sense his gaze on her like a bug under a magnifying glass.

"Nothing," she insisted.

"Evalyn," he whispered. She could feel the heat from his words tickle her left ear.

"You don't honestly expect me to believe that, do you?" He asked while he backed up a bit. "I always know when you are being a little less than truthful with me."

She could hear the lowness of his voice and see the concern in his eyes. Then he grazed his warm hand over hers and she couldn't hold back. She tried. She grabbed his hands and clung to them, tightly.

"Really, what's bothering you?"

"It's Alzerion," she blurted then bit her lower lip. "I fear that I made a huge mistake." She swallowed and closed her eyes. She could feel a slight burning.

"What do you mean?" The king shifted his stance to keep his view partly open. "Evalyn—"

"It's a long story, and it might amount to nothing. No use for both of us to be worried."

"Evalyn, it's hard for me not to worry when you look like you may burst into tears."

The queen stared at her feet and then looked at her husband, trying to compose herself. Finally, she sighed.

"I paged Alzerion late last night. It was practically morning. I felt something was wrong. I don't quite know how to explain it, but it was this distressing feeling, so I was going to have him do a quick check about the palace. However, he never came when I paged him. Since it was so early in the morning, I thought maybe he went to visit his family or was just busy. I even thought maybe he was just asleep after the excitement from the day before, but anyway, I didn't go to his room to check."

She paused for a moment. She saw his brows furrow and his head bend inward toward her.

"Like I was saying," replied Queen Evalyn when she noticed her husband was not going to reply. "It was late, and I eventually went back to sleep. Just a little bit ago, Isabella told me that Alzerion wasn't in his room. So, that's why I'm worried, because what if he has been gone this whole time?"

The queen couldn't hold back the pain any longer, and she let out a slight whimper as tears pricked at her eyes and started to slowly roll down her cheeks.

He patted his wife on the back. "Evalyn, it's not your fault. You didn't know that he would have gone somewhere. Right now, we have something greater to worry about."

"What could be worse?" She tried to wipe away her tears.

"Well … remember how Alzerion acted last night? He—"

"Oh, Francisco, I forgot! How could I have been so foolish?"

"Now, dear, I wasn't trying to get you more upset. You can't blame yourself. However, we do need to find him."

"Do you think that maybe he went to visit his parents?"

"I don't think so, no matter how upset he seemed yesterday. Remember, Alzerion and his father don't get along. In fact, his father basically left his upbringing to his mother. Now, Alzerion likes his mother, so he might visit her, but it's unlikely because she's here." The queen steered her vision to the short woman sipping what looked like cider as she swayed back and forth to a man playing the violin.

"Maybe all we need to do is relax," replied the queen, who was slowly calming down once more. "I mean, Alzerion is responsible and will probably be back soon."

"I hope you're right," said the king. "You know what's at stake. We should stroll around, no matter our worries. We don't want the people to think us rude, or worse, that there *is* something wrong." Queen

Evalyn nodded as she took a deep breath and descended from the throne.

The king wrapped his arm about her waist and escorted them toward the middle of the room, by the rugged looking man playing the violin. As King Francisco spun her around and they waltzed with the other couples in that area, she couldn't help but to let her mind wander. She couldn't forget how much Alzerion really meant to them, and the future of Bachusa. She let out a sweet smile as she glanced at the golden crystal chandelier. The lights shimmering against the stone walls reminded her of the impression of water glistening in the sun.

Once the song ended the king was stopped by a landowner. He wanted to discuss growing patterns so she split up and watched a cheery bunch discussing the latest play they saw. The queen was feeling her spirits return, but she still had a small part of her mind on Alzerion. She was talking to a noble woman when someone tapped her shoulder. Queen Evalyn turned around and saw Isabella. Isabella looked a bit pale and kept diverting her gaze down.

"What's the matter, Isabella?"

"Ma'am, it's not good." It appears that Alzerion is not the only one missing," she said briskly.

Queen Evalyn grabbed Isabella by the hand and pulled her to the side, away from anyone who might overhear their conversation.

"What do you mean? Tell me at once!"

"It's … Aironell. She's not in her room. Maybe she went with Alzerion?" Isabella suggested, then gulped.

"She's missing? No, no, no." She paced around Isabella while digging her nails into the skin around her fingers.

"Your majesty? Maybe it is some sort of coincidence?"

She loved Isabella for trying to calm her, but she knew better. Now it was time to panic. Her lips parted to reveal a half smile and then she turned on her heels and strode toward the thrones. Instead of sitting down she smoothed out her hair around her crown, took a deep breath, and turned to face the room. Isabella followed her and stood at attention nearby. Queen Evalyn pressed her fingers against her vocal chords and muttered an incantation.

"Dearest subjects," Queen Evalyn's voice boomed. It adjusted to reach just the right volume without sounding like a warning. "The king and I have enjoyed our gathering, but I have just received word of some pressing matters. King Francisco will say his closing remarks and we look forward to our next town gathering."

King Francisco sauntered toward his wife, faced the crowd and gave his formal good-bye. As he did that the queen forced her diplomatic smile as she shook hands with her subjects as they passed by her and the king.

Queen Evalyn could feel her cheeks getting warm, and her cerulean blue eyes stung. The moment the last person left the Great Hall, she closed the door, she pressed her eye lids closed, firmly, and blinked. Tears started to cascade down her face as she opened them up. It was like a volcano of hot tears erupting all her feelings and fears. Her beautiful eyes were a bit pink and puffy from crying. King Francisco wrapped an arm around her shoulder.

"Your Majesty, I can send the Royal Army out as a search party if you'd like? We need to stay positive," Isabella bowed her head.

"I think dispatching the army is a great idea," the king stated. "In fact, Isabella, please go now and do that. Alert Quairken, he will know what to do and how to contact the men."

Isabella nodded and left.

King Francisco's muscular arm turned the queen around, and then escorted her to the throne. Queen Evalyn watched as her husband sat down on his throne, next to hers. She saw him staring at her. His eyes narrowed like those of an animal surveying the environment. She needed to regain her calm before she could do anything. She did smooth out her gown and sat down, too.

"Dearest," Francisco broke the silence, "what's wrong? When we parted earlier you seemed to be in better spirits. Now, you look like you are carrying the weight of a thousand mistakes on your shoulder. I want, no, I need to know that you are alright."

She could hear the concern in his tone. She dabbed the wet spots on her cheeks. "Thank you for always being so good to me. There is cause to worry. Actually, if I didn't blame myself, I'd say there is cause to be frantic," Queen Evalyn replied, looking at her husband.

"Alright," he said as he shifted a bit on his throne beside her. "Tell me what happened."

"Isabella went upstairs to wake up Aironell and get her dressed for me, and she had some difficulty."

"What do you mean? Are you trying to tell me she couldn't dress a one-and-a-half-year-old when Alzerion, has no problem?"

"It's not that, dear. It's much more troublesome. She went into Aironell's room and, well, she wasn't there." Now the Queen's tears continued to stream down her cheeks.

"Wait! You mean Aironell is not in her bedroom? Where in the world would she be?" His voice rose.

"I don't know," she sobbed. She just felt the hot tears pouring like a bad rainstorm. She couldn't seem to make them stop, no matter how many times she tried to take a deep breath. Pain and anger oozed off of the king. There was nothing she could do. How she wished she had made a different decision.

"Evalyn, we will find her. I hope I'm not upsetting you, more?"

She could hear his tone shift from anger to sincerity and she looked into his eyes. King Francisco took her hands in his, pressed his lips to her hands, and kissed them gingerly. She felt the warmth of his face against her hands and felt some of her fears steady. This helped her to regulate her breathing. She slowly took her hands back and wiped at her eyes. The king handed her a handkerchief from a small pocket.

"Isabella suggested maybe she's with Alzerion." She sniffled and wiped her tears with the handkerchief.

"I'm not sure. Alzerion would know how worried we would be. Could he have such a lapse in judgement?"

"I don't know." She was there but not really. It was like all the thoughts had finally invaded her whole being. She felt numb. She heard Francisco exhale and watched as he rubbed at his chin.

"At least we sent out help," Francisco broke the silence. "You know Quairken is very good at tracking, too. I am confident that he will find them, whether they are together or not." They sat side by side in stoic silence.

While most of the town was present at the palace, there was a small group of people who did not attend the royal gathering. Alzerion laid on the sofa and did not feel as scared as he did. He was still worried but not quite as frightened since Warren and Ulbrick were not going to kill them. He sat up and watched Aironell, who was still sleeping. He sighed and shook his head. In the passing years Aironell would not know the truth about any of this. None of it seemed right.

"Alzerion," said Warren. "What are you doing?" he asked with narrowed eyes.

"I'm just sitting here," he replied as he turned to see Warren coming out of one of the bedrooms.

"Really, do you always just stare at children?" he asked with a chuckle.

"I'm watching over her. That is my job. When I'm worried or need to think, I can look at her, and everything else just melts away. There's a sort of soothing quality about her. She manages to give me new insights. It's something I can't really explain."

"You have no idea how ridiculous you sound," Warren said with a hearty laugh as he sat down beside Alzerion.

"Anyway, what did you need?"

"Oh, Ulbrick wanted me to see if you were up yet."

"I see. Does he want to properly threaten me today?" Alzerion spat out. He saw Warren's smile vanish and it was replaced by a stern look. *Maybe I should have been more discreet in my distaste for Ulbrick? I guess I'll find out.*

"It's not like that. You know what he has planned as of now. All we ask for is your help."

Alzerion gave him a scrutinizing look, but Warren didn't flinch. Maybe Warren was just trying to watch out for him, like a big brother.

"Alzerion, we just have to be careful. Ulbrick worries about when Aironell comes of age and she is tasked to marry. When the time comes, we want to know that she will cooperate with us, that's all."

That seemed a bit reasonable, he thought. He knew that with his help he might be able to keep the princess safe, but it was a gamble.

"You have no idea just how valuable you actually are," Warren continued. "I mean, you have a strong relationship with her now. Just imagine how strong that bond will be then. She will do anything you ask."

"I feel like a dirty rotten snitch, though," Alzerion said with a downcast gaze at the floor. He spotted the etching of the grooves in the floorboards. "The king and queen have done so much for me, and this is how I repay them? I join forces with a man who wants to bring about the demise of their rule."

"You make things sound so sinister. They will understand because you're protecting their daughter. Nobody has to die for Ulbrick's plans to work. Plus, you might be able to still help them while remaining on Ulbrick's side. For Ulbrick, the ends justify the means. I had to learn that because I had to do things I knew I couldn't do. So, I got the job done my way and still managed the outcome he wanted."

"The ends justify the means, eh?"

"Exactly," said Warren. "See? I can teach you some things."

"Yes, but what's the catch?" he asked with his eyebrows raised a bit.

"Nothing. Except that perhaps we could be friends. When you serve Ulbrick, there's no time for friends. At least, where I'm concerned, and I don't always make the time. However, I can see us getting along quite well."

Alzerion merely stared at Warren, unsure if whether or not he was being serious. Yet he could not detect a glimmer of false sincerity, so he let out a half smirk.

With that, Alzerion said, "Fine, we can be friends. I guess we'll both need the company, and we'll already spend our time together."

They both simply shook hands and talked, for a bit. Alzerion never had something like this. Sure, he would talk to Aironell, but she could not respond to him. Finally, Alzerion thought, *Maybe, just maybe I can have a real friend.*

A bit out of breath from trekking through the different parts of Bachusa, Quairken had the army stop to catch their breath. A few of the men propped their back up against the wall of some of the town buildings. It had been a long day. After much searching, Quairken finally had a lead. An elderly man, selling pamphlets thought he saw a boy that fit Alzerion's description. He did not know where they went but remembered seeing him at some point.

"Men, let's spread out and search the town."

"Quairken, we already searched."

"Is that a groan?" Quairken towered over the soldier who spoke with his thick arms crossed in front of his chest. "Ihon, do you want to return empty-handed and explain to the king why his daughter and our commander-in-training are still missing?" His eyes bore into the teenage soldier.

"No, sir!" He jumped up and straightened his lanky posture.

"I know it has been a long day. I know we searched the town, but a witness swears he saw Alzerion. That means we look again. Understood."

"Yes, sir." Just as Quairken was about to send them in groups, he heard shuffling of feet on the cobblestones. He spun around, hand on the sword at his waist. There he was. Alzerion holding the princess. There they were set against the dark backdrop of the night sky, like a model waiting to be sketched. He watched as Alzerion took a few steps closer and Quairken could see the dirt smudges plastered on Alzerion's face.

"Sir," I'm glad we found you. We were just about to do another round of searches."

"I appreciate your hard-work and effort. In fact, I am grateful to all of you," Alzerion proclaimed while looking around at the whole group.

"Why don't we make our way back?" Quairken placed an arm behind Alzerion and ushered him. "Would you like me to hold Aironell for a bit?"

"Thank you, but I think I'll keep carrying her. She is sleeping and I don't want her to wake until I get her home."

Quairken nodded and then he led the army back to the palace. As they walked, Quairken kept glancing, sideways, checking on Alzerion. His gaze was like a ghost. It was like he was there but not, like there was a vacancy.

"Alzerion, are you alright?" He had to know. He felt like he would burst from the sounds of the boots hitting stones.

"Of course."

Quairken scrutinized Alzerion as they continued the trek back to the palace. He did not believe Alzerion.

With eyes furrowed, Quairken asked, "Are you sure?"

"Quairken, I appreciate your concern; but I don't want to talk about it. It was quite a trying day."

Quairken cocked his head back a bit, then bit at his cheek. He took a breath and said, "Of course. I-I hope you realize that the king and queen have been so worried. You may not owe me an explanation but you sure owe them one." He hoped he didn't sound too hurt, but Alzerion's comment stung a bit.

"Thank you for the warning." Alzerion kicked the last pebbles before they headed onto the dirt path ahead of them. "I'm just not in the mood for an interrogation. I know how that must sound."

"Well, if it helps, I won't do that to you. I mean technically, you're my superior," he replied with a little laugh as he clapped Alzerion on the back.

"That is true. Weird but true," laughed Alzerion.

"I know things don't always make sense, but I trust the king's judgment. What's more, I trust you." Alzerion stopped and stared.

"What's the matter?"

"Thank you. It means a lot to know I have such strong allies."

"I will always have your back. Let's keep moving. The sooner we get you guys back the happier the king and queen will be. Plus, I know I'm beat so I know the rest of the men would love to get some rest."

They continued up the dirt paths. When they reached the palace, the Royal Army headed to their quarters. Quairken looked at Alzerion, patted his shoulder, and strolled into the palace toward his room with Isabella.

Alzerion walked through the big front doors with Aironell. He followed West Wing corridor and approached the king and queen's bed chamber. Then he adjusted Aironell in his arms, knocked on the door, and waited.

"Enter," came King Francisco's deep, commanding voice.

Alzerion ambled into the room and then stood before their bed. He stood like a statue next to a circular table maybe two feet from their bed.

"Alzerion…Aironell you're safe!" The Queen shrieked.

She stood up in her floor-length emerald green silk and lace night-gown and bolted toward them. She took Aironell, hugged and kissed her, and then hugged Alzerion. The king, in turn, embraced his daughter.

"I'm pleased that you two are alright, but my wife and I were very worried," he said with narrowed eyes and a deep tone.

"I could only imagine. I'm very sorry," Alzerion apologized. He watched as they couldn't take their eyes off of Aironell. "I know you both must be very angry, but I assure you that my goal wasn't to worry you."

"Alzerion," the king sighed. "It has been a long day, and yes we are upset, but we should all get some rest." Alzerion watched as the king smiled at Aironell and rubbed her back.

"Tomorrow," the king continued as he shifted his gaze back to Alzerion. "Tomorrow you can tell us what happened and where you were."

"I think that is a great idea," the queen chimed in as she looked up for the first time since they entered the room.

"Very well," Alzerion said as he moved a bit closer. "I'll put Aironell to bed. Then tomorrow we will both be clean and well rested."

The queen was a bit hesitant, but then she kissed Aironell on the forehead and handed her to Alzerion. "Please go *straight* to her room."

Alzerion held Aironell, nodded to the king and queen, and then left their bed chambers. He walked to the East Wing corridor and entered Aironell's room, which was the second door. Alzerion went straight for the washroom to bathe Aironell. He used lavender body wash and shampoo on her. When he was done, he ruffled through her drawers and found a light pink chiffon nightgown with red lacing, then changed Aironell into her new clothes for bed.

Alzerion sat her down and waved his hand, and crackers appeared. He gave the crackers to Aironell and watched her while he ate his own. While Aironell was still occupied with her snack, Alzerion decided to take a brief shower in the washroom. He finished quickly, then snapped his fingers and he was in a navy-blue shirt and dark gray flannel pants for bed. He came back out and saw that Aironell was playing with some of her crackers. She smiled as the cracker pile fell over, and Alzerion laughed.

Then Aironell said, "Alz-on."

That made his lips curl into a wide smile. In the past few months, Aironell had started talking, babbling mostly, but she always had trouble saying his name. *It probably had something to do with the 'z'.*

"It's time for bed," he told her.

Her curls bounced about as she shook her head and continued eating her cracker. Then Alzerion cleaned up the mess and picked her up.

"Alz-on, bed."

He walked over to her crib and laid her down, placed her light pink blanket with red roses embroidered over her, and then read her a book. At the end of the story, Aironell was fast asleep.

As he kissed her on the cheek, he said, "I'm sorry, sweet little princess. I hope someday you can forgive me."

Alzerion was not usually this emotional, but as he said those words, a tear formed in his eye. Then he wiped his eyes, walked to the door, turned off the light, shut the door, and headed up East Wing corridor. As he walked down the corridor, he realized what he needed to do. Then he turned right and opened his bedroom door. He shut the door and started piecing together part of a plan, and when the night waned a bit, he decided to go to sleep.

The king and queen were still distraught from what transpired the day before. They readied for the day and walked down West Wing corridor toward the Royal Dining Room. They entered and sat at the table. The cook maids brought the queen her tea and the king his coffee. They both ate the delicious food in silence waiting for Alzerion to come and explain himself.

Meanwhile, as he was extremely tired from the night before, Alzerion wished he could keep sleeping. Instead he woke up and heard the birds chirping. He went straight to the washroom. When he got back, he put on his black and red royal robes and left his room. He started making his way down East Wing corridor and came to Aironell's door. With a quick motion of his hand, the door opened instantly, and he walked into the princess's room.

He came right up to her bed to see her sweet little face. She sat up in her crib and smiled at Alzerion. She started clapping her hands and said, "Alz-on, Alz-on," in a happy tone.

Alzerion went straight to work and undressed her, putting a pretty floral cerulean blue dress on her. Then he brushed her dirty blonde hair and put a blue ribbon in it. Finally, he was done getting Aironell ready, so he carried her down East Wing corridor toward the West Wing corridor and the grand staircase, putting her down once they were outside the doors to the Royal Dining Room. Alzerion stood in front of those doors and was worried, more about what he was going to say than anything. All he knew was that the king and queen should never know what sinister plans were against them and their daughter. Then he put his hands on the door, hesitated a moment, and then pushed it open.

Aironell bolted in her tottering manner, toward Queen Evalyn, who picked her up as her long, willowy trumpet-shaped sleeves cascaded downward, and she gave Aironell a big embrace. She made certain to position Aironell away from the black necklace that draped over her open neckline. Instead, Aironell sat contentedly on the queen's lap. Then he watched the king, bend over and kiss Aironell's little cheeks, and as he did so, his family pendant brushed against her hair. Then Alzerion strolled over and sat down at the table.

The queen gave Alzerion a small smile and said, "Good morning."

"Thank you," he swallowed. "Good morning to you both." Alzerion looked to both of them.

"What's the matter?" The king inquired while Aironell started to bounce on the queen's knee.

"Nothing, sir."

King Francisco's eyebrow raised a bit. "Alzerion, we may be annoyed, but we don't want to be rude. However, we have some questions."

"Of course," Alzerion moved his hands to his lap, so that they could not see him picking at the skin around his fingers. He took a few slow breaths in through his nose. "It wasn't planned, Your Majesty."

"We didn't think it was," King Francisco admitted. "Alzerion, we only want to know where you were."

This was the moment that Alzerion was dreading. He gulped as he stared at the king who was currently standing behind the queen. He had no idea what to say. *What could possibly explain their absence from the last day?* What could seem convincing and then it hit him. The story flowed through his mind faster than he ever could have expected.

"Well, the other day, when I looked so upset, I decided to go for a stroll around the town. I took Aironell with me so that I wouldn't feel so alone. We just finished our walk and were starting to head back when this fight took place. It started as a mild disruption that turned forceful. It was dangerous as anyone near was being sucked in. A nice married couple saw us, pulled us out of the way, and allowed us to stay with them until it all was better and there was peace on the streets."

"Aironell and I were very tired and fell asleep. It turns out that we slept most of the day away. The people fed us, and when we were ready, I decided to continue our journey back to the palace. That is when the Royal Army found us and escorted us the rest of the way back."

When he was finished he could not believe the words that came out of his mouth. Alzerion never knew why, but he was always able to tell a believable lie, when it mattered most. However, this particular story was his best yet, and if he did not know any better, he probably would have believed it.

"Well, it seems like you two had quite the adventure. But next time go to sleep instead of wandering off," insisted the queen sternly, handing Aironell to King Francisco to hold for a bit.

"Of course, Your Majesty," answered Alzerion. With those words, he strode toward the door.

"Wait, Alzerion," said the king. "Where are you going?"

"I was going to resume my usual duties. I have to go alert Quairken to call the troops for practice."

"If we let you go, you're not going to wander off again, right?" asked the king with one eyebrow raised.

"No, sir, I'm just going to get my job done."

King Francisco exchanged glances with the queen, and before they could interject or keep him longer; he bowed and left the room. As he walked to the door to leave he gave one last glance back as he pulled at the doorknob. *If only they could think of this as playing a game of hide-and-seek.* He knew he couldn't say that to them. Then they would really worry that he lost his sanity, but with that Alzerion left the room.

THE DECISION

The queen craned her neck to the king and he gingerly brushed the side of her cheek.

"Francisco, were we overreacting?"

"I don't think we were. This is our daughter that was missing, plus our future commander of the army. We had a right to be worried. I think Alzerion was just trying to return to some sort of normal."

The queen walked to her husband, picked up Aironell, and cradled her. She brushed Aironell's curls away from her eyes and kissed her forehead. Then the King and Queen put her on the floor to play, and they sat down and finished their meal.

Meanwhile, Alzerion paced the halls. His mind felt like it was pulling double duty. So many possibilities. *Ugh. But how to make them agree?* He scratched his head and forced a smile as servants passed him. When he came to a decision, he peeked around the hall corner, empty. He moved to the hall closest to the Great Hall, and slid into the corner. The king and queen were busy listening to town troubles. Soon, they would be done. Again, his gaze roamed and nobody. He ran up to the closed door and pressed his ear against the wooden door.

He heard a man babbling on and on about which crops yielded a better supply. Someone else jumped in and said it was due to lack of water access. Alzerion rolled his eyes. He wanted to speak with them-before he lost his nerve. There was shuffling of feet as he heard a shrill voice. His eyes bulged as he rubbed his ears. Some dispute with a neighboring market seller. Alzerion backed away from the door and sat on a little bench. Cheeks puffed out like a filled pastry, he tapped the sides of his cheeks. The door creaked open. *Finally*, he grumbled. The last of the townspeople left and Alzerion nodded as he passed and entered the Great Hall.

The king and queen leaned over eyes on the princess. His gaze fixed on her as he stood in the middle of the Great Hall. It was for her. That's what he kept telling himself. He was in this situation to keep her safe. It was like being a scout, spying on each side. As long as Aironell stayed safe.

"Alzerion, Alzerion!"

"Yes, Your Majesty, what can I do for you?" He shook his head-attention focusing on the queen.

"Did you need something?" She looked at him with such focus. He felt like an insect being inspected, closely.

He held his breath for a moment. Exhaling, he bowed his head. "There is something that is bothering me." He had to face them.

"Tell us," demanded King Francisco. Both eyes watched him as he strolled closer.

It was not something they would want to hear, he knew that. He had to convince them. Arms folded behind his back, he paced. There was a pressure rising in his stomach.

"Please don't be upset." He kept shuffling.

"Alzerion, we won't. Please tell us what it is you came here to say."

His gaze lingered on Aironell sitting in her ornate little seat. Tapping her tiny fingers.

"We need to protect Aironell," he just blurted it out. "Some safety precautions like more guards or even distancing her. I have ideas." Breathing deeply, he shifted his gaze up at the king, first.

King Francisco leaned forward. He ignored Aironell's little coo and gazed at him. "I'm curious to know what you came up with." He reached for the queen's hand and squeezed. Queen Evalyn's gaze shifted from the princess to them- only casting her gaze elsewhere to grab hold of the king's arm.

"I, um, I think we should side with caution." Voice getting more matter-of-fact as he spoke. He felt his leg muscles tighten as he stood his ground. "It may sound drastic but I believe distancing the princess is best."

"What, *exactly*, does that mean?" The queen's grip tightened around the king's muscled arm.

King Francisco slid his hand between the queen's hand and his arm. His focus never wavered from Alzerion. "Alzerion, I think some distance and time might be just the thing."

Alzerion straightened up as his breaths steadied. Hands clung to the fabric of his pants as he waited. The queen didn't say anything. *Maybe she was thinking about it.*

"My idea centers on a wide distance. Perhaps sending her away. Safe. Not in Bachusa." He caught the queen's grimace. "I know that sounds a bit extreme," his hands danced about while he spoke. "Aironell clearly isn't safe, here." He moved a few paces closer and cleared his throat. "Your Majesties, what if he could find a new 'home' for the princess. Somewhere she can be cared for-protected-loved."

"That's *our* job," the queen's voice faltered. "Francisco, we can't."

The king's nostrils flared as he gently rubbed his hand against her cheek. He leaned closer and pressed his forehead to hers. "Dearest, we must do what it takes to keep her safe."

Queen Evalyn shook her head. Breaking her connection with the king. She stood up and grabbed Aironell. Rocking her slowly, as she pressed her close. King Francisco opened his mouth, but it closed just as quick. Instead he darted his gaze back to Alzerion. "Explain, please." His voice was low.

Alzerion shifted glances between the queen and the king. "A safe haven. Somewhere not in this realm. The Other Realm, perhaps."

Silence. Queen Evalyn paced around as she lightly bounced the princess. The king, however, didn't break his gaze so Alzerion continued. "Think about it, your majesty." He took slight steps as he laid it out for them. "Aironell would stay away until she's sixteen. She can't take the throne until she's of age. Her safety here has already been rocky, at best." He swallowed.

"Francisco, you cannot possibly be entertaining this?" She shot him a glare as she continued to hold Aironell close. "She's our daughter."

"Exactly," the king snapped back. King Francisco stood practically flinging himself away from the throne. His eyebrows furrowed. "Evalyn, I know that. I know of all our hopes. Our dreams for her," His voice cracked. He cleared his throat as he strode over toward the queen.

"Then how can you think Alzerion's proposal a good one?" The queen's eyes teared up- lips trembled- as she kissed Aironell on the head.

Alzerion gulped. This was a sight. In his years here, they never fought. Not really. Not like he remembered from his own parents. He jabbed his thumbnail into his index finger. *Please, please let them understand. Let them get through this difficult part.*

"If you love her, you won't do this."

The king looked like he had been stabbed, right in the gut. His face reddened. "How dare you think I don't love her. If I could love her into safety, I would." He paced back and forth and then faced the queen. "But we can't, Evalyn. Knowing that makes me, ugh." He backed away from them. "Alzerion's proposal isn't great. I admit that. But this is the reality. We can't keep her safe." He spun around and faced the queen. Wincing, he continued. "Sending her away. This safe haven. That will protect our daughter. Our *only* child. Our heir."

King Francisco rubbed his nose and then turned to Alzerion. He swallowed. Took a breath. "How do we do this? Someone must go with her, I assume."

Alzerion nodded. His mouth was taut as he glanced at the queen, still clutching Aironell. Little princess, smiling away at her mother. He felt a twinge in his chest. He pushed up his sleeves as he looked back at the king. "First, we need to have two trustworthy people go with her. Loyal. Caring. They put the Crown above all else."

King Francisco's face was firm, unyielding but he nodded. Alzerion continued. "They will act as her parents. Teach her manners and magic." He paused.

He ran through the checklist in his mind. He hit on all the points. *It was for her, that little girl to grow up and rule; one day.* Now they had to agree. Queen Evalyn still had a sour expression. King Francisco ambled over to his girls. Alzerion looked down. Giving them a bit of privacy.

It was silent. No boots against the floor. No yelling. Then there was the sound of sniffling. "There, there," the king's voice was soft. Calming.

Alzerion glanced up, smiling. King Francisco had his arms wrapped around the queen, rubbing her head. He glanced back down.

"Alzerion." A voice, after what seemed like hours. He looked up and moved toward the queen. "I don't like this plan." There was quiet hesitation. "My heart says no, but if I think logically, then I can see the intentions."

Alzerion clasped his hands, tight. Nodding as she spoke. A weight lifted within.

The king moved his arms around Aironell, as he pulled her into his chest. "We should get on with it. Aironell will need her things packed." His watery eyes wavered on the princess.

"Of course. I will ready her things." He turned and left the room. Once he was in Aironell's room he waved his hand and some bags cloth bags appeared. He went to work.

Meanwhile the king wrapped his arms back around his wife. Aironell squished between them.

"I'm sorry," the queen's voice was uneven. "I didn't mean to say—"

"It's forgiven." He placed a soft peck on her cheek as he bounced with Aironell. He moved, slowly, toward his throne. "It was the grief talking." She bounded toward him and clutched his hand as she sat on her throne.

"I just want what's best." He could see her eyes fighting the pull of tears. He sat down and handed Aironell to her. The queen clung to her. "Momma loves you," she whispered.

He patted her shoulders. "While Alzerion is packing, we should bring in the servants."

Her eyes darted at him. "Already?"

"We must. The servants will need to know. Then we can make our choice."

The queen closed her eyes as she rested her head against Aironell. "I just want to soak up every last moment with her."

"We will," he swallowed. "We will feel worse if we don't give this the consideration it needs." Aironell grasped at the queen's fingers as she giggled.

She sighed. "You're right. Bring them in."

King Francisco snapped his fingers and motioned his hand out toward the small brass bell positioned in the opposite corner. The bell rang out. Then silence. He leaned toward his wife and whispered in her ear.

She nodded. "I couldn't agree more."

Soon there was commotion and shuffling of feet against the floor as the door creaked open. Any servant living in the palace was there.

King Francisco stood and looked out. "We have an important announcement." His voice was firm as he kept scanning the crowd before them. "I'm sure you have heard about the most recent kidnapping of the princess."

There were low murmurings among the group as they looked to each other.

"We vowed to protect her. We made a decision." His eyes lingered on Isabella and Quairken, for a moment. His mouth flattened. He scoured for the right words.

"How can we help?" Isabella bowed.

"I'm sure we could always increase guards around the princess." Quairken stood, solid next to Isabella. Other servants chattered suggestions.

The king spoke deeper. Silence crept across the Great Hall. "You are all so kind." He pressed his hand against his heart. He inched closer to the queen, who was cradling Aironell. His gaze focused on his little girl. "We are sending Aironell away."

"What?"

King Francisco moved behind his wife and peered out. So many voices. Worry. Confusion. The only certainty was that he had to clarify. "No details will be given about where she will be going. Just know that she will be safe. far from Bachusa. Freedom. No burdens or pressures from those who plot against us. She will survive."

The voices from the servants rose. King Francisco gripped the queen's shoulder as he stared out.

"When will she return?" Quairken stepped forward. He clung to Isabella's hand.

"Not until she's of age," said the queen.

Quairken went to speak, but this time no words came out. Instead he shook his head and looked down. Isabella rubbed his back as she pulled him closer.

"We wanted you all to know. You may go about your duties." King Francisco watched as they exchanged glances and spoke. He clambered past his wife and a few servants until he placed a hand on Isabella and Quairken. "Wait."

They turned around. King Francisco watched as the rest of the servants left. He motioned toward the queen. He heard her dress ruffle as she approached.

"We didn't mean any disrespect, your majesties," Isabella spoke softly.

"Nonsense," Queen Evalyn smiled. "You both are not in any trouble."

Quairken's head tilted as he glanced from the queen to the king.

The king smiled at them. "We have chosen the two of you to go with Princess Aironell."

"Us?" Isabella's voice wobbled.

"You both possess great loyalty," King Francisco said. Queen Evalyn took a quick breath. "We believe that you both will love and nurture her as we would have."

"Of course, your majesties," Quairken nodded.

"We will cherish her." Isabella added as she placed her hands on her cheeks.

King Francisco patted the queen on the back. She kissed Aironell on her cheek as she stepped toward Isabella, placing Aironell in her arms.

"Take care of our little girl." Her ones were soft but stern. There was no missing her meaning.

"Of course," Quairken replied. He gazed down at Aironell cradled in Isabella's arms.

Alzerion stepped out for some fresh air. The crisp air washed over him. He needed it. A reprieve from the commotion. The palace had been total chaos. Servants prepping. The king busied himself with the finer details of finding Aironell's safe haven. Townspeople asking questions like; why he hadn't been in town or where has the princess been. He ran his hands through his hair. *It would pay off.* At least that was what he told himself.

Today was going to be tough. He closed his eyes. Letting in the silence- the calm- as another breeze wiped at his face. Alzerion breathed in and out. He opened his determined eyes and headed back in. An instant rush of emotions was everywhere. Plastered on the servants' faces. Hanging in the air. He picked up his pace as he entered the Great Hall.

He noticed the king and queen were already on their thrones, and Aironell sat on Queen Evalyn's lap. He walked over to his seat to the right of the king and sat down. The queen had a somber expression. He felt it. It cut deep into his heart. Silence passed until the doors flung open. Isabella and Quairken bowed and then came closer.

"Thank you, once again." King Francisco held out his hand to Quairken.

"Of course, your majesty." Quairken nodded.

The queen's eyes were puffy with a slight discoloration. She sniffled. "I pray that time moves quickly."

Alzerion quietly strolled to the other side of the queen.

"Be good, little one." Alzerion rubbed her chin.

Aironell grabbed his finger and giggled. "Alz-on."

He felt exhaustion wash over him as he held out his hands. The queen placed Aironell in his arms. He gazed upon her and a crushing force pierced him. He forced a smile as he held her up over his head. She giggled as he soared her through the air. Finally, he brought her in and hugged her. Alzerion handed her back to the queen.

She hugged and kissed Aironell. Tears flowed down her face as she made her way to Isabella. "Don't be scared, darling. You *will* see us again." She placed Aironell in Isabella's arms.

King Francisco wrapped an arm around his wife. He pulled her in, close. The king looked to Alzerion, handed him an envelope, and nodded.

Alzerion, clutching the envelope, handed it to Quairken. "This should cover any expenses." Then he waved his hand and their bags appeared. Each one full for the journey. Alzerion honed in on Quairken, "Take care of her. We are all counting on you."

Quairken nodded, "Yes, sir." He bent his head toward Alzerion. "Watch out for the king and queen, eh?"

"Will do." Alzerion and Quairken gripped each other by the forearm.

He craned his neck to look at the king and queen. The queen's face was buried into the king's chest. Sobbing was all he could hear. Alzerion let go of Quairken and stepped back. He watched as they gathered their belongings. Then Quairken nodded. Isabella held Aironell close. Alzerion lip trembled as he raised his hands. He made an arch up and around them. There was a silvery light that shone through, like a swirling storm of silver and white. Quairken and Isabella stepped forward and were gone.

Alzerion sat on his bed. He felt drained physically and emotionally all the time. He clutched his hair against his left temple. Months passed. Alzerion was grateful to be done with his schooling. Instead there was, Ulbrick, *ugh*, he groaned. Alzerion flung himself back. Head hitting the fluffy pillow. He found he was stretched thin, even with no school or the princess to watch over. *Aironell.* That piercing feeling against his skin. Down to his bones. Just about four years. So much time. Army trainings.

Meetings with Ulbrick and Warren. He sat up and glanced out his window. He didn't need to look out to see the consequences. He could feel it. It rippled through him like the weight of rocks crushing down on him. Bachusa was hurting. Aironell's return would set things right. *Maybe a visit. He was overdue. Two years since he last checked in on them.* He took a breath as he made up his mind.

THE COVER-UP

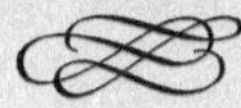

Isabella stood against the doorjamb watching Airon. She was dancing as she watched the television. *Sweet little princess,* she thought. She saw Quairken wrinkle his nose as he walked past, her gaze momentarily followed him. Watching as his rock-brown khakied bottom went into the kitchen. Isabella strolled to Airon and handed her a bowl.

"Thank you, mommy." Her voice was so sweet. Her face lit up as she grabbed the cracker shaped like a tiny bear Isabella blew her a kiss and followed after Quairken.

Isabella strolled the short distance from the living room to the kitchen. Instantly distracted by the scent wafting off Daniel's pale blue shirt. *Earthy tones mixed with mint. Mm.* She loved how the clothes here were much more flattering. There he stood by the little white kitchen table. A talk was coming. She could sense it.

"Isabella, I'm concerned." His voice was low. He moved closer to her.

She rolled up her blue plaid sleeves as she sat on a stool at the kitchen island.

"Qu, I mean Daniel." Such a hard habit to break, even after nearly four years. "Daniel, why haven't they contacted us?"

"

"Right?" He tapped his fingers on the wood of the kitchen island. "We have had no news for almost two years."

"Exactly," replied Isabella. "It doesn't seem like them not to wonder about their daughter. It has been a little over four years. Should we be fearful that Bachusa has been taken over by the growing evil?"

"Honey, we shouldn't worry, not yet. Odds are they will send Alzerion, and it's not likely that all three of them would have been killed." He paused rubbing a hand against his chin. "Alzerion, well, he's a fighter and quite good at persuasion."

"What does that have to do with anything?" she raised an eyebrow. "Who cares if he's a good talker?" She slid her hands against her black jeans.

"It's obvious," he said. "They would never do something drastic without talking with him. It's likely that things are just getting worse and their attentions are needed elsewhere."

"I hope you're right about this, Daniel." Isabella got up and faced the big window. Her hands clasped behind her back, she stared. Then she paced back and sat in a stool next to her husband. They were interrupted by the sound of the doorbell.

"Were you expecting company?" Isabella glanced at Daniel, searching for an answer.

"No, I wasn't. I can't imagine who this could be."

As they started walking into the living room, Airon stood up and ran to the door.

"Honey, let your father answer the door," Isabella warned.

The last thing she needed was for something bad to happen to Airon.

"Oh, please. I want to get it," Airon begged with her hands folded under her chin as her eyes sparkled.

"Well, alright," said Daniel.

"Hun," Isabella said, glaring.

Daniel whispered to her, "It's hard to say no. Plus, we will be right here."

"Go ahead, Airon," Isabella said with a forced smile.

With those words, Isabella and Daniel moved closer to the door, just in case. Airon reached up on her toes and pulled the door open. When the door opened, Isabella was beaming.

Alzerion. Isabella was speechless as Daniel shook his hand. She couldn't get over it. He was taller. Fuller. She gulped as he ran his hands through his brown disheveled hair.

"May I come in?" said Alzerion. "You know, it's not very polite to make people stand in the doorway."

His voice was deep, yet pleasant. She blinked, twice. Taking in his appearance. He even came dressed in dark blue jeans and a black sweater with a white collared shirt to accent.

"Of course," Airon opened her arms. Alzerion nodded as he passed and stepped into the living room.

"Thank you." Alzerion kept his gaze on Airon. "You look like such a little princess."

She giggled as she spun around. The hem of her ivory and light-pink laced dress spinning.

Daniel grabbed her hand and they sat down on the sofa. Isabella just soaked it all in.

Alzerion knelt down next to Airon and said, "What's your name?"

"My name is Airon. How about you?"

He grinned. "Alex."

Airon leaned closer. "Do you like to play games?"

"Of course, I do. What kind of person wouldn't?"

She giggled. "Would you like to join me for tea and cookies? I helped make the cookies, and I've been told that this is what you do when there's company."

"I'd love to," Alzerion replied with a small smile.

Alzerion stood up and Airon took his hand. She tugged him toward the little mahogany table set up for tea, off to the side of the room. She chatted for an hour. Isabella licked her lips and rested against her husband, as they continued to watch.

"Airon, thank you for my tea."

"How about the cookies?" she stared right at him.

He laughed. "They were yummy. I love chocolate chip."

"Me too!" She took a bit of another cookie. Crumbs falling onto the table.

"Thank you for letting me join you," he spoke in hushed tones. "But I must speak with your parents."

"Alright." Her chin tilted down, frowning.

"What's wrong?" He handed her a napkin.

Airon wiped her mouth before speaking. "Grown-ups usually only want to see my parents. I just wish we could play."

He chuckled. "I did have a good time. I'm sorry." He frowned. "It's just, well, been a long time since I saw your parents."

Airon nodded. He stood up and looked to Isabella and Daniel.

"Why don't we talk in the kitchen?" Daniel motioned toward the walkthrough. Alzerion followed him in.

Isabella kissed Airon on the forehead. "Enjoy your movie, sweet pea."

As she entered the kitchen and moved closer to Daniel and Alzerion at the little white table. It was the farthest they could get from the living room.

"She really is a charming young lady," Alzerion said as Isabella sat down.

"She's as perfect as they get." Quairken spoke low and quick. Isabella craned her neck to make sure Airon wasn't watching. Satisfied, she snapped her fingers and three cups and a pitcher of water appeared before her.

"I get that feeling," Alzerion leaned back against the chair. Isabella poured the water and handed a glass to each of them. "The king and queen will be happy to know she is doing well." He took a sip.

Daniel swallowed some of his water. "Speaking of the king and queen, why haven't they contacted us or sent you in so long?"

Alzerion halted.

"What?" Isabella fixed her eyes on him.

Alzerion's gaze shifted between the two of them and the opening between the rooms. He tapped his finger against the table as he looked back.

"Alzerion," Isabella whispered. "What aren't you telling us?"

"Are you keeping something?" Daniel raised his brow.

Alzerion sighed. "Alright. You win." He leaned forward. "Things have been tricky in Bachusa. I wasn't able to come sooner. People are pushing back against the king and queen."

Isabella placed her hands over her mouth as she listened. "How did it get so bad?"

Alzerion gestured at them. They both moved in closer. *It was like they were in on some sort of conspiracy,* she thought.

"Rebels," Alzerion said.

"I'm sorry. Don't think I heard you right." Quairken frowned.

Alzerion was still, unnaturally so as he stared at them. "No. you heard correct. There's a rebellion back home. The leader wants to rid the town of our king and queen."

"Wha—"

"Power. He wants control. That's what we are dealing with."

"How bad is it now?" Isabella's lips pressed together as her eyebrows shifted down.

"The king and queen are feeling at an all-time low. But they did stave off a small coup a few months ago. For now, things are…manageable."

"What do you mean?" Daniel tilted his head. His gaze fixed on Alzerion.

Alzerion took another quick sip of his drink. He licked his lips and continued. "The rebels can't just oust the king and queen."

"Wait. Why not? Isn't that how it is done?" Isabella looked to her husband and then Alzerion.

Daniel shook his head side-to-side. "Not always, dearest." He turned to Alzerion. "What is holding them back?"

Alzerion bit his lip and then stood up.

"Well?" Daniel's gaze followed him.

Alzerion paced around the room and angled himself. He took a few steps closer. One hand rested on his hip and the other pointed into the emptiness of the walkway.

"I don't understand." Isabella stood.

"Are...you...kidding?" Daniel rushed to Alzerion and pulled him close. "No."

Isabella saw the veins throb in her husband's neck. She mouthed, what.

Alzerion swallowed. "It's...Airon," he mouthed. Isabella shook her head as she moved closer to them. Daniel wrapped an arm around her. She felt his warmth ash she tried to find the words.

"They won't come for her. They have no idea where she is or how to find her. *She* is what's keeping the rebels at bay. Ousting the king does nothing. He has an heir. They could never hold real power, not as long as there is a spare to take his place."

Isabella took a breath. *At least there was time. Aironell, she had time before any of this would be her burden.* She looked down.

"I never thought it would get like this," Daniel said. "At least she is safe."

"Don't worry. I'm working with the king and queen to try to keep the peace. The army is training, often, just in case. Right now, it is a wait and see kind of situation."

"Of course," Isabella struggled to find the words.

Alzerion patted them both on the shoulder. "At least I can tell them how Airon is doing. That will be sure to cheer them up. They were getting restless for my visit."

Alzerion started out of the kitchen into the dining room. Isabella and Daniel followed close behind. He spun around. "Magic," he whispered. "How has that been going?"

Daniel nodded. "She knows she has special talents. Right now, we are working on getting her to understand that not everyone has the same abilities. It is slow going."

"We don't want her to know too much and tell one of her friends," Isabella added.

Alzerion nodded. "I hope it progresses soon. We are counting on you both to help her with this. She will need to know how to wield her magic." He looked at Daniel. "Just like we wield our swords."

Daniel nodded.

"I must go." Alzerion shook Daniel's hand. He glanced to make sure Airon was still in the other room. Then he waved his arm and disappeared in a puff of red smoke. Isabella walked the short distance to the door. Opened it quietly and then shut it.

REASSURANCE

Meanwhile, back at the palace, the queen sat waiting. She held on to her husband's hand. Her eyes watching the door-never lingering. Every so often she felt the comfort of Francisco squeeze her hand.

"Evalyn, we have been staring far too long." He tried to pull her close but she did not budge.

"Francisco, I-I, just can't." Her voice quaking.

"I'm sure Alzerion will bring us a good report."

She waved at him. still her eyes never left the door. She felt worn and Alzerion held the key to raising her spirits.

"Evalyn, you're not the only one—"

The door creaked open. The queen gripped both sides of her throne. Alzerion walked toward them. She scanned his face. Nothing. *He was too good at keeping his feelings in check.*

Alzerion walked toward the thrones, bowed, and then stood before them.

"Well, what kind of news do you bring?" King Francisco broke the silence.

The queen stared him down, like someone seeking the truth. He took a breath.

"I'm fairly certain that Your Majesties will be pleased with my news."

Queen Evalyn let out a sigh of relief. Like the sucking doom cloud, hovering, was erased. "Please tell us." She grinned.

"It turns out you both have a very sweet, polite, wonderful, and engaging six-year-old."

"That's wonderful!" The king boomed. He looked to the queen. She couldn't stop beaming but finally was able to break her fixed view. She gazed back at her husband.

"How are Isabella and Quairken?" King Francisco asked.

"Splendid. They were concerned about why I hadn't been down in a while. All in all, things seem well."

"How does she look?" The queen clasped her hands together.

"Isabella?" Alzerion chuckled.

"No." She slapped her leg. "Aironell, of course."

"Well, she's cute. Her hair has grown so much. She has bouncy curls."

"Tell us more," Queen Evalyn pleaded.

He pursed his lips. Alzerion scratched his head and then moved within touching distance. "If I may?" He reached his hands out. Neither stopped him so he continued. He placed a hand on each of their foreheads, just below their crowns. He closed his eyes.

The queen's eyes watered. She saw her. Aironell. Her hair. Her soft rosy complexion. Her beautiful cerulean blue eyes. Then it was gone. Alzerion stepped back.

"Thank you." King Francisco smiled. "That was much appreciated."

"Oh, Francisco." Queen Evalyn laid her head on his shoulder.

"I know." He rubbed the side of her face. "She'll be home again. Don't forget that."

She sniffled.

"Is it alright if I leave for a bit?" asked Alzerion.

"Where are you going?" The king asked.

"I'd like to walk through town.

"Of course, enjoy."

Alzerion bowed and left.

A SURPRISE INSIGHT

Then with that statement, Alzerion walked down West Wing corridor and went out the front door. Then he proceeded down Matters Lane and looked back at the palace to make sure nobody was watching him. Next, he turned onto Abandon Alley and came to the house that started all the nonsense.

He knocked on the door and someone unexpected opened it. It was not Ulbrick, whom he disgusted, but rather a short woman in a simple pale blue dress with pudgy cheeks. She also had light brown hair. However, the woman's hair was mousy, graying, and a mess most of the time. He was a bit surprised to see her. He never expected to find his mother here. Has she been watching out for him? Over the years, they rekindled that bond that was once cracked.

"Mother, is it really you?" asked Alzerion.

"Of course, it is," answered Melinda. "I missed you."

"I missed you too, but how do you know about this place?" he asked as he closed the door. They continued as they traversed back toward town square.

"Did you think that I wouldn't know where my son spends most of his days?"

"Well, it never really occurred to me before." Alzerion laughed as he walked arm in arm with his mother. In an instant he felt Melinda stop. When he turned to face her, he could make out the lines of worry crease her forehead.

She stooped toward him and cleared her throat. "Alzerion, why are you helping Ulbrick?"

"Mother, I didn't have a choice," he said in a low tone. He glanced around before continuing. Then he sat at the nearest wooden bench and motioned for Melinda to sit, too. "He kidnapped Aironell, and it was the only way to save her."

"What do you mean Aironell?" Her gaze narrowed. "You never really spent much time around girls, but I'm not complaining. Is she your girlfriend?" she asked with a gleam in her eye.

"Mother, no, that would be wrong. Aironell is only six years old. She's the princess. Don't you remember?"

"Oh, right, yes, of course," she nodded. "Well six would be too young for a girlfriend."

"Don't worry about it. I bet most of the town has forgotten her by now."

"You're probably right." Then her eyes widened. "Wait, does Ulbrick have her?"

"No, she's some place safe. For now, at least."

She looked at him, her eyes narrowing.

"What's wrong?" Her hand pressed his chin upward to scan his face, as a whole.

"Nothing," he shrugged as he stood up.

"You're lying to your mother," Melinda stood next to him. "There is something missing. You seem like you're not really there."

"I feel fine. What do you mean … missing?"

"Look around. Here in town you see it. Life is happening. Over there you can see a young couple having a picnic. By the lilac bushes outside the café, you can see the owner and his wife squabbling. Alzerion, I'm concerned about your lack of a life. You're eighteen and I don't see that you've started fulfilling your basic needs."

Alzerion felt a warmth around his ears. He swore that they probably turned a slight pink color. He gazed around. People looked happy. Why didn't he? He couldn't really tell her. He hated when these conversations came up. He knew what she was going to say.

"Mother, I assure you that I'm perfectly content. There is nothing more that I need or want, right now."

"That's not true, honey. However, I'm talking about love. You know, possibly a wife that will someday give me grandchildren." She grinned as she sat on a marble seat outside the flower shop.

Alzerion looked at his mother and saw the yearning in her eyes. "Mother, I don't know. Most women bore me. There isn't anyone that I have met that I'm interested in."

"I'm sure they are not all bad, honey. You need to at least try. You can't go through life without a companion."

"Why not? I don't need someone. I don't need a woman." His face was flushed and he could feel it creep across his cheeks. He would give anything to end this conversation.

"Alzerion, a woman you love should be like your other half. They are meant to be a partner."

"Let me see if I understand you. If I don't find a woman, then I'll be messed up?" he asked between gritted teeth.

"Well, I guess for lack of a better word, yes. You lack a source of happiness and inspiration. Dear, don't look so skeptical?"

"I'm not sure if I agree with you, that's all. I think it's all a bunch of nonsense." He crossed his arms across his chest.

"Alzerion! I know I didn't raise you to be so pessimistic." His nostrils flared. She was pressing his last nerve. *He spent most of his life with the royal family, not her.* "Nobody knows why but the bond between two lovers, well, it is strange. It brings out a different side of you."

"How could you not know?" He kept gazing down at his boot tapping incessantly against the stones. "You're married, so you must have some clue."

"There is something you must know, dear. Your father is very different than when we first were together. He has become a changed man, determined to do whatever he pleases." He heard the sadness in her tone.

"What do you mean?"

"I mean, I love your father … but the man I fell in love with doesn't exist anymore. He has changed for the worse. I want you to be happy. At one time, your father and I were blissfully happy. I can't even tell you what changed to make it end. However, you're our only child, and I would like to see you as happy as possible."

"I see. I'm sorry, Mother. I can only try, but I'm always busy."

"Alzerion, that is very telling."

"What do you mean?"

"Well, something is clearly bothering you, whether you want to admit it or not."

"I spoke with someone earlier and I felt lonely when I left."

"Well, you should keep talking to that girl because she probably holds the key to your heart."

Alzerion chuckled as he shook his head.

Melinda reached out and held his hands together. "I mean it."

"I know you do. For now, I must go."

"When will I see you again?"

"I have a meeting, but you could always come to the palace or next time in town. You know the king and queen wouldn't mind."

"Very well, dear. Good luck with your meeting, and hopefully I shall see you soon."

With those words, Melinda disappeared in a thick smoke encasement. Alzerion walked back to Abandon Alley.

THE MEETING

Alzerion arrived at Abandon Alley and knocked on the first door he saw. Almost instantly, Ulbrick opened the door.

"Come in, Alzerion. We have much to discuss," he said in his signature hoarse voice.

"Do we now?" Alzerion countered as he walked into the house.

"Yes, we do! Don't mock me. I'm still not happy with you." Alzerion could hear a bite behind his words.

"Why? What have I done?"

"I'm sure Aironell's disappearance had something to do with you. Despite you saying that it wasn't, repeatedly. Don't think that I'm dumb enough to underestimate you, Alzerion, I know better than that."

"So, what if I did do something?" He sat down on the couch and propped his legs on the tiny square table. "She's gone now, and you have the throne wide open. You know as well as anyone the law of the land."

"I do, but what does that have to do—" Ulbrick stopped when he realized what Alzerion was getting at. "You're talking about how the royal child has to take the throne when she's sixteen, right?" Ulbrick bent over Alzerion and swatted at his legs.

"Of course, and according to the law, she has to come back to Bachusa." Alzerion removed his legs from the table and leaned forward, and continued. "In the meantime, you can start planning your next move. If Aironell doesn't return and assume her place as future queen, then the townspeople can revolt. Therefore, you might not have to do anything except simply be patient."

"That sounds like a promising plan," noted Warren.

"Warren, I didn't know you were here."

"Sorry. I was in the other room going through some papers. I think that sounds promising." Warren nudged Alzerion over with a smile. Then he sat down beside Alzerion.

Ulbrick sighed. "Can you two stop playing like little children? Maybe that plan may work. However, I'm going to put more stress on the king and queen."

"Don't you think they have enough to contend with?" pleaded Alzerion.

"Obviously not, and don't forget that you made a deal with us, so you're ours," Ulbrick snapped back.

"Alzerion," said Warren. "It's best not to fight this. In the end, when it's all over, you can be free and will never have to hear from us again."

"As promising as that sounds, unfortunately I will always have to hear about you." He had this dry bitterness in his mouth, as he spoke. "Anyway, how can I forget that you forced me to make a deal with you, Ulbrick? It is something that I'll never forget. However, since I'm here and have no choice but to help, what is your next move?"

"I want the rebellion to spread its seed of chaos and panic, and I need you to take something from the palace."

"That doesn't make any sense. How does that tie into anything?"

"I'd like it to look like someone is sneaking in and out of the palace. This way the king and queen would be on edge, and they won't expect a revolt, when it happens."

"Alright. What do you want me to take?"

"Take the necklace that Aironell used to wear when she was younger."

"You're terrible. Queen Evalyn will lose it if she finds out the Lost Hope was taken!"

"Exactly. I want to make sure nothing goes right for them. That way they will forfeit or even better; make sure that Aironell returns. If she is truly their hope, then they would make certain to bring her back to try to fix things."

"Fine! I'll do it tonight." Alzerion felt his blood start to freeze. He had this coldness that crept over him. He quickly looked around, but no windows were open. *It must be them,* he decided. He felt his lip curl as he gazed at them, flatly, as Warren moved and sat by Ulbrick. The two continued to chat about more logistics to the plan.

Alzerion swallowed, hard, as he stood and made his way to the door. He took one more glance back at them, and he felt this tightening creep over his body. He felt itchy. He knew he had to get away from them. So Alzerion left and once he was outside the house, he waved his hands and in a puff of red smoke, he disappeared.

"Well Airon is content watching her show." Daniel admitted as he strolled into the kitchen.

"Why do you think he left in a rush?" Isabella said while stirring noodles in a medium-sized pot.

Daniel shrugged. "I'm not sure, honey, but he must be busy, which would explain a lot."

"It's just ... odd." Isabella looked up at that moment. She saw her husband was sitting at the small kitchen table, folding the napkins into flowers. They looked like the lotus flowers that could be found floating on the pond, back at the palace garden.

"Isabella, what do you mean, that explains a lot?"

She saw him continue to fold. "Well, other than the king and queen, Alzerion loved Aironell the most. I'm surprised he didn't stay and talk with her just a bit longer."

"I see what you mean. Do you think that Alzerion has just as much on his plate as the king and queen?"

"He must," she replied as she strained the noodles and placed them in a bowl on the table next to the tomato and garlic butter sauce.

"Mom! Dad!" came Airon's voice from the living room.

Isabella quickly grabbed a towel to dry her hands and then walked to the door. She cracked it open, to see Airon. "Yes, sweet pea? What can we do for you?"

"Who's coming?"

"Honey, what do you mean?" Isabella saw Airon look around. Her gaze was focused on something, but she didn't know what. "Airon, what do you mean?"

Airon paused, momentarily. "I feel it, Mother. Somebody is coming. You usually tell me that I should trust my instincts."

At this moment Daniel strode in. Isabella tilted her head toward Airon, and Daniel nodded.

"You should *always* trust them, dear, but I'm not sure who is coming," Daniel patted her back.

Isabella smiled a bit as she knew that Airon was finally starting to hone in on her magical abilities. Then, after a brief moment, there came a knock on the front door.

"See? I told you someone was coming," Airon said as she jumped up and down. Then she ran to the door while Isabella followed close behind her. They opened the door and in front of them stood a new face. She looked nice enough.

"Hey, there. I'm Mrs. Turner, and I'm your new neighbor." Isabella noted that she had a silvery voice. It was rather pleasant, clear, and light-hearted.

"Oh, come on in," Isabella ushered her forward with a wave of her hand. As she escorted her into the house she saw that Mrs. Turner wore a stylish pleated dress and designer ankle boots. "I'm Mrs. Henderson, and this is my husband, Daniel, and our daughter, Airon," she pointed as Daniel walked over to join them. Daniel gave Mrs. Turner a quick shake of her smooth hand.

"It's nice to meet you. My husband and I just moved in. I thought it would be nice to introduce myself to the neighbors. Also, I have a little girl, too. Her name is Emilia. Maybe the girls can play together some-time?" Mrs. Turner smiled, wide. Then she tucked a loose strand of her black hair behind her ear.

"Oh, of course. That would be great." They looked down at Airon who was beaming.

"Oh, thank you. My husband and I don't want Emilia to have a hard time making friends." She clasped her hands together. "Anyway, I will call about the play date, but I probably should get going, seeing as it's late and we should be eating dinner soon."

"Of course, no problem."

They said their good-byes and closed the door.

BREAK-IN

Back at the palace, the king and queen were talking. Alzerion walked past their room, heard them, and decided to place his ear to the door to listen.

"It's just ... so hard," said Queen Evalyn in a disgusted tone.

"I know, dearest, but we have to figure something out," King Francisco sighed.

Alzerion noticed a small crack and realized the door wasn't closed all the way. So, he peaked through. He saw Queen Evalyn resting her head on her husband's chest, breathing him in. He knew that the queen always found comfort when she laid her head on the king. If there was anything obvious about their behavior, it was that the king and queen were getting tired and worn out. He could see it on their faces. They both had lines that greased their forehead and this heaviness about their eyes. He hated to see them look so defeated. They always treated him so well. He felt this pain in his chest, as he thought about what he was about to do.

In the end, it hurt Alzerion even more because he knew he was adding to their troubles. This whole scenario was his fault. His idea. With his help, their troubles would continue to grow before they would end. He started to walk away to his bedroom, and he knew he did not want to cause them anymore heartache. He continued passed West Wing corridor, entered his room, and sat on his bed.

"All I wanted to do was help them," Alzerion said to nobody but himself. "I thought getting Aironell out of harm's way was best. But now… her parents are in more trouble than ever. All of their problems are my fault, damn it! I have to make things right; I need to figure something out."

Then Alzerion stood up and picked up a pitch-black leather-bound bag. He walked out into the corridor and started trudging through the palace. He went into a room that had been Aironell's playroom, but now it contained all reminders that she ever existed in the palace.

Alzerion peered around the cramped room. He knew what he was looking for, but to find it was a different story. It was a necklace that had been lost since Aironell was at the palace. It was the one he gave her on the day she was born. Somehow, in the midst of all the planning, packing, and trying to protect Aironell, the necklace had disappeared.

It had an ornate exterior. The engravings were quite detailed. The necklace became the symbol for Lost Hope. For the queen, the hope of being with her little girl seemed far away, like something that would never happen again. While looking for the Lost Hope, Alzerion noticed Aironell's baby blanket. It was the one that she loved most. He had given it to her. He hated looking in this room because it brought back sad memories. As if that could not be bad enough, it always made him think about the memories he would never get back.

Alzerion felt this piercing feeling in his chest. Was it his guilt? His own grief? He shook his head. These were the times that he had wondered what it would have been like if he had helped raise Aironell, as was the original plan. The painful memories of his past flooded through his mind and made him want to burst into tears.

By trying to help the situation, he had only made it worse. Suddenly, Alzerion felt a strong urge to turn. He threw down the blanket and spun around. Then he saw it staring at him, taunting him. There on top of Aironell's basinet laid the necklace that glistened and sparkled as light shone on it. He walked over, picked it up, and placed it gently in his bag.

Then he headed out the door and into the corridor. He disappeared in a puff of red smoke out of the palace and landed where all the trouble started six years ago. He stood outside the palace by the window and looked in.

He looked down at his feet and continued walking down Founders Path toward Abandon Alley where Ulbrick would be waiting. He could only imagine the sorrow that would encompass and befall the palace. *What if they found out I took it? They may think I was the reason it was missing.* But when would the melancholic atmosphere lift? When would the cloud of despair disappear and be replaced by bright, cheerful times? Then in seconds, all went black.

AN UNEXPECTED VISIT

After her play date with Emilia, Isabella had Airon change clothes. Airon changed into a black long sleeve shirt that was silky in feel and ruffled like peplum at the bottom. She went downstairs as Airon put on a pair of black, white, and gray colored leggings with a pair of short black boots that ruffled at the top and had a bow near the foot. Airon played by herself in the living room. The doorbell rang.

"I'm going to get it, Mom," she called.

"Alright," replied Isabella, as she sat at the dining room table. She had a clear view of Airon.

Airon opened the door. She froze. Isabella saw her kneel down and then scream. "He's hurt!"

Isabella got there first. It was Alzerion lying there on the front porch.

"How bad is it?" Daniel probed as he got there.

Isabella looked at Alzerion and saw the gashes and rips to his clothes and the blood.

Airon was kneeling, with a hand to his forehead, as a tear pricked the sides of her eyes.

"It's Alex. I don't know what's wrong, but he looks hurt," she answered as she fought back the tears.

Isabella moved forward with eyes wide, as she continued scanning the sight before her. She shook her head and asked, "Airon, please go and get a bowl with warm water and some cloths."

"I don't want to leave him," she replied with eyes just staring at Alex.

Isabella moved toward Airon and placed a hand on her shoulder and continued, "I know sweetie, but we have to move him and clean his wounds.

Airon gave Alex one last look, stood up, and said, "I'll get it. You can count on me."

Daniel forced a smile as Airon walked by him and dashed into the house. He looked around the neighborhood to be sure that nobody was watching. Isabella covered her hand over Daniel's hand. Her hand glowed lavender.

"How do you feel?"

"I hate doing this. I know the magic you gave me will only last until we take care of Alzerion, but still."

Isabella nodded. Her husband did not possess his own magic. However, they agreed that at times she would transfer some to him when needed. It usually was when training Airon on using her magic. This was the first time in a while they had to do this.

Then Daniel waved his hand and said, "Up."

Alzerion's body slowly levitated off the ground.

Isabella nodded and walked through the front door, first, then Daniel motioned his hands forward and Alzerion's body slowly levitated through the door and into the hall.

"Watch he doesn't hit the banister," Isabella reminded. "Try angling him a bit."

Daniel moved his hands to the right and Alzerion started rotating. Daniel watched for Isabella's next instruction and asked, "Is he going to hit the bronze mirror or hall table?"

Isabella quickly glanced to the side and shook her head, "He's good, but you may want to glide him back toward you. Maybe glide him into the dining room and then you can move him straight into the living room. That way he won't hit the closet door."

"Good thinking," he replied as he waved his hands toward himself. Alzerion's body slowly floated a couple inches into the dining room.

Then he pressed his hands forward. Isabella walked into the living room as Alzerion's body made it in nicely and stood at one end of the beige couch.

Daniel followed behind and moved Alzerion to the side and slowly lowered his body onto the couch.

Isabella, who stood by his head, knelt down and just gazed at him for a moment and then said, "Daniel please move the coffee table closer, for when Airon gets the bowl. Also, please check that we closed the front door. I think we may have left it open amidst all the chaos."

Daniel walked to the table, slid it closer to Isabella and left the room.

Isabella placed her hands at the giant rip on Alzerion's shirt and saw a gash with blood. She noticed multiple bruises, cuts, scrapes, and a few gashes. As she waited for Airon she couldn't stop her mind from racing. She grabbed the hand closest to her and gave it a squeeze, fighting back her tears. Then she heard the bang of the front door close. She heard Daniel stroll back into the living room. Isabella held her gaze down at Alzerion. He walked to his wife and gingerly patted her back. After another moment, they heard Airon run down the stairs. She walked into the living room, placed the bowl on the table and knelt down beside Alzerion's head.

Airon grabbed a cloth and handed it to Isabella. Then she placed the last one on the table. She dipped hers into the bowl and slowly dabbed the cuts on Alex's forehead. Isabella nodded at her and then set to work cleaning the gash in his side above his ribs.

Daniel grabbed the last cloth and knelt down by Alzerion's legs. He slid his tattered pants up to his knees and he dabbed at the cuts on his legs.

"Is he going to be alright?" Airon's voice wavered, briefly, but it broke that silence.

"Oh, dear, I hope so," replied Isabella with a forced smile.

Isabella glanced at Airon and could see she was a bit teary-eyed. She took a hand and wiped away her tear and then gave her a hug. "He will be alright just you see."

Airon smiled and continued dabbing at the wounds.

Isabella continued working, too, but couldn't help the intruding thoughts. Thoughts of better days of seeing Alzerion safe and always helpful. Now to see him at eighteen and unsure if he would live, frightened her. The tears that felt like tiny little drops started to cascade down her cheeks.

"Airon, honey," said Daniel. "It looks like we are about done here and it *is* getting late. Why don't you head up to bed?"

"I don't want to go, daddy. What if you need my help, again?"

"I know you want to help, but we are done. Your mother and I just have to get him to the spare bedroom and change him into clean clothes."

"Her eyes shifted back down to Alex and with one last smile she stood up and said, "Sure, Daddy."

He walked with her to the stairs, gave her a hug and kiss, then she headed up the stairs.

Once he knew she was out of earshot, he walked back to Isabella, knelt down beside her and said, "Hun you seem to be taking this really hard. Are you alright?"

She could hold it all back no longer. She flung her arms around him and just sobbed. Daniel patted her back while they hugged.

"It'll be alright," he reassured, "Alzerion is such a strong person."

Finally, Daniel parted from her and sat. He waited for her. Isabella was taking some deep breaths and replied, "I just couldn't help but think about how happier things used to be. How could this have happened to him, Daniel? What do you think happened to him?"

"I'm not sure," he answered. "Things must be worse than we realized.

"Daniel, I just wish we knew what was going on in Bachusa."

Daniel put his arm around his wife and squeezed. "There, there. I know. I wish we did too, but this is not our fault. Let's just do the best we can and make sure we keep him alive."

"I think we should contact the king and queen," replied Isabella, sniffling.

"No, the only time we're supposed to do that is when Airon is older. We can't risk everything that Alzerion has tried so hard to do."

Isabella nodded and then looked back at Alzerion. She grazed the back of her hand over his forehead and then heard a groan.

Alzerion slowly opened his eyes.

"Alzerion, you're awake!" exclaimed Isabella.

"Mother, what happened?" Airon asked as she ran downstairs. "I heard you scream."

"W-What? Where am I?" asked Alzerion, flustered.

Airon walked toward him, head bowed, as a slow smile parted from her lips.

"You're alright," Airon said as she stared at him.

"H-hey," Alex mustered. "I'll be just fine."

"We were so worried about you." Airon placed her hands on her hips as she looked down at him.

"You're safe," assured Daniel.

Airon put her hand to his forehead to see if he was sick, Alzerion touched her tiny hands and forced a smile.

"Why smile when you're hurt?" asked Airon.

"It's not too bad," he winced. "I'm just glad to see you again."

"I don't understand."

Alex narrowed his eyes and then forced a smirk.

"How about we let him get some rest?" Isabella suggested before Alex could say anything. "Airon, why don't you go back to your room for bed? We will get Alex upstairs to sleep."

Airon nodded, smiled at Alex and said, "Good night."

Then she walked up the stairs and into her room.

"She's adorable," Alzerion blurted out as he flinched.

"Yes," agreed Isabella. "Now, how much damage is actually done here?"

"What do you mean?" he asked through gritted teeth.

"Do you have any other deep cuts?" Daniel retorted. "We did our best at cleaning out the wounds we found."

"No," Alzerion said frankly. "Just bruises. I'm mostly sore. Can you help me sit up?"

Isabella crouched behind him and gently propped him up with her arms. Daniel grabbed the fluffiest pillow he could find, walked to the other end of the couch, and placed it right up against Alzerion's back. Then Isabella slowly moved her arms from behind.

"How does that feel?" Her eyes fixed on him.

"Hurts a bit. Here," he pointed to his side.

"Yeah, you had a rather nasty gash there," Daniel said. He walked around the table to the other side.

"Why don't we get you upstairs?" Isabella suggested. "It may be more comfortable. We can add as many pillows as you need. I can add some bandages, as well."

Alzerion nodded. Isabella and Daniel stood at each side and wrapped their arms around him. They guided him from the couch, past the coffee table, to the stairs, and up to the guest room, which was at the top of the stairs.

THE RECOVERY

It must have been a dream, a terrible nightmare. At least, that was what Alzerion thought. Then he felt a shiver and woke with a start. He did not recollect where he was at first. He noticed his clothes were different, and he pushed the blankets away from his chest and sat up.

Underneath his flannel shirt, he could feel the bandages around his chest, and he unbuttoned it to have a look. It was painful to sit up, but he knew he had to get better.

He heard what sounded like the creaking of wood so he glanced up at the door. Unsure as to what was going on, he closed his eyes and focused his mind. He saw the door in his mind and an image of Airon materialized.

First, he smiled, put the covers back on, and then said, "You can come in, Airon. It's not polite to linger."

She pushed the door open and he saw her. Airon stood still for a moment, bit her lip and frowned. She peered at him.

He propped his back against the pillows behind him and glanced at her outfit. It was a knee-length light gray dress with black leggings and cardigan; then he smiled. *She looks presentable,* he thought, watching her with curiosity.

"What?" he asked. "Did I do something?"

She opened her mouth to speak, but nothing came out so she shook her head, slightly.

Alzerion held out a hand toward her. She went to grab it with a shaky hand, but instead just gazed at his hand.

"Airon, take my hand."

"I-I—" she stammered.

"You can do it," he smiled wistfully.

He held his hands palm up, this time, and she grabbed hold of him. He gently urged her closer, and with his other hand, patted at the bottom of the bed. Airon let go and climbed into the bed and sat near his feet.

A few moments of silence passed, and Alzerion took the chance to think about what to say. He had some questions but didn't want to overwhelm her. Not yet.

Instead he said, "I get the feeling you have something on your mind."

"Well, you surprised me," she admitted.

He raised a brow. "How so?"

"You knew it was me. How?"

"I guessed," he lied. "If it had been your parents, they would have knocked or just came right in. Instead, you tried to make as little noise as possible by slowly opening the door."

"I don't see how that would make a difference. I was trying not to wake you in case you were still sleeping," she frowned.

He grinned and motioned for Airon to come closer. She stood up in the bed, wrinkled her nose, but then she carefully walked over his legs and sat next to him. She bit at her lip and bent her head down.

Oh no, don't be upset, Alzerion thought.

"It's no use trying to be quiet anyway. I'm a light sleeper, Airon."

The two sat in silence for a few moments. Alzerion noticed that she was looking at the bruises on his arms.

He smiled and said, "Yes?"

"Nothing," she said. "I was just wondering how you're feeling. You were badly hurt."

"I'm feeling better than I did. Still a little sore but otherwise much better."

"How did it happen to you?" she asked as she moved her feet under so she could kneel.

"Well, I got into a fight. I had something valuable, and I guess someone really wanted it. Where I live, people are struggling just to survive. They took one look at the object and tried to take it, but I put up a fight."

She shook her head. "I'm sorry. They could have killed you, and for what?"

"Technically, yes, they could have, but I'm stronger than I look."

"Airon, I have a question. How long have I been asleep?"

"About three days," she answered. "I should let my mother know you're awake."

With that, she got up and left the room. Once she was gone, Alzerion's smile turned a flat line on his face. He had been out longer than he had anticipated. *Crap*.

A month passed, and Alzerion was still not back in Bachusa. He knew that the king and queen might be worried, so he had contacted them. He knew they would only be happy when he returned. He had not talked to Warren or Ulbrick for fear that they would try to find him. However, in that time Airon turned seven.

Alzerion sat on the back porch overlooking the summer atmosphere. The weather was beautiful and he was currently fixated on the many flower beds that were scattered about. The sweet aromas and the many colors, *Ah,* he thought, *not quite as nice as Gorgeous Garden, but it was well done. Home. I wonder how the king and queen are doing. Ugh, Ulbrick. What will I tell him?* He was sure to get an earful from him for his absence. He enjoyed getting to know Airon better. If it was possible, they kindled some sort of friendship.

He was in a daze thinking when Isabella sat in the swivel chair next to him. He wished that he could stay forever. Daniel was laying out on a lounge chair, when Isabella broke the silence.

"Alzerion, what has been going on at the palace?" Isabella fumbled with the beading on her blouse.

Daniel opened his eyes and sat up on his lounger.

Alzerion shook his head and narrowed his gaze on the two of them.

"All sorts of troubling things," he replied. "But I fear the worst is yet to come."

"Why? What's happening?" Daniel leaned forward.

"Well, I didn't want to worry you two, but Bachusa is nearly ready to revolt. The many townspeople are not happy because someone is making the king and queen look bad. You see, they don't know how to fix the problems, and when they try to help, even worse things happen. Things are getting out of control, and—" he stopped abruptly. He saw Daniel's jaw drop and Isabella's eyes start to fill with tears.

"I had no idea," admitted Isabella. "I can't believe things are that bad. How are the king and queen coping with this?"

"Not well, to be honest. They feel a bit betrayed by the kingdom and people they have always loved and protected. Someone is using them in every possible manner. They are doing the best they can."

"How close is Bachusa to revolting?" asked Daniel, who stood up abruptly.

"Honestly, I don't see it happening any time soon. The group behind this doesn't have the numbers, and I personally think they are waiting for a more opportune time."

"Now I see why you always look so overworked," Isabella sighed.

"Yes, it hasn't been easy, especially because the king and queen are losing hope. Not to mention they miss their little girl. I try to reassure them by telling them how she's doing. I even remind them why this is all necessary for Bachusa, but they feel hurt and defeated by the people."

"Is there anything we can do to help?" asked Daniel. "Isabella and I hate feeling helpless when everything is being threatened and all might be lost."

"You can't think like that," Alzerion voice was firm. "Don't give up hope. The only thing you need to do is raise Airon. Show her everything to make her a good person, and with that a great queen someday. So far, you two are doing exceptionally well. When she is old enough, you should tell her about who she really is and make sure she is great with her magic."

"Well, she already uses magic, just as you instructed." Isabella told Alzerion. "We have been teaching her about the rules, basics, and principles. Our hope is that as she gets older, she will progress nicely."

"Good. Our success might depend on her magical abilities."

"We won't let you down," Isabella promised.

"Excellent, because Aironell's proper upbringing is all anyone could hope for."

"Do you think she will really take the throne?" wondered Isabella.

"Yes, she will, but only after she gets married. However, she will have to fight for her kingdom from the evil within Bachusa that is threatening its very existence."

"You're right about that, but I guess I meant do you think the people would want her? I mean, she wouldn't have grown up in Bachusa, and she would have been away for quite some time," replied Isabella.

"That won't matter," Alzerion reassured her with a wave of his hand. "They will be happy to have the rightful person take the throne. Plus, if she restores the peace then the people will be in her favor."

"I guess you have a good point," admitted Daniel.

"Anyway, how much longer do you think you will stay with us? It's not like we don't want you here, but we don't want people to start to get too suspicious back home," Isabella said.

"Hmmmm … I'm not sure," Alzerion said with a half-smile. "I'll probably leave soon."

Daniel tilted his head. "What will determine when you leave?"

"Honestly, I should have left by now, it's just … hard. I've gotten used to the peace and relaxation. Plus, spending time with Airon makes it even harder to leave. I never knew a seven-year-old could be so sweet and kind."

"I know she really is a unique and amazing child," replied Daniel.

"She'll make a good queen someday. You two really are doing remarkable work. Airon is everything I could hope for plus more. I know I have to go back because if all goes according to plan, I have quite a bit of work ahead of me."

Alzerion stood. "I should pack. I'll probably leave tonight."

Before either Isabella or Daniel could say anything, Alzerion was already in the house. Alzerion was in the spare room, packing for a while. He was finished putting his things together by night fall. He put his belongings in a pile and looked around the room, remembering all the good times he had while staying with Isabella and Daniel. When he was done, he grabbed his stuff and descended the stairs into the living room. Once there, he set his bags on the floor and had the sensation that someone was behind him, so he turned.

Here he found himself face to face with Aironell in powder blue cotton pajama pants with a laced shirt to match. She looked at his bags, sadly, before staring into Alzerion's eyes.

Alzerion felt uneasy about saying goodbye. He realized it would be harder to leave than he had anticipated, once he saw Aironell's sparkling cerulean blue eyes start to tear up. Alzerion, frowned as he walked toward Aironell. He felt a bit more relaxed, but it didn't change what he felt inside. He gazed at Airon with sadness in his cinnamon-red eyes. Then he knelt down and threw his arms around Airon. Alzerion squeezed as he opened his eyes. Isabella and Daniel were watching from the couch. There was a pained expression on her face.

While he hugged Aironell, Alzerion realized how strange things would be for him to leave. He would be returning to a world where she did not exist.

Alzerion started to withdraw his arms, and he saw Aironell's face. She had water droplets in her eyes and tears were streaming down her cheeks. He gave a faint smile, took his hands, and brushed away her tears.

"Don't cry, sweet pea. It'll be alright," he consoled.

"I'm going to miss you," she blurted, sobbing.

"I know." His mouth tightened. "I'm going to miss you too. I have something for you, though."

"What is it?" she asked, sniffling.

"Something to help you remember our friendship. As long as you keep this, you'll always be in my heart," he said as he pushed her hair behind her ears.

Alzerion turned around and rummaged in his bag. He knew it was in there. He felt the metal brush against his fingertips. *Yes.* All eyes were on him, and then he looked back at Aironell. He opened his hands, and there was an ornate necklace. The Lost Hope. Alzerion looked at it as he put it on Aironell and knew how much it almost cost his life trying to flee with the necklace. It would take much more than a beating for someone to take it from him.

The necklace was said to give the wearer more power. Alzerion knew he wanted her to have it, hoping it might keep her safe. He knew she would need a power boost.

Despite those reasons, Alzerion had another reason for wanting Aironell to have it. It was in fact a gift from him. It was his gift to Aironell the day that she was born. It was a family heirloom, and he could not think of a better person to give it to. Now, looking at her, he saw a bright future for all of Bachusa. Once he clasped it around her neck, he took a step back. Airon looked down, touched it, and smiled.

"Thank you," she said sweetly. "It's pretty."

"Of course," Alzerion replied with a smile.

"I really like it, but I'm confused."

Alzerion's forehead creased as he tilted his head. "Confused about what?"

"Well, it looks like someone broke it on you," she said staring down at it. "It is in half."

He couldn't help but to laugh. " No, Airon, this is how it's supposed to look. You see, the necklace is symbolic, and I have the other half right here."

As he explained that to her, he pulled out his half from underneath his own shirt so that she could see that he did in fact have the other half.

As he did that, Isabella and Daniel smiled wide. Alzerion knew that they understood.

Then Airon said matter-of-factly, "Well, I guess if I'm in your heart then you're in mine too."

"I guess so," Alzerion agreed with a chuckle.

Then he gave Aironell one last hug. "I'm sure we will meet again someday."

Next, he hugged Isabella and shook Daniel's hand before leaving. He grabbed his bags and walked to the front door, taking one last glance at the room, and more importantly, the people in it.

As much as he would love to come and see them soon, like he said. He knew that was not going to happen. It pained him to know that he lied to Aironell, but someday when she was old enough to return home, she would see him again.

With those somber thoughts, he forced a smile and waved goodbye, exiting out the front door. When he left, he wandered to an alley and then disappeared in a puff of red smoke back to Bachusa.

THE FILL-IN

Alzerion entered the palace and walked to the family room. There, he found the king and queen chatting away. He watched them for a brief moment and saw how miserable they looked, and it troubled him. Then he took a deep breath, put down his bag, and walked into the room.

"Your Majesties, is everything alright?" he said with a deepened voice. He quickly glanced between them.

"Alzerion!" exclaimed Queen Evalyn. "We were worried sick. Where have you been?"

"It's a long story, my queen," he responded as he strolled into the room and sat in the armchair nearest them on the couch.

"Well, we insist that you start from the beginning, and don't leave anything out." King Francisco's voice boomed. His eyes were firm as they watched him.

"It started two months ago, when I was walking on one of the back roads. You see, I found the necklace the Lost Hope, and I was looking at it as I was walking. There were these people who got the better of me, you know, they attacked me. They thought I had something of value for them. Anyway, they probably would have killed me if I didn't manage to use my magic and disappear."

"Oh my, I'm so sorry, Alzerion," said the queen sadly. "I wish there was something we could have done. I can't believe you found the necklace. Is it safe? How did you survive if you fled while still very hurt?"

"It's alright, my queen. The necklace is fine, and I survived because of you two. Indirectly, of course."

"How so? What do you mean?" asked the king.

Alzerion looked deeply into both of their eyes and smiled. "When you agreed to listen about sending Isabella and Quairken away, to protect and raise Aironell."

The king furrowed his brows. "Wait, what are you saying, exactly?"

"I'm saying that I disappeared to the only safe place I knew, a place that was too far for them to follow me. A place that nobody even suspected. I went to Isabella and Quairken's house, where they nursed me back to health. Also, the necklace is in a safe place. I split it into its two parts and gave the one half to Aironell and I have the other half."

Once he finished explaining, he saw their faces brighten. The look was soon replaced with one of joy, and both the king and queen exchanged curious glances.

"I know what you want to ask me," Alzerion said matter-of-factly.

"Oh, well if you are so clever, why don't you tell us?" the queen said playfully. Her hands folded across her chest.

"Alright, well I think you want to ask about Aironell and know how she is doing. You know details like that, ones that any concerned parent would want to know."

"Well, it seems you know us only too well," retorted the king.

"I'm not surprised at all," added Queen Evalyn. "After all, we practically raised you since you were a child. I hope you know that we take great pride in the things that you do."

"I have grown to understand that you care for me as a second child."

"Well good," the queen said sweetly. "Then you will understand why we were worried while you were gone."

"Thank you for caring. I do understand, and I'm sorry I worried you."

He glanced at the king and queen and smiled. He felt their warmth. He never wanted to hurt them.

"Aironell is a sweet child, by the way," he quickly added.

The queen started to tear up.

"She helped nurse me back to health, as well. The princess is quite the little helper. She has such a kind heart. She is caring, sweet, and good-natured. You two would be so proud."

"Oh Francisco, did you hear that?" the queen asked as she cried. "We have much to be grateful for. Maybe we can find some hope after all."

"I know, dear, I heard. I'm glad that she is doing well, and I'm happy you got to spend some time with her, Alzerion. You were always close to her, and it was you who saved our little girl. She will someday know of your kindness."

"Well, thank you, Your Majesty. It was nice to sit and talk with her. However, I've had a long day. If you don't mind, I'm going to put my belongings away and relax, so if you need me, that's where I'll be."

During the coming weeks, Alzerion got back into the swing of things in Bachusa, and he even eased the king and queen's pain and helped them make decisions. Also, he met with Ulbrick and told him that he got injured training the Royal Army and stayed in the palace to heal. Even though he had to meet with Ulbrick more often than normal, he did not mind it so much anymore. It was his punishment for not telling Ulbrick of the injury. As far as they knew, Alzerion failed in stealing The Lost Hope.

On his most miserable days he clung to his piece of the necklace. It helped him to remember that sweet little girl who had the other half. A little girl who trusted him, no questions asked. All of his plans were to help save Aironell, and he hoped one day she would truly thank him.

MOTHER'S CONCERN

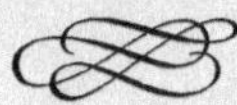

Alzerion took a stroll into town. *Years*, Alzerion thought. He couldn't believe how the time flew, as if it were manipulated by the magical hands of fate. The army kept him busy. Trainings were tiring and long. *At least things seem a bit more settled.* The townspeople seemed different, changed. Less angry. He passed by the little tavern. He peered in the window at people laughing. Air smelled of day's old stew mixed with the smells wafting from the market stalls. He exhaled. So much work. He rubbed his hand against the building as he walked. At least Ulbrick bothered him less. *Thank the stars for that?* He closed his eyes. He pictured Ulbrick huddled up in his house, scheming. *His schemes, ugh. What would that bring?* No. He couldn't worry about that. All he did was worry, according to his mother. A woman. That was what she cared about, for him. He rolled his eyes.

Alzerion rolled his eyes as he opened them. He scanned the scene before him. Things did not seem as gloomy. He smirked. His mother would just have to understand. When it came to romance, he just … didn't care. Only one girl mattered to him, and it was Aironell. Keeping her safe, no matter what. He continued his stroll as he heard a voice.

"Alzerion!"

He turned around and thought, *Really, can my luck be this bad?* He gave a smile, though he knew what to expect in a conversation. How could he not? After all, what did his mother do best if not pester him about his life choices?

"Hello, Mother," he said, kissing her cheeks. "What can I do for you?"

"I just want to talk," she replied. "Isn't it nice out here?"

Alzerion looked at her, brows raised, but thought merely to amuse her question.

"Yes, it is," he answered. "The birds chirping and the warmth of the sun's golden rays, ah. It's quite heavenly." He placed his arm behind her and angled his body.

She moved toward the stone wall. Browns mixed with red colored the wall with the golden sun in the background. His mother plopped herself onto the ledge. He joined her.

"The weather is nice," she agreed.

Then an awkward silence unfolded between the two of them. Finally, after it became apparent to Alzerion that whatever his mother wanted to talk about, she was considering holding off. So, he broke the silence.

"I doubt you wanted to talk to me about the weather. What's really on your mind?" He pulled his one leg in while his other leg tapped on the ground.

"Well, I don't know. I mean, I don't want to become the annoying mother who nags you, Alzerion."

"You don't nag. Alright, maybe you do a bit, but it doesn't bother me much." He flashed a smile with his teeth showing. "You worry about me, that's all, and I know that's normal."

"Well, did you think about our last conversation at all?"

"Do you mean the one where you told me my life isn't fulfilling because I'm single and need a woman?" he asked, trying not to roll his eyes.

"Well, yes." She hesitated. "Should I assume that you have been thinking about it? Since you recited it word for word?" Her arms folded in front of her chest. She tilted her chin down, a bit. He felt like he was about to be scolded.

"Truth is, I have been giving it a lot of thought." He swallowed.

"Good," she said sternly. "I just want you to be happy. You're my only child, and seeing you with someone would ease some of my worries."

"Mother, I am happy. I couldn't be more delighted." His lips curled up. "Seriously, I help the king and queen. I'm in full command of the Royal Army. I even stroll through town, keeping an eye on things." He sat with his chest puffed out. "I know I'm busy but I like it like that."

"That's all well and good, but that doesn't give true happiness." He stared back at her. Melinda grew quiet like the silence that creeps at dawn. Lingering until the right moment. "I wish you would see it differently." She stared off into the crowds of people walking by.

Alzerion's mouth tensed. He pressed his lips together as he gazed down at the cobblestones in front of him. Each wound and curved, running into the next. Melinda was silent, except for her sigh. Then there was a soft touch on chin as she coaxed his face up.

Her smile was faded-weak. "Alzerion," her voice sounded distant. "All I want for you is to find your match. Someone who will just fit with you, in every way."

"Love," he sighed. "Mother, that may take some time. I may never find that person." Alzerion's back curved as he bent forward. He pinched the skin of his throat as he waited.

"I don't believe that is your future. But, you have to be looking. Don't let time or opportunity pass you."

"I promise you that I am. I do look." He crossed his arms. "I'm just not tempted by anyone. I'm not that impressed by what I see." Alzerion raised his chin as he looked at his mother.

"Alzerion, I understand that it takes time and many people are just there, but you need to make more of an effort. There are plenty of young ladies who want you," she pleaded. "Those ladies over there are interested." She pointed toward a group of three chatting by the produce market. "I overheard them talking when I found you."

"I don't want some random stranger. I'm looking for something different. I want someone who wants more from me than to use me. Either that or some just want something else entirely."

"What do you mean?"

"Um … it's not something I feel comfortable saying or discussing with my mother." He felt a warmth wash over his face. He gulped.

"Try me. Just tell me." He could tell that she wasn't going to let it go.

"Alright," he replied in a defeated manner. "Some women might want me for my looks or appearance. They look at me like I'm a three-course meal, and they are ready to devour me." That heat crept across his face up to his ears. He was sure his ears were a shade of pink.

"Well," she swallowed. "I didn't want to hear that."

"Not all women are true. Some like my position. You know… what I can offer them." He paused as he tapped his feet against the brick wall. "That's why I'm a little reluctant to waste my time. However, I do promise to keep my eyes open. If I meet someone I feel is worthy, you'll know, I promise."

"Well, I guess if you are willing to try, then I will try. I will respect your wishes, my darling boy." She placed an arm around and pulled him in for a side hug.

He laughed. "I haven't been a boy for some time."

"Nonsense," she waved her hand at him. "You will *always* be my boy."

He stared out toward the palace. He heard such sincerity in her voice. *It was sweet*, he thought. He felt a hot stinging feeling prick the corners of his eyes. Alzerion stood up. Turning, slowly, as he caught sight of a couple. They strolled down the road, arm-in-arm. He bit down on his lip.

Then he looked back at his mother. "Of course, at some point I'll get married. I do want a family. I'm just not at that point, yet."

"Fine, I can understand and respect that. Just remember you're not going to get any younger. Don't wait too long."

"I know," he said voice low. He cleared his throat as he gazed back at the palace.

"Is it time?" Her head tilted to the side.

He smirked as he stepped forward and hugged her. "Unfortunately." He pulled back and waved. Melinda nodded and then he left.

As he trudged back to the palace his mind felt jumbled. Finally, he strolled to Gorgeous Garden. He wandered soaking in the beauty of the flowers. A sweet scent tickled his nose. *Ah*, he thought, *roses*. Flashes of moments from when he was younger. Playing with Aironell in the garden. He rubbed his hands down his face. He sat envisioning better days. He gazed up at the sky. He closed his eyes, tight. How he wished he could get back some of that fun or maybe just maybe, he could have some brighter days ahead.

A TRUTH REVEALED

The day was going to be great. How could it be anything less? Aironell knew that it would be another fun-filled day with her best friend. It was summer. *Flowers carpeting the ground*, she thought. The water from the pool that sparkled in the sunlight and birds chirping. She threw the blankets to the side and ran to the window.

There, she was able to see the golden rays of the sun shining down, casting a glittery scene. A sweet smile spread over her lips as she smelled the scent of the roses. She never quite understood why but that was her favorite. There was just something about them. They made her feel comforted. She inhaled the sweet scent and then rummaged through her closet to pick out her outfit. She held different clothes up, weighing her options. Finally, she was satisfied with a black romper that had red roses all over the material. She pinched some of the fabric around her stomach. *Ugh too loose*. She picked up a dark gray belt and placed it around her waist. Then she put on a nice pair of black flats.

She looked into her floor-length mirror and moved side-to-side to decide if this was indeed what she wanted. *Maybe just a little cardigan to add a little something*, she thought. So, she picked up a gray lace cardigan that came up to her elbows. After she was satisfied, Airon sat at her vanity and brushed her pretty dirty blonde curls.

Her fingers glided across different clips and bows, until she found the perfect one. It was a sparkly gray clip with small gems, and in the middle of the clip was the design of a rose with red gems. Her curls frothed over the clip, and her fair complexion made those dirty blonde curls look just like she was a model.

After she had her hair done, Airon picked up her favorite necklace. The necklace was a gorgeous shade of white gold. It was something she had for years now. She knew the man it came from; however, she had not seen him in many years. She only ever stopped wearing it once. Anger kept her from wearing it, for a time. Alex did not keep his promise; he did not come and visit again. But then she felt terrible for not wearing the gift he gave her, and it had been around her neck every day since then.

The half-heart necklace always made her smile. She vowed that she would never forget Alex. He befriended her, though she was only a child. His kindness was something she wouldn't forget. With those thoughts, she put the necklace on. Then she stood up, took one more look in the mirror, and ran downstairs. She stood in the hallway near the front door.

"Mother!" yelled Airon. She moved about trying to see where she was. "I'm going outside for a while. Emilia and I want to soak up some sun."

"I'm in here," Isabella called back from the living room. Airon followed the cadence of her mother's voice. She was seated on the couch flipping through the pages of a home magazine.

"Mom, I'm headed out."

Isabella set down the magazine and looked up. "Oh, Airon, you look so beautiful." Her face brightened. "You have grown into quite the young lady." There was a gleam in her eye.

"Thank you." Airon grinned. She practically glided as she moved toward Isabella and sat beside her. "I owe everything to you and Dad." Airon leaned in and wrapped her arms around her mother. "You guys are the best parents anyone could ask for." Airon pulled back and stared back at her mother.

Isabella's eyes glistened. Airon sensed something. Unsure why but she felt like her mother wanted to say more, but didn't. Then Isabella's mouth twisted into a smile. *Still, it seemed out of place*, Airon thought.

"That means a lot, dear, thank you." Isabella grabbed Airon's hand, gave it a gentle kiss, and stood up. While she turned a frown shone on her face.

Airon caught the downcast look. "Mom, are you alright?" Airon wrinkled her nose as she, too, stood.

Isabella rested her hand on Airon's back. "I'm alright, sweet pea. I just have some things on my mind."

"Is there anything you want to talk about before I go? I don't have to leave just yet," Airon said as she pointed toward the door.

Isabella pressed against Airon's back propelling her toward the hall and the front door. She pulled Airon in for another hug. "Not right now, dear, maybe later." Isabella stepped back. "For now, go have fun with Emilia, but be back by six." Isabella pointed her finger at her. "Your father and I have some things we want to discuss with you."

"Should I be worried?" Airon tilted her head to the side.

"Of course not," Isabella laughed. "On the contrary, you should look forward to it."

"Well, alright, if you say so. Goodbye, I'll see you later then." With those words, Airon walked out of the living room and out the front door.

"Isabella," Daniel said, coming down the stairs and into the living room, "I overheard the conversation." He shook his head.

"What? Did I say something wrong?" She pursed her lips as she planted her weight on her right leg.

"I know, it seems like just yesterday the king and queen asked us to watch their little girl," she said as she strolled toward her husband and grabbed his hand. "But she is not a little girl anymore."

"True." Daniel's eyes gleamed. Then he wrapped his fingers around hers, gave the lightest of squeezes, and brought them to his lips. "We will finally go home." He was shaking her hand in his.

Isabella nodded. Hand-in-hand she escorted him to the couch where they both sat.

"Da...Quairken," Isabella held his hand against her chest. "I know you're right, but I can't help but think it'll be hard. It's going to be an adjustment. I mean, we did raise her. It isn't just Aironell's life that will change, but *ours* too."

"Isabella, I know, but it's time. She's sixteen, and I think it has been more than enough time. The king and queen already know we will be returning tonight, and now all that is left to do is talk to Aironell."

"There is one more thing I do want to discuss," Isabella mentioned as she slowly stood up. "Aironell is not going to take this news well, and I don't blame her. How could she?"

Isabella noticed that Daniel's gaze focused more on her. She started pacing back and forth.

"I mean, it would be difficult for anybody to believe they are a magical princess from another realm and that the fate of an entire world rests in their hands," Isabella blurted out as she continued to pace.

"Alright, you've made your point," he replied as he walked toward Isabella.

"But she'll be fine." He placed one hand on each of her shoulders.

"She will be able to deal with the news. It's not like she doesn't know she is magical. We just have to tell her that she's destined to rule once she finds her prince charming, to sweep her off her feet," he finished with a half-smile that showed his teeth.

"Hun, I appreciate you trying to make me feel better, but you know it doesn't work that well."

"I know, but you can't fault me for trying, right?" he asked as he wrapped his arms about her.

Isabella gave him a quick peck on the cheek.

"What was that for?"

"Because I love you. I love how you try to keep me sane," she laughed.

Daniel joined her, and then just as quickly as the laughter began, Isabella stared down at her feet and started fidgeting with her fingernails.

"Isabella, my sweet, what's wrong?" he asked with one eyebrow raised.

"Daniel, I find that no matter how sensible or not, I worry about Aironell," she took a deep breath. "Don't forget she was raised in this world, so after hearing she's a princess, it will all sound crazy. In this world, that is the epitome of fiction. However, I do feel this world has rubbed off on me a little. I feel like her mother, and because of that, I feel leery about her being married off. I mean, she's sixteen, and that seems so young."

"Isabella, this world has changed you," Daniel said as he straightened his stance. "Honey, maybe here that seems odd, but you know better than I, that in Bachusa she is considered an adult. The facts are, well, this is all custom. As a royal, she will be expected to do her part. That means sixteen is a marrying age."

"I know, and I am happy to be returning. I just hope all goes well." Isabella started to pick at the skin around her nails.

"Honey is there anything else you wanted to talk about? You seem a bit unsettled about a lot more than just Aironell. I sense there is something you're withholding."

With hands on her hips, Isabella paced between the middle of the room and the entryway to the hall. Finally, she faced her husband. "Well there is something, but it doesn't seem like the right time to discuss it. In fact, this is definitely not the best moment for what I want to talk about."

"Isabella, you should tell me what's on your mind," he said in an even-toned voice. "I want to ease your mind and hopefully that will end these concerns you have."

Isabella relaxed her hands by her side, looked at Daniel and she could see his brows raised. Within a moment she watched as he moved closer to her.

"Quairken, I-I, well… want to have a baby," she blurted as a slow smile formed across her lips. "It may sound crazy but I always wanted us to have one, just the timing was never right, and then the king and queen asked us to watch Aironell. But now that she is old enough and we are going home, I would like to try for a baby of our own."

Isabella wasn't sure how he would take it, so she closed her eyes for a brief moment to focus her mind. When she opened her eyes, he was grinning from ear to ear.

"Honey, I would love for us to have a child."

"Oh, Quairken, thank you so much," she beamed as she hugged him. "It was all she could do not to jump in place and run around.

"Let's finish our task here first. Let's head upstairs to the attic. We will need to finish cleaning it out. Then we should be sure to pack anything that we want to take with us back to Bachusa."

"Yes, you're right, dear," she said with a nod.

Then they both walked briskly into the hall, up the stairs, and then Quairken pulled the chord from the ceiling above to let the metallic attic stairs descend.

Meanwhile, Airon sat outside by the lavish pool at Emilia's house. She was basking in the sun as the light sparkled on the water.

"It's so nice out," Emilia smoothed out the ruffles on her midnight black skirt.

"I know, it's great, and by the way, I just love your outfit," Airon said. "Those black heels match it so well."

"Thanks, the floral corset tank is new, and it has a front zipper that makes it easy to take off." Emilia winked.

"Well, then it's perfect," Airon giggled. Airon watched as Emilia sat up on the lounge chair, and ran her painted nails through the bottom of her black hair.

"So, are you going to walk by Evan's house? Don't forget I have to leave a bit early today. My mother wants to have a family dinner."

"Oh, that sounds fun. Well, it kind of sounds ominous."

"That's what I thought." Airon gasped. "I hope there isn't anything wrong. I don't want to worry about that." She shook her head. "Let's get back to talking about the plan with Evan."

"I want to stroll by his house, but I'm not sure. What if he thinks I'm a stalker, or what if he only wants to hook up? Airon, I actually do like him, and I don't want to come off odd."

"I know you like him," Airon sat right next to Emilia and gave her friend a soft pat on the back. "He seems to be genuinely interested in you, I promise."

"Well, alright," Emilia shifted side-to-side in her chair. "You've never steered me wrong, so let's do it." Emilia bounced up and motioned for Airon to follow.

The wind blew Emilia's straight black hair as they set off to Evan's house."Ugh! No, no, no."

Airon glanced to see Emilia's hands flailing about trying to fix her hair. "Emilia, everything alright?"

"No. I mean, I don't know. Should we be doing this?" This looked like something out of their favorite kinds of movies. Airon couldn't help but to laugh, a bit.

"What's so funny?" Emilia bit her lips and waited.

"Nothing. I swear," Airon wrapped her arm around Emilia's slender arm.

Emilia took a breath and leaned into her friend. Airon could hear how fast Emilia's heart was racing. "So, what is it that you like about Evan?" Whatever it took, she would help her friend.

"Oh, well. I like that he seems nice. He always makes it a point to talk to me at school."

Airon grinned as she listened to Emilia chatter on. Finally, Emilia rested her hand on Airon's. "Airon, do you think you'll ever get a boyfriend? I mean wouldn't it be fun if we both had one at the same time? Think of the outings we could have."

"I'm sure at some point I will. I want somebody to love but who understands me." Airon watched as Emilia's eyes had this glow to them.

"Well, that's very romantic. I mean, it happens. I think that's so sweet."

"I agree that is sweet, but we have to be realistic too. I don't see many guys, and the ones I do see I'm not that impressed with."

"Well, I hope you find someone. We are young. You just can't be too picky." she said with a chuckle and then stopped. "Airon, I worry about what Evan might expect. Clarissa said—"

"Well, you can't believe everything you hear, especially if it's from Clarissa." Airon gave her friend a hard stare as she slowly started walking. "She has made some bad choices. Ugh and she is almost as notorious as Abigail Bates."

Emilia twitched her mouth and nodded. "That's true but I do know that some of that talk wasn't true." She clasped her hands under her chin as she spoke. "Roger was so sweet, she told me. The rumors spread based on what he told his buddies." Airon looked disgusted. "Seriously, Airon, it was like his evil twin took over or something. I see it with my brother, Greg, and his buddies."

"True," Airon's eyebrows pulled in. She shook her head. "That's why I'm in no hurry, Emilia. I'll know when I'm ready. Airon focused at the concrete sidewalk before them. She couldn't explain it, but she just didn't feel anything. The guys Emilia tried setting her up with were too immature. Maybe she was cursed or something. She sighed.

"Airon, I know. But it is a great feeling." Emilia beamed as she twirled around.

"Why, so I can look exactly like you?" Airon joked.

"Huh, do I really look like I'm freaking out?" Emilia stared wide-eyed and bit her bottom lip. Airon could see the weight of concern so she ran in front of Emilia.

"Emilia, just relax." Airon laughed.

"That's not funny." Emilia stood with arms crossed and a slight pout.

"You know I wasn't trying to upset you. Do you need a minute?" Airon leaned closer.

Emilia closed her eyes, tight. Then took a deep breath. "I-I think I'm alright." Emilia started pacing and shaking her hands. She looked like someone frantically waving about.

"Well we are at Evan's house, and I'm sure you don't want him seeing you like this."

"You're right!" She let out a sigh. "I' m better."

"Good. Now what would you like to do?"

"Airon," Emilia focused in on her. "Do I look alright? Hair? Outfit?" Her hand flung to each as she spoke. "I don't want to look a mess, but I also don't want to seem like I was trying too hard."

"Hahaha. You want to appear like it was effortless to look that good." Airon pursed her lip as she stood with her arms crossed.

"Well, hell yeah!"

"Alright. You succeeded. Emilia there's no reason to be nervous. You look great and Evan will be so happy to see you. How about we walk by his house, you know, casually. We will need to get his attention."

"Yeah, that could work!" Airon sensed that a little encouragement was all Emilia really needed.

"You know, if we act all cute, maybe that will catch his attention." Emilia beamed.

They walked by, and saw Evan through the front window; but Evan did not see them. They strutted by, a second time, chatting, and giggling; a bit loudly and from the living room window, Evan came into view. His arm stretched over his head. Then his face turned. He glimpsed us as we walked. Airon caught a sly smile and then he was gone. In less than a minute, he was outside, moving toward them.

Emilia turned to him. Airon gave her friend a reassuring pat on the back. It served another purpose. Airon closed her eyes, for a moment. After she patted Emilia she opened her eyes and could hear her friend's thoughts. *It would be temporary,* she told herself. Just enough to help her out.

Emilia blushed, slightly, as he strolled over. Emilia's thoughts were crowded. Strong. Wow, Emilia mouthed.

Ahh, he was a vision. From his beige cargo pants to his tight navy-blue shirt. Boy did Emilia have it bad. From what Airon gathered Emilia wanted nothing more than to be alone with him. She stood and simply watched. She pressed down on her lips so she wouldn't laugh. She could feel the tension within Emilia. She was nervous. Her friend seemed a little different. Not her usually care-free bubbly self. *Hmm.* She wondered how she could lose her senses.

"H-Hey. How are you?" Evan asked as he leaned against the beige fence in front of his yard.

"I'm good." Emilia moved closer to Evan. Her face seemed to light up as she spoke. "We were just heading back to my house. We thought a walk and some fresh air would do us some good."

"Well, a walk is always nice." Evan straightened up. "Actually, if it's not too much trouble, can we talk? I mean, we could go on a walk together and talk if that's easier."

"That sounds perfect. Maybe another time, though," Emilia winked.

"Oh, ok. I'm sorry. You're busy."

"Don't be silly," Airon finally spoke. It was her chance to help. "We're not busy. Emilia has nothing but time to talk. In fact, I should be going."

Emilia grabbed Airon by the arm and pulled her off to the side. "What are you doing?" Her voice lowered to a frantic whisper.

"I know you really want to spend some time with him. This way it doesn't look like you're too eager." Airon whispered in Emilia's ear. "Plus, I have that family dinner tonight."

"Oh, yeah that's true. Are your sure about this?" Emilia's eyes darted to Evan and then back at Airon.

"Absolutely. Later, I want all the details." Airon nudged her toward Evan.

Emilia gave her a hug. "Thank you." Then she took a slow breath and walked toward Evan.

Airon stood for a little bit longer and watched the two walk away, laughing. The sound of the two of them brought a smile to her face. Then with those thoughts, Airon started walking home.

"Quairken," Isabella called, "did you find the trunk?"

"Of course, I did." He walked toward Isabella in the attic.

"That's good. I wasn't sure if we would even remember where we placed it considering it has been so long since we even needed it."

"That's true, but the trunk was here beneath the old living room set."

"Well, let's open it," Isabella urged as she clasped her hands together.

"Isabella, I don't know."

"Quairken, why? It's not like we have anything to worry about," she patted his arm.

"I love you, but what if Airon doesn't understand? I worry that despite all our best efforts, what if we have failed? I know I'm kind of panicking, but you did earlier, so I guess now it's my turn to second-guess."

"Quairken, how would we have failed? Aironell is sixteen, and she's beautiful, smart, kind, caring, and everything else that will make her a good queen. She communicates well with others, and she even has a great handle on her powers. She is more than we could ever have hoped for, and I think her parents and Alzerion will be more than pleased with us. We did our job and most important of all, she is still alive."

"Isabella," he said as he put his arms around her waist, "I know we did our best. I know we raised her well, but what if in the end, she can't beat the evil that threatens Bachusa? In truth, she wasn't raised there, so she doesn't quite know how to handle that world."

"Just relax, as you always tell me to do," she replied. A small smile crossed her face.

Isabella's hands moved from his waist to around his neck as she gazed into his eyes, tenderly. Then her right hand moved away to graze his cheek. She smiled and let her lips give him a reassuring kiss.

Quairken grinned when she pulled away. "You always do know how to calm me down." He winked. Isabella laughed as she shook her head.

"Well, I should. After all, we have been married for far too long—not that I'm complaining." There was a twinkle in her eyes.

"You're right, though. Everything will be fine. Yeah."

"Exactly and I'm looking forward to telling Aironell the truth."

"I'm glad you are. He cleared his throat. "I guess one of us should be."

"I mean, I was dreading it, but I since realized something. The sooner Aironell knows who she really is and all about her past, the sooner we can return to Bachusa. It has been an honor to raise the princess, but I miss our home." Her breath caught in her throat, just a bit.

"Well, I can't disagree with you on that. I am happy to go home as well. In fact, just hearing the name Bachusa brings back memories of fonder times."

"I know what you mean," Isabella said. "It does bring a smile. However, I do hope things have gotten better since the last time Alzerion was here."

"Oh wow, that's true. I hope things did too, for everyone's sake. What with us bringing her back to her kingdom."

The two walked down the stairs and into the living room.

"I agree, Isabella. It isn't like Alzerion not to have contacted us since he left." Quairken sat down on the couch and motioned for Isabella to join him. "He must have been busy."

"That's true, but I just hope he's alright. You know he how gets."

"I know what you mean," he answered with a sort of smile.

Airon opened the back door. She heard talking so she followed the voices through the kitchen, then dropped her bag on the floor in the hall. Within a few moments she strolled in from the open entryway to the living room. As she got closer she heard an odd name. Alzerion. *What's an Alzerion?*

"Who's Alzerion or what is that?" Airon asked as she stood in the doorway of the living room with arms folded across her chest.

"Oh, darling, you startled me," Isabella said as her hand clutched the shirt up against her heart.

"I'm sorry. I just got home and I heard you. But who is Alzerion? I've never heard that name."

Isabella and Quairken's gaze kept shifting from each other and then back to Airon. Isabella motioned to the couch, and Airon sat down between them.

"Well," Isabella hesitated. "In order to tell you that, we have much to discuss first."

"Alright, but you are starting to scare me. Mother, what's wrong?" Her eyes drooped in as she listened.

"The thing is," Daniel added. Airon looked over to him. He fiddled with his wedding ring, "Alzerion is a dear friend of ours. There is so much that you don't know."

"Please tell me. I'm not understanding." She whipped her head from her father and then her mother. Waiting for one of them to start making sense.

Isabella gulped. But she broke the silence. "Airon, Alzerion is … Alex."

"Alex? Alex who? Wait, you don't mean—"

Isabella smiled, nodded, and pointed to the half-heart necklace around her neck. Airon looked down at the necklace. She felt the cool metal against her skin. Airon just stared, between blinks.

"He gave you the necklace," Isabella spoke with such calm. *It was unsettling*, Airon thought.

Airon glanced back down, pulled on the silver chain around her neck, and smoothed her fingers over her necklace. *Could it be?*

"No." She shook her head. "Alex gave it to me, not some guy named Alzerion. Alex!" She stood up and started pacing in front of the couch. "It was Alex, yeah." Her head bobbing as she moved.

"Sweet pea, his real name is Alzerion," replied Daniel. "I know this must be difficult but we have so much to explain."

Airon halted. She was trying to soak it all in; but something was off. This didn't make sense. *Why would he have gone by another name? What was she missing?* Airon's hands graced the sides of her temples, and her fingers pressed, firmly, as if she was trying to will the pieces together.

"What he means is, that there is a lot that you don't understand. Things are not as they seem. We had to protect you from the evil that wanted you dead."

Dead. "Hold on," Airon's hands stretched in front of her like she was putting up a barrier. "What evil? Protect me?" She stared at them with raised brows. She took long slow breaths. Airon leaned forward, with hands on her knees, as she steadied her breathing. Then she stared back.

"There's so much that even we don't know about. I'm sorry but it was our duty, our job, to raise you to—"

"Wha-what does that m-mean?" Airon continued as she gripped her arms together, tight; like the weight of it all was crashing in on her.

"What she means is that we are not your parents. My name isn't Daniel. It's Quairken." He swallowed. "I'm a soldier where we come from."

Airon continued to stare. Lower jaw slowly buckling, trembling but making every attempt to hold firm. She could not believe her ears. Again, she started pacing back and forth in front of them. She bit her lip to choke back the tears. *How could this be? They lied to me about everything. Why?*

"Then who are you?" Airon gave a cold look to the woman she thought was her mother.

"Isabella. We are sorry for all of this. We love you, Airon. But there's more we have to tell you."

"More? How could there possibly be more?" Airon was slowly gaining her voice back. Then she let out an audible breath, as her hand splayed across her chest.

"Airon is not your name," Quairken said. "It's Princess Aironell of Bachusa."

Aironell stood, still. Unmoved. After what felt like an eternity, she took a breath and slowly sat down in a chair across from them, sagging into it. So many thoughts. Questions. Feelings.

She fought back the tears of anger and let her eyes bore into them. "Why?"

"What do you mean?" Isabella gulped. She shifted in her seat.

"Why did they get rid of me? Didn't they want me? Didn't they, love me?"

"Aironell, they love you very much," Quairken stood and moved toward her. He stopped and knelt down in front of her. "Things were chaotic when you were born."

"It's true," Isabella added. "They did not want to lose you, but they knew that your upbringing was crucial."

"The fate of Bachusa rests in your hands," Quairken's voice was low.

Aironell looked down at her hands. Her fingers were pinching the skin around her nails. Quairken reached out to lay his hands over top. She stopped fidgeting and looked into his eyes. She saw him clear as day. She could see that his eyes were a mess of guilt, sorrow, and sincerity. She sniffled.

"So, they do love me?" Her face felt pinched as she spoke.

"Of course, they do," Isabella strolled toward Aironell. She knelt down at her side and placed an arm around her shoulders. "Your parents never would have done this if it wasn't in your best interest. It was the recommended way to keep you free from physical harm."

Aironell's eyes glistened as she looked, slowly, to each of them. She took slow breaths to hold back the tidal wave of feelings inside. She didn't want to appear unstable. "Then whose idea was it? Who thought I was better off without my parents?" Her voice rose.

"Alzerion." Quairken cleared his throat as he stood up. "He convinced them that it would keep you safe. I know it is a lot and you probably don't understand."

She stood, completely still. Mouth falling open as her gaze fell flat and fixated on the picture of their so-called-family portrait. It hung above the couch. A memory that once made her feel happy. But now… no. She felt this numbness. It crept through her body until it hit her brain. A numbness that washed over her thoughts.

Then all that remained was a slight burning within. She couldn't tell why, at first, but then she knew. "I don't believe this!" Aironell bolted across the room and stood in front of that mockery of a family portrait.

Head sank as she twirled around and sat on the couch. "He only befriended me out of pity. He knew he ruined my life." She saw feet moving toward her out of the corners of her eyes. Within seconds Isabella and Quairken both sat next to her.

"Alzerion wasn't trying to ruin your life." He patted her back. "He spent his whole life keeping you safe. He befriended you not out of pity or duty; but because he enjoyed being around you. If you need proof, it is in the necklace you wear. It came from him. It's a special gift. It's a family heirloom."

"It's all true," Isabella's voice was calm and soothing as she held Aironell's hand.

Aironell nodded as she pondered all that they said. This Alzerion, maybe had her best interest at heart, too. "Wait, can we back it up a bit?"

"Of course." Quairken responded. "What can we clear up?"

"I have so many questions and things running through my mind. I realized you said something before, about, me. I'm a princess?" Aironell scanned Quairken's face for any hints or change of expression. He was solid like a wall that didn't or wouldn't yield. "Aironell, you heard correctly."

Isabella gave her hands a light squeeze. Aironell nodded slowly, trying to take it all in. "We come from a beautiful magical place called Bachusa." Isabella smiled and continued. "You're the sole heir to the throne."

Aironell's jaw slowly gaped open. Wow, she mouthed but no words came out. She didn't think they could stun her anymore.

"Aironell," Quairken smiled. "We believe you will do a fine job in Bachusa. Isabella and I have raised you to possess all the traits you need."

"I know this must be a lot for you to absorb." Isabella gave her a sympathetic smile.

"Well, I guess you were right. I am different than most people."

"Aironell, being different makes you special and unique. Your powers are part of who you are."

Aironell nodded and then looked up glancing between them. "Why... now? What has changed that you are telling me all this, now?"

Quairken cleared his throat and clasped his hands together. "Well, um, we were instructed to wait until the time was right."

"What makes this the right time, though?" Aironell watched him awaiting his response.

"We had to wait until you were of age. In Bachusa sixteen is that age of adulthood." Quairken steadily exchanged glances with Aironell. She noticed that his gaze was soft.

"What?" Aironell blinked rapidly as she wiped around her lips.

"Now we can go home," Isabella's voice bubbled as she smiled, wide.

"Wait, by home you mean Bachusa?" She pointed her hands around. Realizing she had no clue where that was.

"Yes," Quairken nodded. "We packed everything so you wouldn't have to."

With those words, Isabella snapped her fingers and their luggage appeared before them. Quairken stood up and walked over to the bags, then picked his up. Isabella got up and did the same thing. Then they both looked and waited and watched her. She stayed rigid as stone, refusing to move.

"What if they, um, you know, don't like me?" Aironell shrugged her shoulders.

"Who?" Isabella raised her eyebrow.

"My parents. What if they don't like me?" Her voice cracked.

"Aironell," Isabella gently placed her hand under Aironell's chin and slid her face upward. Isabella smiled. "They will adore you. Don't worry. Everything will be fine. Promise. They will see just how wonderful you are."

Aironell sighed and turned to Quairken. He, too, was nodding.

"Alright, but what about, *him*?" She spun to look at Isabella. She bit her lip to keep her chin from trembling.

"Darling who are you talking about?" Isabella placed her hand on Aironell's shoulder, and they locked eyes. Isabella's gaze was deep and sincere.

Aironell cleared her throat and mustered, "Alzerion."

Quairken stretched his legs as he ambled to the middle of the room. "What about Alzerion? He will be there, if that's what you're asking."

"I remember that he was nice to me," Aironell smiled as she twisted her index fingers around her necklace. "He played with me. He said we were friends. I remember that we were inseparable when he was here.

The thing is … what if I'm not what he's expecting? What if I'm not what he was hoping for?" Aironell grazed her nails against the couch.

"What do you mean?" Isabella voice probed.

"What if I disappoint him? If he has such high hopes for me. I mean what if he finds me lacking, in some way? I just don't want to upset him if I turned out different than expected."

"I see," Isabella smiled as she patted Aironell on the shoulder and then moved to Quairken's side. She glanced up at him.

What could they be thinking, Aironell wondered. It was like they were sharing a silent secret and she wanted to know. Maybe, for now, it was best that she didn't, besides, she just learned so much at once. She wasn't sure she could take any more.

"I doubt you could disappoint him," Quairken reassured.

"Why? I'm the reason you all have turned your life upside down. That includes him."

"He thinks the world of you," Isabella blurted. "When you were a baby, he was charged with the task of taking care of you." Isabella beamed as her hands twisted around each other. "So, early on, he felt this obligation to care for you."

"I just don't want to disappoint him or my parents."

"You won't," Quairken nodded.

"However, we should be going," Isabella motioned.

Both Quairken and Isabella stared at Aironell, waiting.

Aironell stood up and paced the room. She looked all around her, and saw the walls that at one time in her life contained her story. She had grown here. She experienced life here. Aironell shook her head, glanced down at her feet, and wiped a tear from her eye. Then she took a few breaths and strolled toward Isabella and Quairken.

Aironell forced her mouth to curve up. Ready or not things were about to change. All she had to do was embrace it and make the most of this new life. She nodded and picked up her suitcase. Isabella smiled and patted her on the shoulder.

Then the three of them stood in a triangular pattern and Isabella waved her right hand. Suddenly, they were immersed in a puff of red smoke, and Aironell couldn't see a thing. All that was left was to hope that no matter what, she would be alright.

HOMECOMING

Meanwhile, the king and queen had the maids do an extra special cleanup around the palace. The palace was buzzing with excitement. Alzerion observed with a fixed stare. Glancing around did nothing. None of the maids would stop whisking about long enough to tell him anything. They zoomed left and right all through the Great Hall. This was way more cleaning than they did for their own anniversary. *Huh.*

His one eyebrow was raised slightly, as he rubbed his hands on his chin. He shook his head and quickly took a sip of his tea. "Your Majesty, are we throwing a party?"

"Oh no, of course not, Alzerion," Queen Evalyn took a sip of her tea. "Why do you ask?"

"Well, um—"

"Go ahead." Her voice had a bit of harshness to it. Like she had other matters to deal with. Alzerion scooted down a seat or two to be closer to the queen.

"Honestly, I don't want you to be offended," he whispered. "However, you have the maids doing a lot of cleaning. This is kind of out of the norm." His gaze stared back at the maids. He shook his head.

"Oh, didn't Francisco tell you what's going on?"

Alzerion snapped his attention back to her. The queen beamed from ear to ear. He raised his brow.

"No, he didn't mention anything to me. What's going on, Your Majesty?"

"Alzerion, I wish I could tell you." The queen shifted her gaze to the scone on her plate. Before she took a bite Alzerion caught a glimpse of her scratching at the back of her neck. He sat back and as she ate her scone she averted his gaze. Something was going on and he wanted to know.

"Nobody is hurt, are they?"

She swallowed her bite and waved him off. "Of course not. We are all fine and well."

"Then why can't you tell me what's going on? You know I don't like being kept out. The suspense is killing me," Alzerion pleaded. He stood up and circled around to the other side of the table. Walking always helped him when he tried to keep calm.

"I know, but I can't tell you. If the king didn't say anything to you, then he must want it to be a surprise. I can say that you will find out soon, I promise."

"You know I *hate* surprises." He folded his arms in front of his chest.

"I know," she chuckled. "But you should head out. Don't you have some training planned for the Royal Army tonight?"

"Yes, I do. I almost forgot. Your Majesty, I can't believe you're going to have me leave without telling me this … surprise."

The queen smiled. "Have a good practice, Alzerion, and try not to think about it."

"Yeah," he said flatly. "Practice, though, will not go well. Conditioning is never a fun thing for the guys or me."

With that, he walked away from the queen and went down the hall. He continued out the big front doors and once outside, he took a deep breath. *Ugh, please don't let this be something bad.* However, he continued to take some breaths.

In came all sorts of wonderful aromas from the beautiful bushes in the front of the palace. He closed his eyes. *Aironell.* Then he opened them and realized that time had the last laugh. It was a cruel thing. *She's all grown,* he thought as he clutched his necklace; hidden beneath his shirt. He scowled at the thought of what was to come. She would be courted by many suitors. His face twisted as he crossed his arms. *A cruel thing indeed. She would return just so he could lose her all over again.* He felt a sudden ache in his chest. Then he heard a sound that broke his reverie.

At first it was faint, but then it grew louder. He realized it was a voice calling his name. In fact, it was the king who stood in front of him, trying to get his attention.

"Alzerion, what are you doing?" King Francisco was firm.

"I was thinking, Your Majesty, and I got lost in my thoughts," he admitted.

"I see. Normally I wouldn't care, but aren't you supposed to be training the Royal Army, now?"

"Yes, sir." He nodded. How could he let himself get so distracted?

"The men are still waiting for you. They sent for me when you didn't show up," Francisco said flatly.

"I'm truly sorry, Your Majesty. I'll head there now," Alzerion replied as he started walking toward the training field.

"Don't take too long tonight," the king called after him.

Alzerion turned around, "Why not, Your Majesty? I should probably make up for the time I lost."

"Well, you could do that, but there's a surprise back at the palace for you. Honestly, I think you'll be pleased."

With those words, Alzerion tilted his head. The king was in on this trick. He smirked as he turned around and continued on. At least the king wasn't angry for his lateness. He hiked down the path and veered around to the field by the barracks.

Aironell still only saw red. The smoke slowly dissolved revealing the room around her. What she saw was something she thought only existed in her dreams. She was in a gigantic palace with walls that were covered with filigree. The room was large with a fireplace and various shades of red all around. In the center were the king and queen dressed so elegantly that they could have come straight from a fairytale. She glanced over at Isabella and Quairken, both of whom smiled and bowed.

"It has been a long time," King Francisco held out his hand.

"It has indeed," Isabella shook the queen's hand. "I can't begin to explain how great it feels to be back in Bachusa, Your Majesty."

"You have no idea how long we have dreamt of this moment," Quairken shook the king's hand.

"We know," Queen Evalyn spoke with such softness.

Aironell felt the melody to the queen's voice. She continued scanning her surroundings.

"We dreamt of this moment for quite some time." The queen breathed. "However, we don't know how it feels to be whisked away from home and then come back after such a long time. Honestly, I can't even imagine the feeling. The king and I are glad you are back; all of you." Queen Evalyn let her gaze linger on Aironell.

Aironell turned around and let her eyes linger on the royal couple. Aironell was silent, unsure what to say. It all felt too quick. She did not get enough time to process, before she was brought here. Then the queen smiled at her and waved her over. Aironell moved within arm's reach.

"We are glad to see you, Aironell," Queen Evalyn gingerly tucked some of her hair behind her ear. "It has felt like forever since we saw you last." Aironell heard the hint of her soft voice tremble.

"I-I don't know what to say," Aironell glanced at each of them.

"I know." King Francisco patted her hands. They were firm but not rough. "It's hard because you don't have memories of us. This whole arrangement has been difficult. We look forward to learning more about you."

"Quairken. Isabella. How about you go and put Aironell's things in her room?" Queen Evalyn instructed. "Then maybe put your things away. I'm sure you would love to see your room and finally relax for a little bit."

"Yes, Your Majesty." They picked up all the bags and turned to leave. Before they left, they gave Aironell a smile, then they left.

"Now, why don't you sit with us? We can have tea and treats." The king's voice was deep and smooth. "Maybe reconnect, if you're up to it?"

The queen sat down on the ruby red couch. The king sat down beside her. Aironell turned and faced the ruby red armchair near the king and queen. They watched her. She could sense it, even if she didn't see them. At least they seemed pleased to be with her.

Queen Evalyn placed a snowy-white teacup on a saucer in front of Aironell. She snapped her fingers and the silver teapot floated and slowly poured steaming hot tea into the cup. King Francisco held a plate of something that smelled sweet to her.

Aironell pursed her lips, "What are those?"

"Why they are chocolate scones," Francisco held the platter toward her. "They are quite delicious."

"Thank you." Aironell grabbed one and took a bite. They were yummy. Then she took a small sip of the tea, as she blew on it. It tasted sweet but unlike anything she had ever tasted.

"Do you like it?" Evalyn watched her carefully. "It's a family blend of licorice root and chamomile."

"It's definitely interesting. A subtle soothing quality that is sweet." She took a few more sips. "I think I could get used to it."

"Excellent," Evalyn smiled. "Well, Aironell, we want to know as much as we can about you."

The king nodded.

"Oh. I don't know what to say. I don't have much to tell."

"Honey, anything you say will be new to us, so anything will be great," Queen Evalyn clasped her delicate looking hand to her chest.

"Alright," Aironell bit her lip. Her fingers slowly twisted around each other. "I'm sixteen. I, um, I—"

"That's a start," King Francisco's eyes softened. "Take a breath. You're doing fine."

"He's right. Why don't you tell us about school? Do you have any friends?" Evalyn smoothed out the bottom of her dress.

Aironell took a few slow breaths. "School is great; I love it. I have lots of friends. They come to me for advice." Aironell felt a heaviness. *Emilia.* She realized she would never see her again. Never get to tell her what happened. She slumped in the chair.

"That's good that people come to you. Aironell, are you alright?" The queen leaned forward.

"I just realized I won't be returning. It's all new to me." The king's eyes looked solemn. Then he blinked.

"I love helping others find happiness. Interactions could be complicated."

"Well, that seems to be the case, generally. We see complicated daily in our line of work," replied Queen Evalyn.

"I know that's true. I remember meeting Alex, but I think Isabella said his name was, Alzerion." She said his name slowly. She wanted to be sure that she said it right.

"Ah yes," King Francisco nodded. "Alzerion is one of the good ones, but complicated."

The queen smiled. "Of course. He's just busy at the moment, but when he comes back, he will want to see you."

"So, you didn't have a boyfriend?" Francisco asked as he sipped some tea. His eye quirked up.

"No, of course not." She blushed. "I never found someone who was a perfect fit for me. I know what I want and well, I wasn't keen on anything less."

"Oh, she is definitely your daughter." The king laughed as he shifted in his seat.

Queen Evalyn pursed her lips as she pushed his arm. "I can't believe you said that." She turned her attention back to Aironell. "We want the man you choose to be the right one. I mean, here in Bachusa, you are considered an adult. As our heir to the throne, the man you pick will help you rule the kingdom. Your choice is rather important."

"Oh, well…no pressure or anything." Aironell gulped.

"We don't want you to worry about that." King Francisco swallowed. "We will support any choice you make. We're just saying that when you're ready to decide, you should do so with much thought. People here can be more manipulative than what you were used to. What with being the future queen and all, just be cautious."

"I promise I won't make any hasty decisions." Aironell set her cup down. "I never have in my life, and I don't plan to start now."

"Good," said the queen. "But sometimes things don't always go according to plan, dear."

Meanwhile, over in the training field, Alzerion heard panting. Some swearing as the men ran their laps. The sweat poured off of them like sweaty shirtless blurs. Until they started to finish.

"Come on, finish strong! You can do it!" yelled Alzerion.

He was trying to give the men a decent workout. Normally he would have worked out with them. He didn't know what that surprise was but he didn't want to need to shower from all the sweat.

"Sir, that was torture. Can we call it quits for tonight?" pleaded Castro. He was bent over hands on his knees. Strength and the ability to push forward. He knew that Castro showed promise, but he needed to master that. Some dropped to the ground and laid on their side. Catching their breath. He knew the army needed to be better, stronger. Whatever it took to be sure that Ulbrick wouldn't defeat them.

"We'll stop soon," he told them, his voice booming over the field. "Not because you're all tired but because I have to return to the palace at a reasonable time. The king said I have a surprise, whatever that means, so I will be cutting practice short tonight."

"Alright," said Castro. "When will we be done?" He spoke through ragged breaths.

"When I say you're done! Come on, men, I'm disappointed that you're all tired already."

"In our defense, we did a lot of workouts in a short timeframe."

"That's true," said Alzerion, "but—"

Something caught Alzerion's eye. He saw a light on at the palace. He squinted for a better look. As he stared, he saw two silhouettes in a window upstairs.

He turned back to Castro and the men and said, "Well, you are all in luck. You're done now."

With those words, Alzerion quickly put on his white button shirt, navy blue tie, and black sweater. The men didn't stop to ask. They headed to the barracks. *Who could be in those rooms? Could there be someone trying to break in and steal something?* Then with those thoughts, Alzerion disappeared in a puff of red smoke. He landed in the hall and outside the two bedrooms he saw them walk in. He strolled up to the door that contained the two silhouettes, opened it, and his jaw dropped. He was not expecting to see Isabella and Quairken, and then his eyebrow rose. He inched closer.

"W-What are you doing here?" Alzerion stammered.

"Alzerion! It's so good to see you and that you're in good health!" Isabella hugged him. His arms hung at his sides.

Alzerion's eyes surveyed the area while he was rooted to the spot. He didn't know what to think.

"We thought you would be glad to see us," Quairken tapped his arm.

"I am happy to see you, both. You seem well. Where is Aironell? Did something happen?"

"Oh, Alzerion, she's fine," Isabella lifted her chin as she spoke. "In fact, she's downstairs with the king and queen. They are having a nice time getting to know each other better."

"Oh," Alzerion bit his bottom lip. "Is she well?"

"Of course, she is. She even asked about you," Quairken nudged with his elbow. "She never forgot you."

"Well, that's rather surprising," Alzerion cleared this thickness from the back of his throat.

"I guess it can be seen that way," Isabella replied. "She always hoped you would return. Anyway, the king and queen were glad to see her."

"I can only imagine. They waited a long time to see her." He spoke like he was in some sort of a daze. He was replaying memories in his mind and trying to push them away.

"Aironell has turned into quite a lady," replied Isabella sweetly.

Alzerion just looked at them. "I see."

He looked down at his hands and was momentarily lost in thought. It was by his hands that Aironell was whisked away and forced to leave in the first place. He could not help but feel like this was his fault, even from the first day. If he watched her better, she never would have been taken by Ulbrick. She would not have been bait to lure him. Now, Aironell was back, and he was not sure what to do. He frowned.

"Alzerion, why don't you go see her? I'm sure she would be excited." Quairken leaned in and placed a hand on his shoulder.

"She would be delighted," said Isabella matter-of-factly.

A smirk escaped Alzerion's face, and he felt a warmth in his heart. He put his hand on his necklace and pulled it on top of his shirt. Isabella and Quairken looked at the necklace. Isabella's mouth opened.

Isabella broke the silence, "Obviously, you two will surprise each other. She thinks the world of you, Alzerion. She's nervous to meet you, again. She is convinced that you will be disappointed in her."

Alzerion's expression darkened. "Oh, Isabella, I could never. I'm just happy she's safe; I mean, that was the goal after all these years. Her safety means the world to me, and I'm glad all is going well."

"Well, she has had a lot to shock her today," replied Quairken. "She found out she was a princess, today."

"That must have been hard for her."

Isabella looked down, "It seemed too harsh to tell a child every burden. Nevertheless, she is strong and quite the sorceress."

"I'm sure she will get accustomed to being a princess. Anyway, I'm going to my room. I'll see you two later. Tell the king and queen that I'll be down for a bit once I'm finished. I just need some time to be alone and think."

With those words, Alzerion left down West Wing corridor and went straight to his room. Once there, he closed his door and sat at his desk. Alzerion started leafing through papers as he thought about Aironell, and then he found what he was looking for. It was a letter from Ulbrick. Only he could make Alzerion feel like a failure, even when everything was working out well.

Dear Alzerion,

The princess should be coming home soon. She is of the appropriate age. We need to meet up soon to discuss what our next move should be. We need to figure out what to do about Aironell. Also, we have to finalize our plans for the future of Bachusa. All in all, we have much work that needs to be done and tended to. See you soon, obedient servant.

Ulbrick

Alzerion sat and read the letter at least a dozen times. It pained him. The words clung to him. Dredging up every insecurity he held. *Aironell.* She made it this far. Now the real work started. Keeping her safe, especially once everyone knew she was back.

Alzerion slammed his fist against the wooden desk. Flexing his fingers out as he gripped the wood beneath his hand. Ulbrick's words cut into his very being. He was persistent. Alzerion swallowed this sourness. The truth was bitter, but Ulbrick had to be watched.

His head lowered and slowly shook. Aironell just arrived and already there were forces against her. He fought the churning feeling in his stomach as he straightened up.

Downstairs in the family room, Aironell listened to what the king and queen; her parents were telling her. *It was so weird. She was a princess. Wow.* That was going to take some adjusting. After the latest topic, her eyes wandered across the room. Someone was coming. She always could just feel when someone was near. Aironell's gaze locked in at the doorway. There Isabella stood. Her body rested against Quairken. Aironell tracked them as they moved into the room. Isabella took a few deep breaths. Quairken continued pushing them forward with his hand against her back. *Something was off. She could sense it.*

King Francisco looked over and saw them standing near. "I thought you both would have liked some time to yourself."

"That was rather generous, your majesty." Isabella pursed her lips.

"Is there something wrong?" King Francisco tilted his head toward them. Aironell couldn't believe how firm he looked, like iron.

"Nothing, Your Majesty," Isabella bowed. Casting her eyes down to the ground. Aironell frowned. *Lie. Isabella was hiding something.* She bit the inside of her cheek as she kept observing the exchange.

Aironell rubbed her hand off the base of her neck. "Please tell us. I'm not sure what, but there is something you're not saying."

Isabella kept her gaze down at the ground. The king shot a look at Isabella and then over to Aironell.

"Are you sure about that?" Queen Evalyn shifted as she pulled at her dress.

"Yes …mother, I'm sure." Aironell cleared her throat. She tested how it felt to say. *Awkward.* No, she couldn't do it, not yet. It felt wrong, especially in front of Isabella. The woman who she thought was her mother all this time.

Isabella gave a wavering smile. She looked back at Aironell. *There it was*, Aironell saw the pain. I'm sorry she mouthed.

Isabella nodded. She took a breath. "It's Alzerion."

"What do you mean?" Queen Evalyn pursed her lips as she waited "He's not here. He's out training the Royal Army."

"He was just talking to us, Your Majesty," Quairken placed a hand on Isabella's shoulders.

"He might have returned," King Francisco said. "I told him he could have a short training session. I hinted that there would be a surprise when he got back: your arrival."

"Well, I'm glad you did. Alzerion will be excited at his surprise." The queen beamed as she clapped her hands together.

"Actually, well, you see, we saw him upstairs," Isabella finally looked up. Her eyes shifted back and forth between the queen and king. "He was not in a rush to come down."

"Quairken nodded. "He didn't seem pleased that we were here, with Aironell. I'm not sure why." He straightened up.

"I told you he would not like me," Aironell sighed. She flinched at the thought and shook her head.

"Darling, that is nonsense," Queen Evalyn grabbed Aironell's hand. She squeezed it, ever so lightly. "Where is he right now?" She turned to face Isabella and Quairken.

"He went to his room instead of coming down here." Isabella picked the skin around her thumbs.

"I see," King Francisco stood. "Well, I'm going to check on him." He moved off to the side. He disappeared in a puff of red smoke.

He appeared outside Alzerion's room. He took a breath and quietly opened the door. Alzerion sat at his desk with his hands on his head. Elbows propped up against the desk. He knew that Alzerion was over-worked, but so were they all. The king watched for a few moments. He stepped a bit closer with arms crossed. "Alzerion, why won't you come down and see Aironell?"

Alzerion spun around in his seat. He rubbed his jaw as his eyes never left the king's face. "I will. I just can't yet."

"Why, though? This is the day we have all been waiting for. She's here. She's safe. It is all thanks to you." King Francisco waited, but Alzerion said nothing. He seemed distant. "Aironell blames herself."

Alzerion locked eyes with the king. "I can't imagine why."

King Francisco sat down on the empty seat next to Alzerion. "She said she knew you would be upset or disappointed with her."

"I could never be disappointed in her." He sighed.

"Alzerion, I must admit that you are unusually quiet. What's wrong?"

Alzerion ran his hands through his disheveled hair. "I'm- I'm." He cleared his throat as he rubbed his lips together. "There's nothing wrong. I'm just a bit tired." Alzerion rubbed a hand against his forehead. "Is she, really upset?"

King Francisco nodded.

"I don't get why. She doesn't know me, not really. Hell, there's not much to know."

"That's not true," King Francisco patted him on the arm. "You're a great person. She remembers you from when you stayed with them."

"She does?" Alzerion's head pulled back. His face still.

King Francisco nodded. He stood up and strolled toward the door, then turned. Alzerion sat there and half-smirked. It faded faster than it formed.

"What's wrong, now?"

"Nothing. I'm just thinking, that's all."

The king's gaze bore into Alzerion. His arms crossed.

Alzerion walked toward King Francisco, with his head low. "What will I say to her? She was young when we last spoke. How will she react when she finds out what I did?"

"You kept her safe," the king's tone was light. "Why would she be angry at you for that?"

"I…don't know." The king observed Alzerion. He couldn't shake the feeling that there was more going on. Alzerion wasn't acting like himself.

The king leaned in and broke the silence. "Alzerion meet her. There will be time for you to worry later. You might find that she enjoys your company and that you don't have to worry." He held out his hand.

"Alright," Alzerion sighed as he looked up at the king. He nodded and left his room. King Francisco followed right behind him. They came to the grand staircase, and Alzerion halted. He took a breath and continued.

Once they reached the family room the king strolled in and sat next to Queen Evalyn. He waited for Alzerion to follow.

Alzerion stood in the doorway and looked around. He smirked. Aironell was here at last, reunited with her parents. She looked so grown up. He felt a bit flushed and then looked away. He glanced down at his hands and the ring placed on his finger. It had a *U* insignia and a snake. It was the emblem of Ulbrick and his rebels. For him, it was a constant reminder of the snake lurking under the surface. Ulbrick and his plans. *Ugh*, he rolled his eyes. He snapped out of his thoughts once he heard her voice.

"Is he not coming? I knew it. I warned Isabella and Da—I mean Quairken that he would dislike me." Her voice was sweet. It sounded like a melody. But there was no mistaking the pain that cracked through her words. He licked his lips as he continued to watch.

The queen exchanged glances with her husband.

"Aironell, he doesn't dislike you," the queen leaned over and rubbed her arm. "He has been waiting years for your safe return."

"Your mother is right," King Francisco grinned. "I'm sure when he's ready, he will come see you."

He saw Aironell looked down at her feet. The king glanced back at the doorway, at him. Alzerion gulped. The king was firmly staring at him. He didn't like how Aironell seemed, hurt. She had this pained expression, almost like disappointment, as she looked down. He did not want Aironell to think he hated her, but he was torn. Should he move closer and speak? *There were so many choices*, he thought, as he watched.

He saw her eyes as she continued to look down. They were even more spectacular than he could remember. The hints of cerulean sparkled like that of water glistening under the sun. Except now, they looked sullen. They were heavy and misty.

Her beautiful curly, dirty blonde hair brought out her fair complexion. He waved his right index finger in a circular motion, and a red rose appeared in his hands. Then he approached Aironell. The rest of the room scanned his every move.

Alzerion stopped right beside Aironell. He straightened his posture, "I kept my promise." His voice oozed warmth.

Aironell looked up. Alzerion and his red rose were inches from her body. Aironell looked at it and then up at him. Alzerion desperately wanted to know what she was thinking. Aironell stood. She glided until she was in front of him. He noticed that her eyes locked on his. "You, um, you're, I mean you are Alex." She circled around spying each side of him.

"I am." Alzerion licked his lips as he continued to hold out the rose, as if they were the only two in the room.

"May I?" Aironell pointed at him. Unsure what she wanted, Alzerion found himself nodding. *Dummy, what did you agree to?* Aironell's smile was sweet and wide, as if her whole face was smiling. She continued to pace around him, but this time she reached out her hands. Within moments, she gently slid her hands up his arm over each ripple of muscle. Her fingers danced across his skin with such delicate speed. They traced the lines of his cheeks and her hand cupped right under his chin. Alzerion gulped, loudly, that he was certain everyone else could hear. He pulled her hand down and took one step back.

Alzerion bit the side of his lip as he took a deep breath. "You're supposed to take the rose. It's a gift."

Aironell reached her hand out and took the rose. Then she brought it closer and gave it a whiff. "Thank you. It seems so familiar."

Alzerion swallowed. "They were your favorite. I would place them around your room." He quickly glanced around. The king and queen sat nestled on the couch, while Isabella and Quairken stood off to the side. Everyone was watching. Waiting. Not sure if she sensed the awkwardness, but Aironell broke the silence.

"What promise were you talking about?"

"No need to worry. I will tell you, in time," Alzerion smirked.

"Why bring it up if you didn't want to tell me?" Aironell furrowed her left eyebrow.

"Mmm, we don't know each other. Not well." His head moved side-to-side.

"What does that have to do with anything?"

Alzerion shook his head, "You can be difficult."

"It's just—"

"Why don't you sit and join us," King Francisco motioned. Aironell breathed out and sat down in the armchair. He strolled over and sat on the armchair across from Aironell. They were separated by the fleur-de-lis table.

"I thought we were going to have to send you both to your rooms," the queen laughed.

"I'm sorry," Aironell tapped her fingers on her lap. She turned her gaze back on Alzerion, "I didn't mean to sound harsh."

"No apologies are necessary," he gave a curt nod as his lips twisted into that crooked half smirk of his.

"Alzerion tends to be rather a riddle-master," Queen Evalyn joked as she took a sip of tea.

"Quite true," King Francisco beamed. "Sometimes it's almost like a game of chess. Who can puzzle out the other first. He isn't into sharing."

Alzerion grabbed a fresh cup of tea from the table. He Craned his neck over the cup, and blew at the steam; slowly. He glanced at Aironell. Her eyes bulged a bit, but still had this steady sharpness. He swallowed another sip and wiped his mouth. "I prefer to keep things to myself. Once I know you better, I am more forthcoming."

Aironell straightened in her seat. Her gaze softened. "Can I ask if you are well?"

"Quite well, but why do you ask?" Alzerion's eyes pinched in. His foot lightly tapped on the floor.

"It has been some time since I saw you last. I remember that you were injured and were recovering."

"Oh, that was a long time ago," chuckled Alzerion. "I've long since healed."

Her gaze flicked up as she crossed her arms. Her eyes narrowed. They looked like daggers waiting to slice. "That's not funny. All I wanted to know was that you are keeping yourself safe."

"I'm sorry," Alzerion stopped laughing. He bit the inside of his cheek. *Way to go, genius.* "I've kept out of major trouble."

"What do you mean by major trouble?" Aironell gazed down at the rose in her hand. She pressed her thumb and index finger together, with one of the petals firmly squeezed between them.

Alzerion ran his hands through his hair and leaned back in his chair.

Should he answer all these questions? Why was she so interested in him? He opened his mouth to speak, but then closed it just as fast. He didn't want to overwhelm her. Alzerion wrinkled his nose and scratched the side of his head. "I don't know if anyone ever told you what my job entails."

Aironell shook her head as her fingers danced across the rose petals.

"Well, let's just say that I have a knack for getting into tough spots."

Quairken coughed. "Sorry." He nodded at Alzerion.

Alzerion slowly turned back to Aironell. "I was sent here as a child for a proper education. I wasn't the easiest, I will admit." He paused. Aironell made no move to say anything, so he continued. "So, I found myself receiving physical training, with the Royal Army." Aironell was no longer fiddling with the rose, but rather her gaze shifted to him. He felt a warmth on his cheeks. He breathed out.

"There was talk about my being groomed to become the commander of the Royal Army. So, I studied, went to school, and trained as hard as I could. Things changed when you were born."

"How so?" She tugged at hair as her fingers wrapped a lock around her index finger.

"There was such excitement when you were born. Your safety became our number one goal. I was tasked with keeping a close watch on you. It was my duty to protect you at all costs."

Aironell nodded as she looked around the room. "I see. So, what you're saying is that from time to time, you do deal with chaos that could land you in a sticky situation."

"Exactly." Alzerion shifted in his seat. He heard the king clear his throat. He almost forgot that they were not alone. Alzerion stood up and strolled behind the couch to gaze out the window. He heard the queen speak.

"Well, I don't mean to ruin this wonderful moment, but it's getting late. Why don't we get some sleep?"

"That sounds like a good idea," the king agreed. Alzerion turned around to face them.

"Of course," Isabella bowed her head. "Come, Aironell, we will show you to your room."

Aironell nodded and strode toward Isabella. She took one last glance around. "Goodnight." King Francisco and Queen Evalyn strolled to Aironell.

Aironell hugged the king and queen. She went to Alzerion and reached out her arms to hug him, but instead he shot his hand out. She grasped his hand. He felt the warmth of her touch. Her skin was smooth like folded silk. Aironell lowered her eyes and walked toward the door, where Isabella and Quairken waited. With that, Aironell followed Isabella and Quairken upstairs. The king and queen left to go to their rooms, and Alzerion followed suit.

HEIRLOOMS AND ADVENTURES

The sun rose a mix of pink and yellow-orange. Such vibrant colors shone through her room. Aironell rolled on her side, peering out the window. What could possibly be better? Aironell felt lighter, somehow. It was like she was never gone from this place. She stood up in a hurry but remembered her parents were in a morning meeting, so she sat back down on the soft bed.

"Hmm, what to do?" She tapped her fingers against the silk bed sheets as she looked around.

She wanted to do more than study the history of Bachusa. Those large tomes sat, over there, by a quaint little fleur-de-lis shaped book-shelf. It hung behind—yet still close—to her little table and chairs. "Well, I do still need to explore," she said with a sly smile on her face.

After a few minutes, there came a knock on her door. "Come in."

The door swiftly opened and Isabella stood with a small silver plate of something delicious smelling. She walked to Aironell's bed and sat down by her. Isabella placed the plate beside them on the bed.

"What smells so good?" Aironell sniffed around the plate.

"Those are new from the kitchen. Not sure if they have a name yet." Aironell sat mouth practically watering, as she glanced over at her. "It is some sort of dough that has been fried and tossed in powdered sugar."

Aironell's eyes widened. "May I take one?" Her hands reached for the plate even before Isabella nodded. It was warm, fresh. It had this soft textured feel to it. Aironell raised it to her nose, tossed her head side-to-side, and then took a bite. She could have melted into a puddle of sweetness. "Oh—my—goodness." She spoke between bites. She knew it was not behavior for a princess, but she couldn't help it. The sweetness of it just melded together.

"I guess you like it." Aironell nodded as she handed a piece to Isabella to try. "Now I see what everyone in town has been talking about."

Aironell finished the last bit of hers as she saw Isabella scanning the length of the bed.

"Did you sleep well?" Isabella smoothed out the pillow off to her other side.

"Yes, I did." Aironell wiped her hands together, getting any last bit of dusting off. Her eyes shifted as she held her breath. Isabella laughed. It wasn't harsh sounding but light, warm-hearted.

Aironell tilted her head, "What's funny?"

Isabella placed her hand to her chest and cleared her throat. "Sorry. It's just, well, you reminded me of when you were a little girl."

Aironell wrinkled her nose, briefly, and observed Isabella. She revealed nothing but a radiant smile. "How so?" Aironell finally asked.

She softly patted Aironell's hand. "When you were little you would make the cutest faces." Aironell focused all her thoughts onto the words. "Aironell, you were so expressive. It was rather comical." Isabella rubbed Aironell on the cheek with her other hand. A loving gesture—one that happened a thousand times before. Aironell beamed. So many memories they had.

"This is all so strange, don't you think?" Aironell starred down at her hands. They were fumbling with the tie that hung around the waist of her crème-colored nightgown.

"What do you mean?" Isabella narrowed her eyes.

"Well, not long ago, I thought you were my mother. It's not so easy to just, change." Aironell sounded flat—almost mechanical. It was like she was not present—like the breeze from her window could blow her down.

Isabella grabbed her hands. Aironell felt her touch gripping, squeezing, both hands. "Everything will take some adjusting. I'm sure of it."

Isabella watched her. Aironell could see the softness in her gaze. Like she did when she was younger. It always grounded her, when she was scared or unsure of things. Aironell kept steady eye contact. She nodded and pulled her in for a tight hug—arms wrapped around Isabella as she let the scent of vanilla wash over her like a dream. When she pulled away, slowly, Aironell beamed. "I know you're right. You're always pointing me toward what's true."

"Aironell you will feel right at home," Isabella rubbed Aironell's arm as she gave a slight squeeze. "I will need to adjust, too."

"How so?"

"I'm so used to checking in on you and taking care of you. Now that's not my job anymore. I came here this morning out of habit."

"I see," Aironell looked down.

"I'm glad I came," Isabella patted her back.

Aironell smiled sweetly. "Me too. Isabella? Is everyone else, um, awake?"

"Quairken is up and..." Isabella paused when she saw Aironell mouthing the words as she rubbed her chin. "That would be Daniel."

"Oh yes, I'm sorry." Aironell shook her head. "I find that to be one of the hardest habits to break."

Isabella chuckled. "Yes. All of these changes will take time. The king and queen are in the dining room."

"Thank you, Isabella," Aironell swallowed and tried to clear her throat. I wonder if you could tell me, err, I mean, um, if *he's* awake?"

"Your Highness, are you trying to ask me if Alzerion is up?" Isabella forced a blank stare.

Aironell's cheeks flushed. Her ears felt hot. *This couldn't be happening,* she thought. Her eyes shot right to the ground as she rubbed the back of her neck.

"Aironell, don't be ashamed. It's natural."

"Then why do I feel odd asking?" Aironell laid her head in her hands, as her elbows pressed off her lap.

"You shouldn't. After all, you're still his favorite."

Aironell was still avoiding eye contact so she kept staring at her feet, shuffling on the floor. Her face tightened a bit and she sighed. It was like a weight pressing in on her being—it needed to be released.

"There's more to Alzerion. Isabella ran her fingers through Aironell's hair. Aironell shook her head side-to-side.

"I don't understand." She finally uttered as she slowly picked her head up. "It's not my fault I was forced away. I can't separate his nuances."

"That's not what I mean. Alzerion is, well, complicated— no denying that, but when you were a girl, he made occasional visits."

"I know."

"He also wrote asking about you a few times. He even had us send him reports. Alzerion cared so much about your well-being."

"Well then I hope he stays that way," Aironell said, her face growing hot.

"Please don't be angry, Your Highness, but do you, you know, like him?" Isabella stopped running her fingers through her hair.

"No!" Aironell crossed her arms. "I don't even know him, not really. If I ever did, I would need some time." Aironell's eyes darted back and forth as she felt a slight blush creep across her cheeks.

"Well, that's understandable. I bet you'll enjoy his company."

"He does seem like a good person to talk to," Aironell twisted the hem of her nightgown.

"He is," Isabella nodded. Isabella grabbed that powdery plate and stood. "I wish that I could keep chatting, but I must go. I don't want them wondering where I went." Aironell nodded. "There's much work I have to tend to."

She bent forward and kissed Aironell on her forehead, and walked just barely out the door. She paused and twisted her face back in. "In response to your question, Alzerion is awake. He does his letter writing at this time, though." Then she left the room.

Aironell turned to find that precious gift. That red rose. She spied it on her dresser in a narrow crystal vase. It was still beautiful with that sweet, luscious smell, as if she was given it just yesterday. Her lips curved up into a smile. Since arriving in Bachusa, Aironell found that she felt lonely when the king and queen were busy. However, when she thought about things, she found herself doing the unthinkable. She could not stop thinking about Alzerion.

He changed over the years. Tall. Handsome. Mysterious. He intrigued her. She got up to put on a rose-pink lace gown with a corset top. She stood in front of her floor length mirror. Her hands ran along the gold trim cuffs and traced the fleur-de-lis on the sleeves. She smoothed it out. The bottom of the dress and the neckline also had gold trim. Then she put a rose-shaped clip in her hair. The clip was ruby-red with real rubies and tiny diamonds to accent it. She turned her face side-to-side and beamed. This became part of her morning ritual. Aironell caught her breath. She couldn't believe how different she looked.

"You're gorgeous," came a voice from behind her.

Immediately, she crossed her arms. She felt like she had been caught doing something wrong. Aironell turned around, slowly, as the figure of Alzerion stepped closer. She tried to level her breathing. She was hoping that she did not look as flushed as she felt.

"Do you really think so?" Aironell mustered.

"Definitely," responded Alzerion with a confident grin.

He stepped closer once more and pulled a tiny black box out of his back pocket. Her eyes fixed on the edges. They shimmered an inviting gold. She kept staring at the box.

"What?" Alzerion smirked as he thrummed his fingers against the box.

"What's inside?"

Alzerion licked his lower lip. He opened the box and pulled out a silver bracelet. Precious cerulean blue and cinnamon red stones dangled from it. The silver sparkled as the sun gleamed over it from a nearby window.

Still, Aironell furrowed her eyes. She watched as Alzerion's lips pressed together. They slowly moved upward into a curve, forming a seductive smile. He took a deep breath and closed his eyes momentarily. Finally, he made another step closer and slid his hand over hers. His skin was so soft. She swore her heart beat a little bit faster, like a pounding drum. She felt a jolt. Aironell merely, grinned.

Alzerion's fingers raised her hand, while the other hand placed the bracelet on her. When he finished, he moved back a step. She felt his eyes on her. Then he nodded. This time, her heart fluttered. Hell, it was practically dancing in her chest. She was speechless.

"Aironell?"

She looked down at her wrist. Grinning from ear to ear. So many things she wanted to say, but none seemed right. So, she flung her arms around him in a big hug. "Thank you," she whispered in his ear.

"I'm glad you like it."

Aironell squeezed once more and then stepped past him. "It's beautiful."

She winked and dashed to the door. Glancing back for just a second. Alzerion's right eyebrow raised slightly, and his nose scrunched up a bit. *How cute,* she thought. Then she darted out of the room.

Once out of sight, Aironell took a slow breath and made her way toward the grand staircase. She held onto the railing as she descended. She couldn't help but wonder if Alzerion was still in her room or what he thought about her departure. She pushed open the doors and entered the Royal Dining Room. She quickly spied the king and queen sitting, side-by-side, at a small table in the middle of the room. Aironell sat down across from them. She felt quite comfortable in this room. It reminded her of the dining room where she grew up. It was a bit smaller than most of the other rooms, here, but with my charm.

"Good morning, darling." Queen Evalyn grinned as she held up her cup tea.

King Francisco cleared his throat and stared. "You look stunning. So, grown up."

"Thank you, dad." She saw his expression soften. "You-you called me, dad." He reached out his hands and Aironell allowed him to grab her hands. He held onto her. It was an endearing moment. Aironell beamed as she glanced over at her mother, too. The queen's eyes appeared a bit watery and she placed her hands over her mouth. Aironell kept glancing at them both.

After a few minutes she folded her hands back in her lap. "May I ask you something?" Aironell's nails tapped against the textured white fabric that draped across the table.

"Of course, you can," Queen Evalyn spoke as she dabbed at her eyes.

"You can ask anything." Francisco nodded.

There was the creaking of the door opening. Aironell turned as she popped a grape into her mouth. Alzerion strolled toward them. She wiped her mouth with a napkin as her eyes scanned his body. She couldn't help but stare. He was so attractive. So mysterious. So, kind. She loved everything about him. She remembered to blink as she watched him run his hand through his hair.

"Hello Alzerion, would you like to join us?" King Francisco motioned to the chair next to them. Aironell narrowed her gaze. Watching. Waiting. She saw Alzerion look at them.

His gaze lingered on Aironell. She was beaming so hard that she felt like she might burst. Then Alzerion's gazed honed back on the king. "No. I have some business to attend to in town." Alzerion bent his head down low, like a nod.

Aironell's face went still as stone as she gulped. Alzerion turned to leave, but she caught his gaze and then he was gone. She couldn't help but feel this ache in her heart, like she wanted to lie in bed and wallow. Her eyes fixed on the door.

"What's wrong?" asked Queen Evalyn. "You seem a bit out of sorts."

"Oh, it's nothing." The princess shrugged and snapped her attention to her mother.

"Are you sure, dear?"

"I'm positive," she insisted, forcing a smile.

King Francisco licked his lips, grinned, and ate his pastry.

"Well, if you're sure."

Francisco swallowed. "Evalyn, she is fine. Right Aironell? It was just a momentary distraction."

Aironell's gaze darted between the two of them. "Absolutely. I was just distracted." She fixed her eyes on the king, he knew something, he had to. She looked back at Queen Evalyn and smiled. Hoping that they could move on.

"Oh alright. We want to discuss magic with you, anyway," said Queen Evalyn. "Isabella told us you have a good handle on your abilities. Is that true?"

"Oh, my magic. It is true," she nodded. Aironell picked up the half-heart necklace that hung around her neck, "I use this as a power source. It helped when I was learning how to keep my magic under control."

"That was a good idea," Queen Evalyn spoke as she pulled out this satin-red material and placed it on the table. King Francisco started speaking but Aironell heard very few words. Her eyes locked onto the satin material. She needed to know its contents. It wasn't flat. It bulged slightly and had an almost square-like shape.

She heard someone say her name and her gaze snapped back into focus. "Y-yes?"

"Are you alright?" King Francisco asked. Aironell could hear the concern in his voice. "I am fine. I didn't mean to worry you." She looked back at the queen and added, "Either of you. I was admiring that." Aironell pointed to the material.

"Alright. Well, that is a surprise, for you." King Francisco stood and ambled toward Aironell. He sat down in the chair next to her.

"A surprise? Oh, you both didn't need to do that." Aironell beamed as she glanced at the king. "Just being here is more than enough." Aironell leaned forward and wrapped her arms around her father. She squeezed, tight, and left an endearing kiss on his cheek as she turned at a small sound off to her side. Queen Evalyn stood with the mysterious material.

"For you, darling." Queen Evalyn placed it in Aironell's hands. Then she sat beside Aironell, too. Aironell was flabbergasted. *They didn't need to do this. Still. What could it be?*

"Aironell, you are too sweet, but we insist." Queen Evalyn's eyes darted down at the satin-wrapped gift. Aironell grinned as she started lightly pulling at the small opening on the satin wrapping. She felt so happy that her eyes sparkled from the unshed tear in her eye. She slid the last of the fabric off to reveal a book. Aironell grazed her hands over the covers, flipped them over and over. She beamed. Her fingernails caught on the elegant lettering of the titles, The Ancienne Magica de Bachusae volume I and The Ancienne Magica de Bachusae volume II. The books had this rather older yet elegant design that covered the book and the edges.

"We hope you...like it." King Francisco broke the silence. Aironell kept glancing down at the book; thumbing through some of the pages that crinkled with each turn.

"It's a family heirloom," Queen Evalyn added. "It has been passed down for many generations."

"Like it? I-I. I love it! Thank you." Aironell gripped the books close to her chest. She beamed left, to the king, and then right, to the queen. "I can't believe it. My very first family treasure!"

"I'm glad you're excited," King Francisco chuckled. "Your mother and I feared that you might not like them."

The queen placed a hand on Aironell's arm as she spoke. "We just weren't sure if books would be great gifts, but they are more than any ordinary read."

Aironell gently placed the books down and then hugged the queen. "I promise I love them. I will treat them with the utmost care and respect."

"Excellent." Queen Evalyn said. She reached for her glass and took a sip of her drink. "You may have noticed they are books of magic spells, first and foremost."

"I noticed." Aironell was scanning one of the pages. Her head tilted a bit and then she glanced back at the queen. "Mother, I am a bit confused about something."

"What may that be?" she cleared her throat.

"Well, they say volume I and volume II. I assumed they would flow in an order, but they don't."

The queen nodded and the king chimed in. "When we married our family lines were connected. Meaning that our family's magic books were, too. Your mother's family book has much more about the really powerful magical spells and even some tips." He paused and continued, "Does that help?"

"It does." Aironell stood up. "I cannot wait to read them and see what I can learn. What are your favorites from the books?" There was silence. Aironell looked at the queen and then the king. They each avoided her gaze. "What's wrong?"

"Sweetheart," the king started, "Your mother and I both have magic, we do, but, well, we don't use it often. We haven't used heavy magic in a long time."

The queen looked up at Aironell and added, "Your father and I gave you the books not just because it's the proper thing to do. We were told that you love using and practicing your magical craft."

Aironell nodded, "I do."

"That makes us so proud," the queen continued. "There is a wealth of knowledge in those books. Use them wisely and I hope that you make better use of them than we did."

Aironell nodded. "I will. I promise." She had this determined look about her. "I will practice. I know that it can help with matters here.

"That is very true." King Francisco wiped his mouth and stood. "I wish that we can stay and chat longer, but your mother and I have some things to attend to. Will you be alright, alone?"

"I will." Aironell grabbed the books and strolled out of the room and up the grand staircase. She heard the door shut and knew that her parents must have left the Royal Dining Room. She went to her room and placed both books on her mahogany desk. She took a few short breaths and then decided that it was high time for her to explore the palace. There were still a great many rooms that she hadn't seen. She wanted to feel like it was truly home. She strolled toward the frame of her door and stood in front of it while looking left and right.

"Hmm," she thought aloud, "going down the West Wing corridor will take me toward the grand staircase. However, I'm not certain about over here." She craned her head the other direction.

She started in that direction. This seemed more interesting as she knew where the grand staircase led. As she took her stroll, she kept at a leisurely pace so as to observe as much as possible. She let her left-hand glide against the hazelnut-colored walls, and she felt the golden fleur-de-lis embellishments. She walked down the hall for what seemed like forever, soon realizing this was the living quarters for the servants. Finally, Aironell came to another bend in the corridor. She went right to take her toward the outermost portion of the palace.

This corridor was narrower, and the walls were covered with pictures of the kings and queens of the past. There was a light that shone down the corridor from a curved opening where there should have been a door, but instead there was an archway with these beautiful pockets of light. They danced on the walls like how she imagined dancing at a ball.

"So beautiful," she mouthed in awe.

The picture frames were a dazzling gold with what appeared to be black diamonds all around like an accent. After looking at the pictures, Aironell headed toward the opening where the light was emanating from. Aironell cautiously stepped over the threshold, and the sight instantly took her breath away. Aironell blinked twice to be sure that she was not imagining things; but the scene before her resembled that of a picturesque book or painting of landscapes.

She moved toward the railing of the balcony and leaned against it as she surveyed the landscape. The balcony had vines that wrapped around the railing with small red roses that outlined the opening. She caught her breath when she saw the outline of buildings and the stalls from the market on the backdrop of a cornflower blue sky with a radiantly shining sun. The sights that were closer were even more captivating. Her eyes glanced below the floral balcony and saw what was called: Gorgeous Garden.

It was true to its name. Aironell saw ornate fountains, an elegantly carved wooden swing, and benches throughout the area. There was a small wall of stones that were gray, brown, and white that allowed people to look in, however, it mainly served as the boundary for the garden. The white stones sparkled a bit when the sun's rays cast its light. Everything seemed so perfect, especially with the flowers; bushes, and ivy vines.

"Mm," she said to herself happily as the scent of roses wafted toward her.

After standing on the balcony, soaking in all the beauty, Aironell decided to continue exploring, so she went back inside the palace. She walked down a corridor that led her toward the heart of the palace. Then she went down winding spiral staircases and came across more pictures.

She found the pictures of landscapes and family members to be lovely, but she yearned for that same amazement she felt at seeing the balcony and Gorgeous Garden. "Maybe I saw all the wonderful sights already," Aironell wondered as she continued walking.

Then she stood before an enormous door, one she had not seen before. She realized that the door had the same detailed sequence patterned across. It was a fleur-de-lis with a crown inside a heart with flecks that sparkled, just like magic. With her curiosity piqued, Aironell grabbed the rose-shaped handle and opened the door.

The room was quite spacious with shelves upon shelves all covered with books. Some of the books were very old because she saw that some had tattered covers with that old book smell. Aironell could not help but twirl about as she looked up and all around. There were so many books that someone could probably get lost here. She strolled around the room taking in all the sights when something caught her eye by the window. It was jutted out from the windowpane and lined with a satin cushion.

"This is amazing," she exclaimed. "Is that a window seat?"

She walked over and smiled wide when she realized it was a comfortable place to sit with a cushioned seat lined with silk nestled there beneath the window. After sitting in the seat for what seemed like forever, Aironell decided to head back to her room to relax and start going through The Ancienne Magica de Bachusae volume I.

THE MASTER PLAN

In town, the streets were all bustling. Alzerion sat on a bench and rubbed his hand to his head. He couldn't quite get Aironell out of his mind. He couldn't help it, but she intrigued him. Her mannerisms. The way she spoke.

"What's on your mind?"

Alzerion bolted up almost knocking into the person who spoke to him. When he realized it was his mother he just blinked his eyes into focus as he sat back down.

"Alzerion, is something wrong?" She asked visibly concerned.

He gazed at her. "No mother, nothing is wrong. You just caught me a bit off guard, that's all."

Melinda placed her bag of goods on the ground, propped against the bench and then she, too, sat down. Alzerion looked at her and saw lines creasing her forehead. He noticed that her eyes narrowed a bit.

He didn't want to burden her but how could he not tell his own mother. "Have you heard the latest news?"

Melinda's eye glowed at the question and she focused on Alzerion. "What news? I always know town happenings but I'm unaware of something new. What is it?"

Alzerion caught a laugh in his throat. He didn't want to offend his mother, but she reminded him of a little child, eagerly awaiting some prize. "Well, it is big news from the palace, so I'm not surprised you might not have heard. I just thought that maybe, just maybe it had reached your ears."

"No, I haven't heard anything about the palace. So, what is it?" Her hands pressed firmly on the bottom of the bench as she leaned in, digging her nails into the wood of the bench.

"Well," he leaned closer while some people finished walking behind them. "The princess has returned."

"What? I'm sorry I must have misunderstood." She shook her head.

Alzerion watched as she looked around them, like they were conspiring and didn't want to be found out. "Mother, I assure you of what I am saying. The princess—"

"Alzerion, I heard you right, then? I swore that I must have been wrong." Her face grew a bit paler, than normal. "Um, uh, how? When?"

Alzerion reached for her hand. She gazed at him. He could see she had a thousand questions. She stood and paced until she stood just behind the bench, staring.

"Mother, are you alright?" No response. She didn't even budge or look down at him. He ambled to be by her side and placed his hand, gently, on her shoulder and softly spoke, "Mother."

She blinked a few times and turned to face him. "I'm sorry. I'm just not sure what to say."

Alzerion couldn't help but laugh. She narrowed her gaze on him. "I'm sorry, but you are never at a loss for something to say."

"Well, very funny. I find your news to be worth more than a quick reply." Alzerion cleared his throat and nodded. His mother was right. This was serious business, indeed. He bent down, picked up her bag and handed it to her. She fumbled for the strap and once found she draped it over her shoulder. Alzerion motioned for her to go ahead of him and she did. They moved away from where they sat and strolled through the tiny garden.

"Alzerion are you worried? I mean with the princess returning."

He kicked at some of the grass as they moved about. "Oh, no. Well, I don't know. Maybe I am. I-I, I'm just not sure yet. I hate being unsure of things."

"You don't think others will try to act against her, again, do you?"

Alzerion gazed at his mother with a fixed stare. Did she know about Ulbrick and his past actions? He couldn't just ask her in case she did not. "Mother," he cleared his throat. "What do you mean?"

"Well, if my memory is correct didn't she have people trying to harm her?"

Alzerion sighed and nodded. "That is true. We will have to work to keep her safe. However, she does still have the necklace I gave her."

Melinda's face was scrunched up. He circled around so they could make their way back across the grassy area that they just came from. "Mother, I gave her The Lost Hope."

"The necklace that has been in our family for ages?" Melinda paused. He could feel her eyes boring in, inspecting his very core.

"Yes. You said it could go to a girl of my choosing."

"I know. It's just that I was hoping it would go to my future daughter-in-law."

"I know." He swallowed. They were back into the heart of town. He waited for his mother's words. He knew they were coming. She ambled toward Alzerion and they sat down on a bench that overlooked the markets.

Melinda patted his back. "Alzerion, I'm not mad. It's just that, that necklace has magical properties. It's special. What's more, it has been in our family for a long time; passed down through the generations."

He gulped and then gazed at his mother. "I didn't know it was that important. I just felt that she should have it. I can't think of anyone else I'd want to give it too." He stared back down at the ground watching his feet rolling pebbles over one another.

Melinda lifted his chin up and he could see her clearly. She did not appear angry. Her face was calm. "Alzerion, well I sense that things will work out the way they are supposed to." He nodded.

"You seem like there's some burden on you. Are you sure that you're not worried about the princess' return?"

"No, but Aironell will need to adjust. I have to find the best way to help her, that's all." He broke his gaze. He stood up and started pacing and stroking his cheeks. "I find that I keep thinking about whether we are doing all that we can or is she being cooped up inside too much or—"

"Oh Alzerion," her voice sounded light. He looked at her. Her eyes seemed like they were dancing. Her face beamed like she just won something.

He stopped and focused in on her. "What?"

"Honey, it all makes sense now." She was practically bubbling in her seat.

He moved back and sat down next to her. "What makes sense?"

"Alzerion, when did these feelings start?"

Alzerion stared off for bit and then tilted his head back at his mother. "What do you mean?"

"How long have you been thinking about Aironell?"

"I'm always thinking about her safety…it's my job."

"I see," Melinda grinned so much that he swore she might burst.

He folded his arms across his chest as he leaned back against the bench. His eyes narrowed at her. She seemed amused by something. All it did was spur a grimace as he sat. he waited to see if she would say more. But nothing came. Finally, he spoke with a sharp tone, "Mother, what is it? What do you see?"

"Oh, nothing. If you don't understand it's because you don't want to," she chuckled.

He squinted as he slowly took a breath. "Mother, Sometimes I think you're so very cryptic."

They sat side by side, staring off into the town for a little while when Alzerion felt a firm hand on his shoulder. He grabbed the hand, squeeze hard, as he stood up to face the newcomer. He relaxed his muscles when he realized it was Warren.

"You startled me," Alzerion smirked.

"Really? Aren't we a little jumpy today?" mocked Warren.

"You would be too if someone came out of nowhere and laid a hand on you," he playfully shoved Warren.

"Maybe."

"What are you doing here?"

"I was sent to find you, you know, you didn't show up for our meeting." Alzerion saw that Warren looked down at Melinda and back at him.

"Oh yes. I'm sorry. I got distracted for a moment. Warren, this is my mother, Melinda. Mom, this is Warren, a friend of mine."

"Nice to meet you, Melinda," Warren reached over to shake her hand.

"Same to you, Warren," she said sweetly.

"Mother, I have to go. I'm late for a meeting."

"Oh, of course. It was nice to see you, and I look forward to next time."

Alzerion and Melinda hugged, and she even gave him a kiss on the cheek. Then she said goodbye to Warren and disappeared into the crowd.

"Well, your mother seems nice," remarked Warren.

"Thank you. I love her and her meddling ways, but where are we headed?" Alzerion wanted to change topics.

"Oh yes, we need to go to Ulbrick's house."

Warren and Alzerion strolled through town. Alzerion loved how Bachusa was like a gem below the radiant sunlight. He caught the sun's rays hitting the light crystalline stone of the buildings. They strolled through Town Square and he saw merchants selling their products. The sights were always pleasant. The pleasant chatter. The children playing and running around. He stopped for a moment and closed his eyes. Ahhh, his favorite part. All the wonderful smells.

"Is everything all right?" Warren faced Alzerion.

"Oh yes, I'm fine. Why?" Alzerion opened his eyes.

"You just seem to be a little distracted."

"I'm not. I'm just looking around. Don't you just enjoy being in town? Sometimes I feel like I'm not here enough."

"Oh?" Warren chuckled, briefly. Alzerion quickly shot him a scrutinizing glare.

"What?" Warren scratched at the back of his neck, just barely making eye contact. Alzerion grabbed Warren and turned him around, slowly. Making certain to catch the sights before them. Then he twirled his hand in front of them, wafting over the smells from the delicious foods cooking and waiting to be purchased.

"Okay, I get the point. Alzerion, I wasn't making fun of you." Alzerion stared at him with arms crossed.

"Honest. I wasn't trying to start something." Warren patted Alzerion on the back. "The way you see things it's just, well, I don't always see our world the way you do."

Alzerion's relaxed back at his side as he placed one arm around Warren. They continued to walk leaving the sights of the town behind them. "Warren, I know. I'm not mad but, well, there are other things on my mind."

"Like what?" Warren chided. Alzerion just gulped. They headed away from the bustling part of town. Heading to Ulbrick's house. *Should he tell Warren? After all these years Warren had been like a friend. Ulbrick, hell, they would never be friends.* He sighed.

"You've been quiet." Alzerion no longer heard Warren's footsteps beside him. Alzerion turned and saw Warren just standing there, palms up. He motioned for Warren to come closer. Warren stood inches away. "Well?"

"Nothing is wrong. Again, my mind is elsewhere." In the dark narrow alley Warren leaned in, closer. Alzerion could feel his hot breath on his face. Could feel Warren's dark eyes scrutinizing him. Alzerion opened his mouth and closed it right back up like a spring. Now Warren crossed his arms and waited. Alzerion wrapped his arm around Warren and ushered him on, out of the dark alley and onto the back roads. He was almost there, to Ulbrick's house. Then he stopped. He spun and clasped Warren. One hand on each side of him. He saw that Warren was looking sharply at him.

"You're my friend, Warren, and I need to tell you something."

"Well, go on then. I've been waiting. I thought if I had to wait any longer I may die of impatience."

"Warren, I'm nervous to tell."

"What, is it a secret?" Warren whispered the words and then chuckled. Alzerion did not waver in his stony expression. "Maybe you should start talking, Alzerion, I'm starting to get annoyed."

Alzerion cleared his throat. Warren's face twisted. Brows furrowed and lips tightened. "Alright. I just don't want this to be made into a big deal."

Warren straightened his posture and stood, legs and arms crossed with back against the stone house. Alzerion looked left and right. Nobody was there.

Alzerion started pacing in circles. He stopped as he faced Warren as his hands smoothed his hair back. "Aironell is back." Finally, able to breathe after he just laid it out there.

Warren walked, almost sprinted away from the wall toward Alzerion. He grabbed him by the arms. "Are you sure?" Alzerion watched him. A moment passed. It could have been more as Alzerion scanned Warren's expression. Warren held firm to him as he shifted a bit. He never wavered. His gaze was strong and fixed. Warren nodded as the lines of lips slowly parted into a smile.

Alzerion blinked and swallowed hard. "I'm sure." Warren was in a frenzy of excitement. He twirled around like he was celebrating. Alzerion stepped back and his forced smirk faded. "Warren, Ulbrick can't find out."

Warren halted and turned. "What do you mean? He *has* to know. He will be so *pleased* with us."

Alzerion could see the determination in his eyes. "Warren," he clapped his hand to Warren's shoulder like he was clasping one of the soldiers after a good practice. "You know that I want to keep the princess safe, right?"

Warren wrapped his arm around Alzerion in a tight side hug as they continued walking down the back roads. "Alzerion, I know that you have strong feelings for the royal family, but—"

"Warren, there's no but. I hope that I can count on your silence here." He glanced over and saw Warren's gaze shifting. "Alright. I'll do it your way, but if Ulbrick finds out we are keeping things from him, he will end us." Warren pulled Alzerion to face him. "You know that I'm not exaggerating."

"I do. Thank you for your word." Warren nodded as they continued. They meandered avoiding large crowds as they approached Ulbrick's door. Passing one stone house after another.

"Alzerion wait." Warren broke the silence as he stepped in front of him with arm outstretched. Alzerion tilted his head and waited. "I really don't want to cause issues but I was thinking. You should know, well, um, Ulbrick has been plotting."

Brows furrowed down into slits, "What do you mean? Look at me and get to the point. I can hear Ulbrick's steps."

Warren's eyes darted to the door and back. "I shouldn't tell you. I can't. I—"

"Warren, say something, quick." Alzerion slid his hand behind his back into a quick waving motion. He heard Ulbrick's steps get further away, but not much. He bought some time but Warren had to start talking, now.

Warren's head slid down, facing the ground. "I can't. I'm sorry. I can't betray him, you know that. Just know that there is a plan. You have been busy with the royal army, lately, but Ulbrick has been moving right along."

Alzerion's nostril flared. If he could smack Warren he would. "You never said anything," he hissed between clenched teeth. Warren opened his mouth to speak but then closed it.

"Warren will I like these plans?" Then the door clicked open. Alzerion quickly glanced over at Warren who shook his head and then focused his gaze at Ulbrick who stood before them.

Warren cleared his throat, "I found him for you."

Alzerion breathed out his nose as he tried to regain composure. He knew that he had to time it right. Ulbrick can't suspect anything. He nodded his head to the master.

"Come in," Ulbrick croaked in his raspy, hoarse voice. Ulbrick walked inside followed by Warren and he followed suit.

He strode in not really paying attention. His mind was flipping through different emotions and thoughts like one flips through the pages of a good book. *What was Ulbrick planning? How bad was it going to be?* He knew that he would have to endure it. Warren shook his head, right, that wasn't a trick of the eye? He took a deep breath and stood against the crème wall, back straightened and arms folded over his chest. He knew, in his heart, that if he had to make a choice between the royal family and Ulbrick- there was no contest.

Ulbrick patted Warren on the back as he meandered to the couch and sat. Ulbrick looked a bit different. Could be age but he believed it had more to do with all the scheming and plotting, as of late.

"What was keeping you?" Alzerion heard but was still locked in on his thoughts. He felt this nudge against his side. It was Warren. Warren looked at him, sharply, like he was trying to convey a message without words.

He surveyed Warren's face but nothing. Warren then strolled over to sit on the little armchair across from him. Then Alzerion turned his gaze toward Ulbrick. "Sorry. I'm a bit out of sorts today."

"Any reason in particular?" Ulbrick's hands folded on his lap like he was awaiting something.

"Not really. You know just keeping busy." Alzerion did not waver. He kept his face firm like stone.

"Really." Ulbrick spoke between clenched teeth. "I have been hearing differently." Alzerion attempted to maintain his composure. "I'm not sure what you've heard but I assure you that it'll be news to me." Alzerion locked eyes with Ulbrick, who just had that same steely expression. He knew something but Alzerion knew better than to entertain it, unless he had a reason too. He spied Warren out of the corner of his eyes. Ugh he will give us away. Alzerion focused on slowing his breath out of his nose and blinked, once.

As his eyelids opened he locked onto Warren, for a moment, *don't say anything.* As he shifted his head back to Ulbrick, he saw Warren's eyes bulge a bit. He knew that he received his message.

"Hehe. I see. Well we do have much to discuss."

"I did tell him that we had things to talk about," Warren said then swallowed.

Ulbrick snapped his attention on Warren. "This is a delicate matter! You shouldn't have said anything. You didn't have authority." Ulbrick's voice, though hoarse, boomed. Alzerion saw Warren's gaze cower and then look down. Almost like a child being scolded.

"I-I-I sorry." Warren dared to look back at his master. "I didn't tell him any details."

Ulbrick's fist pounded on the table in front of them. "No excuses."

"Well, what are these plans." Alzerion asked. "Better yet, will I approve of them?" Ulbrick gave Warren one last menacing glare and then turned to Alzerion.

"How dare you speak that way." Ulbrick leaned forward and beckoned for Alzerion to come closer. Alzerion moved closer, but did not sit. "Alzerion, I don't rightly care if you approve of the plans." Ulbrick hissed.

"You should if you want my help. I think you didn't tell me because you're not looking for my partnership but rather just someone to mindlessly do what you say."

Ulbrick stood. He glanced down at Warren and then over at Alzerion. "So suddenly you both grew a spine or maybe you're just being too sensitive? How troubling." Then he chuckled as he moved behind the couch and over to a room with the door closed. Ulbrick waved his hand and the door clicked open. "Come, both of you." Warren stood up and walked, quickly, as Ulbrick instructed. Alzerion hesitated but then followed.

He knew this was Ulbrick's planning room. The walls were darker in here with papers everywhere. There were piles on shelves mixed in with books. In the center of the messy room there was a simple battered wooden table. The table was not any different. It was covered will all types of papers. Alzerion walked toward the table and fumbled through pages that had things circled, crossed out, and some papers were crumpled into tight balls.

Alzerion twisted his head to Ulbrick who stood next to him. Ulbrick nodded at Warren who grabbed what looked like a large book. He opened it as he came closer. He set it down on the table and Alzerion saw what looked like an opening in the book. Then he focused his attention on it. It was not a book, Alzerion smirked.

Warren's hands moved nimbly twisting knobs and turning levers until there was a slight click; and then a little metal lid opened. Warren pulled out a wad of papers that were neatly folded. Ulbrick snapped his fingers and the papers floated up and flew toward Alzerion. He grabbed them and sat down in a rickety chair. Alzerion's eyes widened as he slowly leafed through the pages. Speechless, for moment, as he mouthed, wow. He flipped again and he felt something pumping within him. He gazed at both Ulbrick and Warren who stood around him.

Ulbrick pointed his finger at the next paragraph. "If we take the rebellion further, we could incite a war. Then we could defeat the Royal Army once and for all." Alzerion tapped his fingers against the edges of the papers as he read.

"How do you plan on defeating the army?" Alzerion's tone was a bit sharp. "We don't have the numbers and the Royal Army is well trained."

Warren cleared his throat and Alzerion focused on him. Warren's gaze bounced between papers but not at Alzerion. "Alzerion, if you look at the next paper, it shows that we do have the numbers." He gulped. "Ulbrick made it my mission to gain followers and support for the rebel cause." Alzerion couldn't believe his eyes. One hundred and fifty. Did he read that correct? "I've been training the newcomers," Warren added.

"See?" Ulbrick said smugly. "We have a good chance of winning this. What do you say?"

He shook his head. "No!" He stood up and slammed the papers into the table. He paced without stopping. Then he turned and leaned with hands planted against the table. "How do you expect me to fight the people I owe my life too? The king and queen practically raised me. Plus, I'm one of the best soldiers and *I* trained the Royal Army."

"You will do this." Ulbrick demanded. "You don't really have a choice." Ulbrick spoke with his head held high.

"Alzerion," Warren cleared his throat. "We held off on plans for a while."

Ulbrick moved within reach of Alzerion and his cold hand patted his shoulder. "Alzerion, I haven't made any harmful attempts on the king and queen before. I held off long enough and that was out of respect for you."

Alzerion shrugged him off and took a step back. "You don't value or respect me! If you did you never would be suggesting a war."

"Come on, Alzerion." Warren spoke. "Let's stay calm."

"It's too late." Alzerion felt this rage within.

"Enough!" Ulbrick snapped. "Alzerion you will do what I ask. You made me a deal many years ago."

Alzerion's eyes narrowed almost into slits as his nostrils flared. "I'm not afraid, Ulbrick. There's nothing that you can do to me, that I couldn't live with." He stormed toward the door to leave.

"Oh? So, you no longer care about the princess' well-being?" Ulbrick's mouth twisted into a sly smirk.

Alzerion stopped. He spun around so fast. "You really will say anything to keep me from walking out that door."

"Alzerion, please." Warren pleaded. "You know what will happen if you don't help." Alzerion did not say a word. He looked down at the papers. Uncertain. He knew he did not want to push Ulbrick to the point of no return, but how could he condone what Ulbrick wanted.

After a brief silence, Ulbrick meandered around the table and smirked. "Alzerion I know what this is about."

"What do you mean?" Alzerion asked. Even Warren had this blank stare.

"Tell me, is she beautiful? Has she cast some spell over you?" Ulbrick waited.

Alzerion opened his mouth but thought better.

"I don't get it." Warren spoke first.

Ulbrick's gaze darted at Warren. "I'm talking about the princess. I know that she's back. I was waiting for Alzerion to admit it, but I guess he was trying to keep it a secret." Ulbrick hissed. "Did you know about it, Warren?"

Warren gulped. Alzerion shook his head. Warren gulped. "I knew. I'm sorry." He flinched away but nothing happened. Alzerion glared at the both of them.

Ulbrick smirked and then sat on one of the chairs with his hands folded. "I'm not mad. Disappointed but you came clean in the end, Warren. Now, Alzerion, I do believe you said I couldn't do anything to change your mind. Well, I do believe that I have the upper hand." Alzerion's nostrils flared as this bitterness filled inside as he looked over at Warren, who mouthed, I'm sorry. Then he focused back on Ulbrick. "I really do hate you."

"I know." Ulbrick's words had this coldness to them. "Is it your job to keep her safe, just like before?"

Alzerion glared but then nodded, firmly.

"Warren?"

"Yes," he replied. He fixed his eyes right on Ulbrick.

"This will help us gain access to the princess. It has always been Alzerion's job to protect her and now, well he will serve her head on a platter if we need."

"Enough!" Alzerion thundered. "Warren you know I don't want her harmed." Alzerion pleaded, but Warren just looked down at the ground.

"Alzerion, you will do what we need."

Alzerion's face twisted into disgust. Then he frowned. "No. I-I can't." Alzerion's voice wavered for a moment. "I could never harm her. When I agreed to help you, you promised no harm would come her way."

Ulbrick sat with ease. Like nothing affected him. "Actually, I said that she was safe, for now. Well, now things are different. Now she matters. Now she is of age to cause trouble for my plans. Now she must be dealt with."

Alzerion shuddered at the coldness but still held firm. "No! Never going to happen."

Ulbrick rose. "Alzerion enough. We will fight. Go to the palace and prepare as the rebellion will strike within the month. There is nothing you can do to stop me!"

Alzerion glared. He was frustrated with both of them. Warren bowed his head toward Ulbrick. *How could he always do as instructed? Does he have no soul, either of them?*

Annoyance and anguish flooded his face. As his right hand circled above his head, he disappeared in a puff of red smoke and then appeared in an empty hallway at the palace. He slammed his boot into the ground as he turned trying to collect himself. How could he have been so blinded? He knew Ulbrick shouldn't have been trusted, but he trusted Warren to have his back. Turns out old age wasn't going to make Ulbrick soft, just desperate. Alzerion clutched at the half heart necklace and closed his eyes. He knew what he had to do.

AS THE BONDS GROW STRONGER

Aironell laid in her bed wiping the last bit of sleep from her eyes. She was bombarded by a whirlwind of thoughts. *It's too early.* She sat up, slowly, scanning her enormous room. This couldn't be real, she thought. Then there was this chirping. A bird was perched on her window.

It had copper brown feathers, all slicked back, with a white underbelly that was flecked with black specks. It was stunning against the sunlit sky. The chirps were even more amazing. It sounded like a seasoned flutist, serenading her. She sat watching at it, grinning. It stopped abruptly and flew away.

"Wait, where are you going?" *Wow. Did she really think that the bird would listen to her?* She shook her head and started to pull off her blankets, but resisted when she heard laughing. There he was Alzerion. Standing there with that smirk. Like he was toying with her somehow as he stood with his arms folded across his chest as he leaned against the doorjamb.

Her eyes were glued on him but she steadied her breathing just enough to not seem exasperated. "What are you doing here?" She fiddled with the seam of the blanket that covered her.

Alzerion locked eyes with hers. She watched, carefully, as he bit his lower lip. She couldn't help but think that they were inviting her in. *Kissable.* That is how she described them. Every time he laughed or smirked or just spoke it was like they were inviting her in; like magnets.

Alzerion strolled in until he was in front of her. "I just wanted to check on you. Seeing that you slept well." *Did he care about her?* She wasn't sure and she was not going to ask. She was practically melting inside the way his words oozed out. He always sounded charming and sure of himself. She swallowed.

"I am awake. I was watching the cutest little bird, but it left." She craned her neck toward the window. There was a dip in the mattress and she felt this warmth wash over her hand, as it lay on her sheet. She turned back and there he was, inches, if that from her.

"Well, you know what they say, right?"

Not entirely sure of what he said she stared blankly and shook her head sideways. "Huh?"

He slid his hand against her cheek until he was near her ear. She felt this fluttery feeling in the pit of her stomach. She wasn't sure if it was excitement or nerves. He leaned even closer. *Oh! There's about to be a kiss, she was sure of it.* Her insides were screaming at her. Now was the moment she had to decide her reaction. Her lips slowly parted.

He moved a loose strand of hair from behind her ear and then pulled back, a bit, and continued. "They say birds are quite the judge of character. They only get close to remarkable people."

"Are you mocking me?" Her eyes narrowed as she laid her hands over both of her cheeks. She felt the warmth attempting to creep through. She did not want him to know that she was blushing, even if it was just a little.

"I would never." Alzerion smirked. Then he grabbed her hands. He held them tightly in his. She gazed down at her hand in his. "Aironell."

She nodded. Any words she had, were eluding. His other hand cupped under her chin as he gently eased her face to look up at him.

"I am being serious. No jokes. No misunderstandings this time. You are amazing."

She looked into his cinnamon-red eyes and felt comfort. How did he do that? She found him mesmerizing. She felt like he understood her, down to her core. Excited yet nervous. That was how she felt around him.

"What do you mean, I'm amazing?" She finally found her words. She glanced at him and looked away, quick. She was regaining a bit of her sanity. *What was she doing? What was he doing?* The real question she still couldn't quite answer was, did she care?

Alzerion cleared his throat. She saw his cinnamon red eyes soften a bit. This was a look she hadn't seen before. "I think you have been so brave with coming home and meeting your parents, facing the people of Bachusa, and learning how to govern." He took a breath.

Aironell noticed that he seemed a little flushed. She grabbed his hand and squeezed, gently. She wanted him to know that she was here.

"Thanks. Aironell you are very sweet and kind." He stared right into her eyes, now. She gulped. "You are just an incredible young woman; so talented and beautiful and, well, it all makes you remarkable."

Aironell glanced away. She never was good with compliments. She wanted very much to believe him. "Alzerion, thank you." Again, she felt this urge within that he was someone she could trust, plus she liked that his attention was on her.

"You're welcome." She could practically feel the steam from his breath. She attempted not to swoon.

"Aironell?" She nodded. "Am I making you uncomfortable? I don't mean to sound full of myself but you seem—"

"I'm alright." She straightened up as she played with the bottom ends of her hair. "Honestly, I'm not used to all the compliments. They do make me a bit uneasy."

"Why? You haven't been complimented by a man before?" Alzerion playfully shoved her arm and pulled her in for a hug.

"Not quite like you just did," she leaned back and bit her fingernail and then folded her fingers into her palm.

Alzerion watched her. Glad to be seated. She felt so heavy like if she stood she would crumble down on the floor. Finally, Alzerion placed his hand on her upper back and slid her closer. Any closer and she would be on his lap. She just bit her top lip.

"Aironell, what are you going to do today?"

"I'm not sure." She tried to hide her disappointment. "My parents said I can do what I'd like. No magic practicing or lessons in governing. Why?" She tilted her head to the side.

"Just curious." His hands rubbed at his chin. "You should spend some time in town."

"I've already been in town."

"I know, but it never hurts to spend more time there."

"That's true." Aironell paused. Alzerion did not jump on that obvious moment. So, she continued. "Maybe I should do that." She scratched at the back of her neck. She tried not to look upset. The way that he was suggesting things, she thought he was hinting around at asking her on a date. But no. Nothing. Alzerion really was hard to read.

Alzerion nodded. He pushed down on the mattress as if to leave. Aironell held the blanket around her waist with one hand, as she moved to a kneeling position. Then her slender hands grabbed him by the elbow. He was about to stand when he turned back to her. He somehow managed to tower over her with his back arched. It looked like he was doing some kind of pushup, the way he stood. The creases that formed beneath the fabric of his arms rippled as he moved.

"That can't be comfortable." Aironell chuckled. She wanted to mask her staring at him.

"It's not. I didn't want to hurt you." He glanced at her hand, briefly. "Why did you pull at my arm?"

Aironell's hand recoiled back by her chest, as she held the blanket now, with both hands. "I had a question for you. I thought you were leaving."

Alzerion now straightened up as he looked at her. "No, I wouldn't have left without telling you. I'm not rude." Aironell nodded.

There was silence for a moment. "Alzerion, are you sure you want me to go to town just so that I can get better acquainted? What kind of game are you playing?"

Alzerion's gaze scrutinized her. She felt like she was about to be scolded. Instead his eyes softened and he laughed. "So, you think you know me well, do you?"

"Hmmm, maybe a little," she grinned. She managed to wrap the blanket around her body, like a cloak. She attempted to get out of bed but wobbled. Alzerion held out his hand and she grasped it. She clasped, firmly, to keep her body hidden as she scanned his face.

Alzerion placed a hand on her shoulder. "Honestly, I'll be in town today. I was hoping to see you there."

"You mean you want to spend time with me?" She tilted her head. She was just so, immersed in him and his next words.

"Well, yes. I, um, enjoy talking to you." Aironell breathed in and grinned from ear to ear. She couldn't believe it. *Maybe this was his way of taking her out, after all.*

She was now only half aware of her surroundings when Alzerion strode toward the door. Between thoughts of his dreamy demeanor, she heard his voice. As he turned to face her. His voice was deep but made her think of melted cinnamon butter. Smooth and delicious. "Aironell? Aironell? Aironell?"

Oh. He was calling her name. She gazed at him, like she was in a daze, and nodded. Hoping she didn't seem childish.

"Aironell, why don't I go so you can get ready."

"Of course." She nodded. "That makes the most sense."

Alzerion shook his head and smirked. He opened her door and left. Aironell squealed as she released her grip on her blanket. It fell to the ground and she immediately ran to her closet. It was filled with many gowns but she pulled out the one she bought the other day, and draped the baby blue gown over the armchair of her vanity. Her mind was buzzing as her fingers grazed the white lace that embroidered the top of the dress.

She bounded back to her bed. She flopped back and took a few deep breaths. *Alzerion.* How perfect that she would get to spend uninterrupted time with him. Away from her parents. She could not get Alzerion's face out of her mind. He was so handsome. She bolted up and put on that gorgeous dress. She was posing in front of her tall mirror, and checking her sides. She wanted to look perfect. Her hands glided over the light pink roses that decorated the gown, as she smoothed out any creases. Then she opened a little jewelry box on her vanity and grabbed a silver clip. She looked back at the mirror and placed it in her hair to hold back her curls. She touched her cheeks as she looked side to side and smiled.

"You look beautiful," said Queen Evalyn from the doorway. Aironell turned to her mother. She was so busy that she didn't hear her open the door.

"Thank you." Aironell beamed.

Queen Evalyn strolled over to her. She held her daughter's hands up as she slowly twirled her around. "You look lovely." Aironell beamed. "Is there any special occasion that I'm unaware of?"

"Nothing really." Aironell said as she glided toward the window, leaned against the balcony railing, and gazed out. "I'm going into town." She felt her mother's hand pat the top of hers. The queen moved about without a sound. It was a like a special superpower of hers.

"Aironell." There was a pause. Aironell turned to face her mother. She had that look. Lips in a tight line. Eyes that drooped a bit.

"Mother, did I do something?" She thought surely at sixteen that she was too old to have a moment like this; but she was wrong.

"I don't want to disappoint you." Aironell blinked, slowly, and stared at her. "I don't think you should go into town." Aironell shook her head and turned away. Face hard as she gazed out at the town.

She could see the bustling from there. People doing what they wanted. She took a breath. "Why can't I go? I-I-I want to do something more than royal duties and practicing magical spells. Some of which could kill me." Fists clenched as she held firm to the railing. The ebb and flow of the woody vines poked her palms. They were tough, never yielding, the same could not be said for the maroon-colored leaves as the points crushed beneath her grip.

Queen Evalyn placed a hand on her back and rubbed in slow circles. "I know. Trust me, Aironell, I understand the urge to get out but—"

"But, what?" Aironell pushed her hand away as she turned on her heels. She strode to the other side of her balcony and sat on a marble bench. She focused on the lines that divided each stone of the balcony floor. How each one, though a part of the whole, was still an individual. "I don't see the problem in getting out and doing something… fun."

"Sweetheart, please look at me." Aironell hesitated but did as she was told. The queen stood majestic as always. She looked solemn as she folded her hands. "Aironell, I'm just thinking about your safety."

Aironell perked up a bit. "Could I go if I have someone with me?"

The queen ambled to the archway between the balcony and Aironell's room. "If the person is suitable, then yes." The queen disappeared from view.

Aironell walked, briskly, inside. She saw her mother standing by the little oval mahogany table and chairs. She followed. "Mother, what does suitable mean, exactly?"

The queen sat in the chair and grabbed one of the porcelain teacups. She placed the cup near her mouth and chanted something, under her breath. Then Aironell smelled the tea. It was her mother's favorite. A pleasant mixture of chamomile and mint. Aironell sat across from her and waited.

After a few sips the queen glanced at her. "I'm not being snobbish. I don't mean a suitable partner, which wouldn't be a bad idea when considering marriage. No. I'm talking about someone to protect you." The queen blew at her tea, stirring it just so. "Maybe you can get someone from the Royal Army?"

Aironell pressed her teeth against her bottom lip as she grasped a loose strand of hair. It was there, calling her— beckoning her fingers to twist the curls around as she cleared her throat. "Well, I was thinking about going with someone that you would approve."

"Oh?" Queen Evalyn cocked an eyebrow. Aironell picked at the hardened skin around her jeweled finger. "Who did you plan to have escort you?"

Aironell gently pulled at her ear, for a moment, and then clasped her hands together in her lap. "Alzerion." She blurted. "I thought I would go with him and explore more of the town."

The queen's face brightened. She was practically radiating her approval. "Mother, why are you smiling so much?"

"Oh, well, it's nothing... really." The queen waved her hands like Aironell was being ridiculous. "I am pleased with your choice. Alzerion will definitely keep you safe." She took another sip of her tea.

"I know he will, but that's not the only reason why I want him to go." Aironell squirmed in her seat. Her ears had to be pink, bright, fluorescent—pink.

"What other reason do you have?" Her mother laughed, just for a moment.

Aironell felt like the queen's gaze softened. Thankfully. *Whew. Could she sense her deepest truths?*

"He asked me to go with him, and I want to go." Aironell clutched the arms of the chair like her life depended on its softness to keep her from falling. She forced her mouth closed. She couldn't believe it just poured right out.

"Aironell," the queen's voice did not sound angry but pleasant—soft, almost. The queen leaned closer to Aironell and held her hands. Aironell breathed out. "Darling, I understand but..."

Aironell stopped at but. *But what? What could be wrong? He wasn't just in the Royal Army, he was in charge. She couldn't be in better hands. Ugh... his hands. No.No. NO. She needed to focus.*

"Aironell are you alright?" Her mother's left eyebrow rose ever so slightly, as her lips parted.

"I'm fine. Promise." She sensed the queen looking for any doubts or any traces of something more. Well she wasn't going to give her any— no reason for her mother to keep her home.

"Aironell," the queen spoke in this warm tone. She noticed that her mother grinned so wide, that it could have matched her bright eyes. "I don't want to overstep but how do you feel about Alzerion?"

Aironell tightened her grip on the chair. She refrained from denying anything. She opened her mouth but then immediately closed it. She didn't want to come off like a stammering fool. "I guess I find him interesting." She blushed, a bit.

"Aironell is that all?" There was this eagerness in her voice.

"He makes me feel a little special." Aironell met her mother's gaze. Her eyes softened. "He says nice things to me and does sweet little things. When I'm with him I feel like he can see into my soul. I never knew that someone could be so... easy to love." Her gaze shifted away from her mother.

The queen bent to be eye-level with her and wrapped her arms around Aironell. Aironell welcomed the hug. "You don't think I'm ridiculous?"

The queen pressed her knees to the ground as she pulled back. In an instant she held Aironell's hands. "You're anything but. Alzerion is quite the catch. I want you to be sure of what it is that you want."

"He's nice, charming, and, well—"

"He's handsome." The queen laughed. "I'm sorry. I'm not trying to make things awkward."

Aironell nodded and her look of concern was replaced with a smile. "I appreciate that. I needed a good chuckle. Mother, I just don't want to scare him away, you know?"

"Honey, he doesn't scare so easily." Queen Evalyn lifted her chin up. "I think you will be fine." She patted her back, once more, and rose. "Have a good time with Alzerion, dear. Be you. But be safe." With that the queen ambled out the door.

Aironell fanned herself with her hands, quickly, and took in a couple slow breaths. Then she stood up and smoothed out her dress. She snapped her jeweled finger and a pair of shoes appeared. She liked how they matched her dress. Then she walked out the room.

Her mind was a maze. *What should she say? Would he think she looked alright?* She steadied her breathing as she walked down West Wing corridor. She came to the main entrance to the palace, looked over the banister, and all self-doubting stopped. Alzerion stood, waiting, at the base of the grand staircase. He wore his navy-blue jeans and a black long sleeve shirt. Her heart almost raced out of her chest as she saw the muscles bulging at the creases in his shirt. Her eyes continued scanning as she descended the stairs. He stood tall with this playful gleam in his eye. He was all charm; him and that off centered smirk of his. *Ugh*. She could just melt.

"Are you ready for a good time?" Alzerion winked and his hand was held out— waiting. She glanced at him and strolled passed, slowly. She wasn't about to make it that easy for him. She glanced back when she reached the front doors.

Alzerion was watching… with eyebrows raised. She laughed and smiled coyly. "Alzerion you seem so sure of yourself. So sure, that I will have fun; why that is quite presumptuous."

He moved toward her and pushed open the door. "Oh?"

"Well, I guess I'll be the judge of how well you think you know me."

"We shall find out, now won't we?" he teased. Out they went, side-by-side. A bit of silence passed and all that could be heard were Aironell's shoes against the cobblestones as they passed Gorgeous Garden.

"So, are you excited?" Aironell noticed how Alzerion tilted his head and stared. It was like he was examining her next move. She slowed to a stop.

She peered into his eyes. "Of course, I am, but you promised fun, so now you have to deliver, or else." Her eyes narrowed as she pointed her finger at him.

"Hmmm … somehow, I'm not afraid of you," Alzerion chuckled as he grazed his hand over her fingers, slowly coaxing them down.

Aironell straightened as her hands repositioned to her hips. She frowned as her eyes narrowed and her nostrils flared. Alzerion burst out laughing.

"What's so funny, Mister?"

"I'm sorry, but you are," he continued laughing. "You look rather cute pouting." He pursed his lips.

"That's not my fault," she retorted, sticking her nose up to him. Arms folded across her chest, firm.

"You're right," answered Alzerion. "It's my fault that I didn't get to see you pout. However, that superior look you're giving me is more than I can handle."

"I don't think it's funny," she started to walk, faster than before, as she passed him.

She did not like being mocked. In one moment, she thought he was the universe's gift to man and now, well, she was frustrated with him. She heard Alzerion's boots against the stones. He must have been trying to catch up to her, but she did not slow her pace. She was still annoyed with him. Then she felt the warmth of his hand around hers. In seconds she felt the air whirl against her as she spun around; until Alzerion held her tightly against his chest. His broad and well-defined chest. In that moment she felt like she could fuse into him.

Aironell glimpsed into his cinnamon red eyes. She steadied herself as she eased the slight dizziness. Unsure if it was from the spinning or from him. She attempted a grin. He was cute. *No— not cute.* A puppy was cute. A baby was cute. He was something different. *Ugh,* the way he made her brain feel scattered. Attraction.

Something she never thought would happen to her, but she was undeniably attracted to him. She felt the muscles of his arm tighten as she grabbed hold of him. They held her in place which she was grateful for, as she was sure she would fall over. Alzerion closed the gap between their faces.

She could feel the warmth of his skin against her cheek as he whispered in her ear. "Are you angry with me?" His voice sounded worn, cracked. She pulled her head back, to see him. He bit down on his lower lip revealing this pained expression. He was a puzzle. A mystery. Hmm— an attractive mystery.

"I'm not funny looking." She held firm to her arms across her chest.

"I didn't mean for you to think that." His somber gaze lightened.

She fixed him with a glower. "Well, what did you mean then?" Aironell was focused on him. His words. His answer.

She felt his arms relax as he stepped away. "I'll tell you later." His lips curled. Then he turned and started down Founders Path. Aironell sighed. She wanted him, for once, not to leave her hanging.

She shook her head and followed. She didn't want to let this ruin her outing. She made up her mind. Aironell gazed at the bushes, trees, and then she felt this pitting, within, as they came near the rock enclosure. "Alzerion…" Her voice wavered. He must have heard because he was by her side in seconds. She couldn't help but feel this heaviness. It was deep within. Like a boulder crushing, no, gashing at her, rising up in her chest. She clung to her necklace, eyes closed, tight.

"What's wrong?" Alzerion spoke in a low voice.

Aironell slowly stepped back, as if she was trying to escape. Still clutching her necklace like it could ward off this feeling. She felt his strong hand on her shoulder as he scanned her face—her eyes—so distant. As if no time passed, grabbed her hands, so warm, and moved them. He placed them on his heart. It beat, in a rhythmic calm. She glanced up and met his gaze. Alzerion leaned closer to her. His gorgeous eyes were freckled with guilt. "Aironell, what can I do?"

His one hand let go of hers and his fingers danced against her chin. That nagging feeling ebbed, a bit, as she focused on him—every touch. She licked her dried lips and blinked, once, twice. "I-I—"

This time Alzerion bent his head down, toward hers. He pressed his forehead against hers as he looked into her eyes. She felt like he was searching for some clue—searching her very being. It was like some sort of inspection. A few slow breaths.

"I didn't mean to make you worry." Aironell spoke. She took a few slow breaths. Alzerion helped keep her grounded and she was grateful. She stepped back but Alzerion's one hand still held, firm, to hers. His fingers wrapped around hers—like he was the key that fit just right. "I'm better, now, I promise." She saw his eyebrows narrow. "Alzerion, I mean it. I just, well, I couldn't shake this feeling. Thanks to you I'm doing better."

His gaze softened. "What kind of feeling?"

"It's nothing. We should get moving if we are ever getting into town." Aironell attempted to pace, to start moving, but couldn't. Alzerion stood still with his fingers entwined with hers. He was unmoving and unflinching as he watched her. "Ugh. I felt like de-ja-vu. Like maybe I'd been here before. Before you can say it, no, not just from a walk but like something meaningful happened."

His expression didn't shift. She couldn't shake the feeling that he knew something. *Would he reveal anything? Probably not.* Alzerion and his darn secrets.

Alzerion stepped toward her, closing that gap even more. "I'm not really sure what you mean." She turned away from him. "This is a main walking trail from the palace to town. I mean Founders Path is—"

Aironell snapped her focus back at him. "It's what?"

"Aironell." His words were more than charm but calm. His voice was low and solemn. He glanced around and then continued. "Something did happen here; when you were little."

"What was it?" She felt his grip tighten around hers as he ushered her on. Of course, now he was ready for them to keep moving.

"It's not something I like talking about." His other hand popped up. It was like he knew she would object. "I will say that you already know that your life was in danger, here, in Bachusa."

She nodded. "I want to know what happened."

"You are so determined." Alzerion wrinkled his nose and she was sure she saw a grimace escape that handsome face. "You win." Alzerion said solemnly.

"I'm sorry. I don't mean to push, but if it's about me I think I have a right to know. Don't you think?"

Alzerion sighed. "I do." He quickly glanced at her and continued. "When you were little strange things would happen to you or around you. Back there by that area was one of the places I found you, after you were kidnapped for the second time."

Aironell's eyes narrowed. She knew that she was sent away for good reasons but, wow. "Alzerion, why? Why would someone hate me so much? I was just a baby. What could I have done to make people dislike me?"

He patted her fingers as they walked hand-in-hand. "It wasn't anything you did. It's the rebellion. There are forces out of our control and they wanted you gone."

Aironell gulped. "Do they still want me gone?" She spied him biting his lip. In seconds he resumed his stony expression. She looked away and then back.

"I would assume. They didn't get what they wanted all those years ago." She sensed that there was more he wanted to say, but he didn't.

"Alzerion," she paused. "Should I worry about this rebellion?" He said nothing. "Alzerion, please. I'm not that little girl anymore."

He opened his mouth and then closed it. He smirked. "You're right. You're all grown up now."

They walked in silence. Aironell occasionally turned to look at him but his face was unmoved. His gaze was fixed on the path ahead. She noticed the ground shifted—changed. The dirt path eroded into grey cobblestones. The stones felt smooth under her feet—no gashes or cracks. Whoever laid them out had an eye for precision. The stones were placed in this circular pattern that never seemed to end. She caught a scent of what smelled liked cinnamon bread. *Mmmmmm.* They would be in the town soon enough. She had to get her answers before then. She knew Alzerion would not want to discuss it once they got to town.

"Alzerion, I don't mean to dredge up the past or any bad memories. I-I—"

"But you still have questions." He cleared his throat. He flexed his hands and his grip gave way. Each of his steps sounded heavy, like he was taking out some sort of frustration on the ground. His gaze didn't waver, still he focused on the ground as they strolled, a bit slower.

"Aironell, I, um, well," His voice was a bit shaky. It worried her that he wasn't being up front. This time she would lead the way.

She rushed over and stood before him. She rubbed his upper arm. "Alzerion, please." She knew she sounded like she was pleading, but she didn't care.

Finally, he brought those cinnamon-red eyes at her level. They stood silent. Just gazing— at least she was— his felt more like a probe. Like he was probing to see if she really wanted his reply. He shifted his legs and then grasped her hands and squeezed. "You are so stubborn, you know that?"

She swore she detected a slight smirk, but it was gone just as fast as it was there. He tightened his grip on her and pulled. She went soaring forward until she was right up against him—chest-to-chest. She bit her lower lip and gulped.

"Aironell," his voice sounded like a deep whisper. She felt the warmth of his breath against her as her own breathing quickened, just a bit. "It really isn't wise."

She blinked, quickly. "Huh? What's not wise?"

Alzerion bent his head lower. "We shouldn't be talking about this, especially in such a public place." Her eyebrows arched as she tilted her head a bit. "You never know who may hear us."

He was still whispering. Defeat playing across her face. "Don't do that." His expression softened. "I will say that you should be on guard."

"Alzerion, I'm sorry, I just don't understand." She took a slow breath. "I just want peace."

"I know," he sighed. "The rebellion has been causing problems for years. It isn't your fault." She swallowed as her eyes felt this biting feeling.

No, she wasn't sad. If anything, she was annoyed. Alzerion grazed his fingers up and down her hand. It tickled, just a bit; but mostly it was soothing. The way his fingers danced along her knuckles. *Ahhh*. The warmth that emitted when they rubbed at her skin.

"Your parents have been struggling with it since you left. I've been helping, but now you're back—"

"So, now it's my problem?" Her voice trailed off.

She forced her hands free and crossed her arms as she took a few steps away. It wasn't right. Each step she took was firm, against those cobblestones. She noticed that Alzerion didn't follow her, good. *How could she be expected to solve the issue of this rebellion? She hadn't been in the kingdom, long.*

She closed her eyes and stopped. Focused on the feel of her sleeve as she took slow breathes. In. Out. In— ah a breeze. It felt a little crisp against her face but it helped to steady her nerves. Her eyes darted open at the sound of Alzerion's boots against those stones. Her hands still gripped her arms, firm. She whipped around. He ambled toward her.

She glowered at him and he froze— like an insect that was spied under a magnifying lens.

"Aironell, I hope you don't think that I was trying to put it all on you?" His eyes looked pained. He lowered his head as he bit his lip. "I-I. I knew I shouldn't have said anything."

She lost sense of anything but him. Her eyes softened as she stepped closer. Then her hand rested on his forearm. He looked down into her eyes. Neither broke eye contact. "Alzerion." Her voice cracked, once. "I'm not upset at you, truly. I'm just feeling—"

"Overwhelmed?"

Aironell nodded. "Exactly. How can I do something that you all haven't been able to achieve?"

He nodded. In one swift motion he grasped her hands and pressed them against his cheek, then continued. "I'm not sure. Just know that you are not alone. I will do whatever it takes— whatever you need, I'm here."

Aironell let a faint smile creep across her lips. "Thanks. That does mean more than you know."

"One last thing. Your parents will also do all in their power for you. I think you should speak with them about these concerns. Don't let them brush you off." Aironell soaked in every last word, like a flower soaking in water. She nodded. "Aironell, they may have things to tell you that could help."

"What do you mean?"

Alzerion cleared his throat and again spoke in hushed tones. "I can't remember it, exactly, but I remember a friend of your mother's, long ago coming to the palace. She is a seer of some sort. All I remember is that after her visit your parents didn't worry as much. They told me that my job of watching out for you was very important. That you were Bachusa's brightest hope." He let go of her hand and let it fall. Then looked away.

Aironell had a thousand questions. She knew that she would, indeed, speak with her parents. Alzerion didn't know more or wasn't going to say more.

"Shall we continue?" Aironell nodded.

They maintained an even pace. She tried to think about the town, anything to focus on something else. She must have been deep in her thoughts because it was only when Alzerion called her name, that she realized they arrived.

She strolled a few paces ahead and slowly turned as she stuck her nose into the air. *Ahh.* The smells of cinnamon mixed, sweetly, with freshly baked bread and apples. She felt like she was being wrapped in a cocoon of wonder. Her eyes widened at the sights before her. She felt like a little kid, exploring a hidden gem.

She turned to Alzerion, beaming. "Can we go look at the stalls?" He smirked and nodded. She practically bolted. She saw him over her shoulder keeping pace, behind her.

So many people busied about. She heard the clanging of the men smacking the mallets against pieces of metal. Little children running about as they played games. It resembled hopscotch and while others, tag. Aironell spun around as she took in the many buildings. Her feet stumbled as she twirled. Alzerion wasn't quick enough to catch her arm before she stumbled right into the woman at the meat stall. The woman dropped the small parcel. Aironell gulped as the woman flattened her crème-colored apron and whirled around. A spiral of braids the color of auburn whacked her hand as Aironell reached to pick up the parcel.

"Watch what you're—" The woman's shadowed eyes blinked, twice, as she picked up the parcel from Aironell. Her cheeks went flush and then she curtsied, low. "I'm so sorry your highness." The woman held onto that parcel as she kept her gaze low to the ground.

Some of the chatter died down. Aironell saw people bow their heads and merely watched. Unsure what to do, Aironell scanned the crowd for Alzerion. He nodded. What did that mean? Well, he was no help.

"No need to apologize." Aironell's voice spoke with this confidence and softness. "Please let me help you." She reached her hand out.

The woman rose, slowly. "Help, me?"

"Did I ruin that parcel?"

"No-No I could have watched where I was going."

"Please don't apologize." Aironell soothed. "I bumped into you. I was just, well, in awe of town square." Aironell looked around. Those that stayed to watch looked pleased. Some nodded while others mouthed affirmations.

"If you're sure, your highness. Then thank you, but the parcel is fine. Just a bit dusty on the wrappings." The woman started to leave but then turned. "Your highness?"

Aironell turned her gaze, "Yes."

"You're too kind. It means a lot that you'd take time to speak to someone, like me. Not at all what I expected." A thin smile crossed her lips and she disappeared in the sea of people.

Aironell scratched at her cheek. *What was that?* The onlookers went back to doing their tasks. Some even stopped to bow. Alzerion moved toward her and held out his arm. Her hand grasped his forearm. He carefully moved her hand, so as to wrap her arm around his. He escorted her through the throng of people.

"Well done," he murmured as they strolled through the crowd.

"Alzerion, what was that about?"

"Not here." Aironell watched as Alzerion looked from side-to-side. His gaze eased up, a bit, but barely. "I love coming to town."

"It is quite pretty and very busy."

"That's true. I find speaking with the people to be eye opening, don't you think?"

Aironell's brow furrowed. Alzerion's face was expressionless. She sensed there was more to his statement— some underlying meaning— not that he was going to say. "Alzerion, where are we going?"

Again, he was laser-focused. "You'll see."

Wherever he was taking her was out of the main town square hub. She saw the last of the markets and the stalls of trinkets of things to buy. He led her on to where the road shifted into grass. They were walking in more of a field, no, maybe a meadow of sorts. Each blade of grass looked greener than the last and they were cut in perfect harmony. She didn't see or hear anyone.

They continued a stretch longer, and she saw these low rose bushes.

They were a mixture of reds, whites, and pinks. They made kind of like a line; almost like they created this floral lane to walk. Her mouth was gaped open as her eyes roamed from all around. Her gaze caught on these tall, magnificent weeping willow trees. They were scattered around but the tallest one was smack in the middle. She caught her breath. It was gorgeous, what with the weeping vines that had little tiny silvery-purple blooms.

Aironell unraveled her arm and started toward it. She grabbed the lower bit of her dress so she wouldn't stumble, as she ran. Aironell twirled with her arms outstretched, beaming as she caught a glimpse of Alzerion who made his way toward her.

"I guess you like it then."

"Are you kidding? I love it!" She sounded a bit exasperated but she didn't care. She felt the tickle of the silvery-purple blooms against her cheek as she twirled once more. Then she grabbed his hands and coaxed him to spin, too. They twirled until her foot caught on his boot and they fell onto the soft grass. Alzerion held her close, so when they fell his body hit the ground and she looked like her torso could have been lying on him. Blushing, she pulled herself into a seated position. Alzerion placed his weight on his left elbow as he held his head up with his hand.

"What is this place?" Aironell swallowed. "It's amazing." How she wished that her hair was not pulled back in braids. At least if it was down, she could use it to hide behind. However, Alzerion did not seem angry, in fact, he smirked.

"This is Majestic Park." The hand that held his head up adjusted and his fingers lingered against his jawline. "What's your favorite part?"

Aironell's cerulean blue eyes grew wide. It all was beautiful and perfect. "I like it all." A slight chuckle escaped her mouth. "I guess if I had to pick it would be this tree above us. I love the silvery-purple blooms. Whoever designed this place knew what they were doing." She continued to gaze out. "Look at how they shimmer when the sun's rays hit the blooms at just right the angle."

"What would you say if I told you I created this place?"

Aironell straightened her back as she honed in on him. His expression didn't waver. "Are you being serious?" Alzerion nodded.

She scooted herself a bit closer and examined his expression. He wasn't joking. She wrinkled her nose, just a bit. "Why?" She sat, with her legs draped off to the side. She plucked one of the blades of grass and twisted it about.

"I'm not sure I understand."

"Well, I guess I'm wondering why you made this?"

Alzerion's eyes gleamed and he laughed. "I see." He paused. Aironell kept fiddling with that blade of grass but starred back at him.

"I did it to make use of an area that was out of the bustling town." Aironell nodded. "It is quiet, serene, and well, more private." She gulped. He reached his right hand out, palm up, as she placed her hand in his. Fingers closing around hers. "And I made it for you."

"Really?" Aironell perked up, trying to mask being giddy.

Alzerion shook his head. She took her other hand and smoothed a strand of his hair back behind his ear. Then she leaned in, so that she was merely a couple inches away. Alzerion held onto her hand as he sat upright. His other hand eased her chin toward him, slowly. Mesmerized as she was, there was a slight cracking, of a twig, in the grass. She almost missed it, *damn Alzerion, always distracting her*. She moved back and turned. Aironell didn't know who it was that made their way toward them.

Alzerion stood abruptly and bit his lower lip. Whoever this was made him squirm, slightly. It was kind of funny, but she followed suit. She looked back and forth between the woman approaching them, and Alzerion. The woman looked to be about her parents age and had the widest grin she had ever seen. It reached both ears. *Who is she*, Aironell mouthed, but Alzerion glanced back at the woman and took a deep breath.

"Alzerion! I'm pleased to see you and you have an acquaintance." She spoke with such sweetness. She was sure Alzerion would burst. Instead, his cheeks looked a bit flushed. "Are you going to introduce your, friend?"

His nostrils flared as he sucked in so much air that Aironell was sure would make him light-headed. Sensing that he wasn't going to introduce them, Aironell held out her hand to the woman. "Hello, I'm Princess Aironell and you are?"

"Oh, your highness." She gave an elegant curtsy, like she could have done it in a past life. Then she pulled herself back up. "I'm Melinda." Alzerion cleared his throat, again. He clenched his hands that appeared to shake, just slightly.

"Alzerion, what's wrong?" He didn't respond. "Alzerion, please. You're worrying me."

"He is probably just getting over being mortified." Aironell heard the thud from where Melinda patted Alzerion on the back.

Alzerion licked his lips and looked at Aironell. "I'm sorry. I'm just a bit off."

"Why?" Her eyes narrowed.

"That's because, Melinda is my, mother."

Aironell's eyes widened, "Oh, I see. Should I give you two a minute?"

"Nonsense," Melinda beamed. She bounced closer and wrapped arms with Aironell, like they were old friends. "I am always up for a good gab session, you hear?" Aironell nodded. "We can keep things between just us, ladies."

"Like what?" Aironell's lips formed a slow thin smile.

"Mother, let her alone." He sighed. "You know enough."

Aironell giggled.

Melinda gave Alzerion this grimace and then turned back to her, smiling just as before. "What he means is that I know all about you, your highness. I must say that I'm pleased to meet you. But I should be going. I only stopped by to see if Alzerion would be here. This is his thinking spot."

"Oh, I didn't know," said Aironell. Melinda let go of Aironell and stepped back.

Alzerion turned toward Aironell. "I'll be right back." Before she could say anything, he was already by Melinda.

She wanted to know what they were saying. *Maybe if I, just do it once?*

What harm could there be? Aironell calmed her mind and placed both hands in front of her. Her fingers danced in the air as she muttered, amplio sonus. Then she tilted her head to the side and cupped around her ear. In an instant she could hear their voices like they were right beside her.

"Mother, come on. You know nothing was going on."

"Oh, do I? Alzerion, that did not look like nothing."

Aironell focused her eyes on them to glean the full extent of their exchange. She saw Alzerion run his hand through his hair.

"Mother, I know my place, alright?"

"That is so not what I mean?" Her eyes softened as she patted his back. "I want to see you happy, I do. I'm just worried."

He stepped back. "You don't need to be." His gaze lowered at his shuffling feet.

"Promise?"

Aironell could sense Melinda's genuine concern, but why? *What did she think would happen?* She continued to listen. She wanted—no, needed to know more. Alzerion, glanced back at Aironell. She smiled. She hoped that she didn't look as guilty as she felt, in that moment. Alzerion smirked and turned back to his mother.

"Alzerion," Melinda's voice wasn't bubbly. It sounded firm. "I need you to promise. You can't possibly think that anything could come from this, do you?"

"Honestly, I don't know. The king and queen respect me, so maybe—"

"Alzerion this is what I mean by not getting carried away."

"Got it." There was this sharpness to his voice, that she had never heard before. "I'm just the help, right?"

"My sweet son, don't say that. You know I didn't mean it like that."

"Didn't you?" Alzerion placed his hands on his hip and took a few steps away. "Mother, I should get back. I don't want her to think we are talking about her."

Melinda moved around to his front and hugged him. "Just take care of yourself... and your heart." She pulled away. "I've always wanted you to be with someone, I just don't want to see you get heart-broken over someone that might end up in an arranged marriage."

"I know." With that Melinda ambled down the lane of rose bushes and was out of sight.

Aironell bit her lower lip and turned away. She had to play it cool when he got over here. She sat down under that beautiful silver-purple weeping willow, breathing slowly.

Alzerion joined her and sat down beside her. "I'm sorry about that." His gaze lingered on the grass.

"Alzerion, don't be. She seemed sweet."

He didn't look at her. "Sweet? No, it was kind of humiliating." He gripped the nape of his neck.

Aironell felt this weight in her chest. She fiddled with her necklace, whilst her eyes never moved from Alzerion. "How come you never mentioned your mom?"

"It never came up." He was there but it was like he wasn't. His voice sounded like someone she didn't even recognize.

"Alzerion, is something wrong?" He finally looked up. He locked eyes on hers and he shook his head. Aironell stood with arms crossed. "So, because your mother never came up you didn't mention her and now you're ignoring me?"

"Aironell, it's not—"

"No. That's not a good enough reason." She turned away and stormed off.

She felt his firm grip on her elbow, pulling her back as he spun her around. Then he pulled her in. They were face-to-face. His eyes looked distant and pained. She realized his mother's words must have hurt him. She wanted nothing more than to bury her face in his chest and stay there.

"Aironell?" She kept gazing into his eyes wishing he would see what she couldn't put into words. She felt his arms around her, squeeze, ever so slightly. "You're cute when you're mad."

She detected the faintest smirk. She would have been glad to see him getting those negative thoughts out of his mind, except that she didn't find his comment funny.

"Let me go."

"Do you *really* want that?" Alzerion asked. His lips parted, slightly, as he rubbed his left-hand fingers along the curved neckline on her back. His other hand pulled her in even more, leaving no gap between them.

Aironell gulped. "It's too hard to stay angry with you."

"Good." His warm breath tickled her nose. Alzerion sounded like himself again. So confident. A moment went by and she just couldn't wait. So, she took matters into her own hands.

Aironell pulled her hands up and slowly rubbed the back of her hand down his face, resting near his mouth. Her eyes locked onto his lips. She leaned her head closer and pushed her lips against his. It was a light peck. She started to pull away, for a breath, when she felt Alzerion's hands grasp her back and pull her back in. She barely took a breath as he bit her lower lip. She cupped his chin. The kissing continued in a rhythm of quick nips of the lip followed by a crushing force of his lips against hers. Her mind was a whirlwind of thoughts. When he nibbled at her lip, she gasped for her breath.

"Are you alright?" Alzerion panted. His eyes lingered until she nodded. He cleared his throat and then licked his lips. "I'm sorry about that. I, um, got a bit carried aw—"

Aironell placed her finger over his lips. "Don't apologize. If I didn't want you to kiss me I wouldn't have let you."

His smirk covered his face. This time Alzerion grabbed her face and smashed his lips into hers. She had no words. She felt like she was melting into him. Words couldn't do it justice. She felt the pull of her necklace tugging closer to Alzerion. She quickly glanced down between kisses and saw that their two half-heart necklaces connected. Then sparks emanated to the sky. Alzerion pulled away for a second. The sparks stopped. Aironell pulled him back in and continued kissing, and the sparks continued.

Meanwhile, Warren was on the hunt for Alzerion. He was nowhere to be found in town, so he figured he would search his secret sanctuary. Warren made it to the outskirts of town and saw him. He saw Alzerion.

His face turned gaunt. *What did he do?* He knew Ulbrick would be furious, but he had to tell him. He feared Ulbrick's wrath more than anything. Warren turned his back and headed to Ulbrick. He found Ulbrick in the planning room amidst the piles of papers.

"Ah, Warren, any news I should know about?"

Warren gulped. He knew he was about to cross a line. "Actually, I do have some news. I don't think you're going to like it very much."

"What kind of news?" Ulbrick snapped. His voice sounded even more grating than usual.

"I saw Alzerion kissing Princess Aironell."

"No! Grr!" Ulbrick knocked over the closest pile of books.

Warren gulped. "There's more. There were sparks."

Ulbrick turned his cold stare on him. "Warren, I don't need the details."

Warren sighed. "No. Not *sparks*. I'm talking like fireworks in the sky."

Ulbrick started pacing and muttering stuff that sounded like gibberish. "I'm sorry I don't follow." Warren shook his head.

Ulbrick plopped himself in a chair and waved for Warren to sit. Warren hesitated, but did as he was instructed.

"That means the necklace is becoming like one."

Warren scratched at his chin. "Huh?

"The necklace that Alzerion wears is special. It has magical properties, and it appears that Aironell has the other half. If he chooses her, and I mean truly chooses her, then we are going to take quite a loss. That necklace is powerful."

Warren saw the veins on Ulbrick's hands bulge, as he tightened his grip on the chair. "What do we do?" Warren's tone was a bit sharp.

"Well, there is only one thing to do, and that is to tell Aironell about Alzerion." Ulbrick patted Warren on the arm. "When she finds out, she will be so angry. Hell, she might not even trust him. With love severed then Alzerion might finally side with us."

"That just might work," Warren admitted. He saw the evil grin plastered on Ulbrick's face. "But don't you think that is a bit harsh?"

"Don't tell me that you're going soft on me now, are you?"

"Of course not, sir." Warren clenched his jaw.

"Good, then you know what to do. I'm counting on you."

As the sun started to wane, Alzerion knew he had to get Aironell back. Her parents would be furious if he kept her out too late. She was a vision of beauty with the weeping willow swaying in the background. He sat with his arms wrapped around her. Her head nuzzled up against his chest. He loved being so close. He knew what his mother said, but she was wrong. Aironell had kissed *him*. He didn't push her. He didn't make the first move. There was something beautiful in that. He bent his head down and laid it against hers.

"I never want this night to end." Aironell sighed.

He nuzzled his cheek against her head followed by a light kiss on her forehead. "I know what you mean." It was like he waited for this moment, his whole life.

Duty and expectation. That always was put first, before all else, but now—maybe he could try something new. Dream a different dream or want something that he thought was out of his grasp. His thoughts came back into focus when he felt Aironell move. She sat up, back straight, as she placed her hands on his chest. He felt the warmth of her hands seeping beneath his shirt. He licked his lips. Then she smiled and batted her eyelashes. He shook his head while laughing. "No. Stop it."

"What?"

Ugh. She was playing with him. She was just lucky that she was so cute. He pressed his hands against her waist and pulled her closer, until her hands buckled and wrapped around his neck. He pushed his lips against hers as his hands moved from her waist and grazed the whole of her back. His whole body felt at ease. Once again sparks flew up from their necklaces. He pulled back and watched them hit the sky.

"We really need to get a handle on that," he joked. He slowly pulled her arms down. "However, we should head back to the palace."

"Yeah. Let's get right on that." She whispered in his ear.

"Don't tease." Alzerion held out his hand and she grabbed it. He helped her stand up. "Not that I want to, but we should head back to the palace."

Aironell scrunched her face and he shook her head.

"Look, I know what you're thinking, but we will be in so much trouble if we get back after dark." She folded her arms across her chest and pouted. "Your parents may not let me spend time with you, if we don't be smart about this. You wouldn't want that, would you?" He held out his arm to escort her back.

"I don't like your smug tone, but you do make a valid point." She grabbed hold of his arm and Alzerion escorted them out of Majestic Park.

"Aironell, I promise I'll come see you first thing in the morning."

"You better." She grinned. He shook his head as he headed toward the palace.

A SEERS WORDS AND WARNING

Queen Evalyn sat and sipped her tea. Eyes closed as the rich cinnamon sloshed around in her mouth, with cloves. Her posture perked, just a bit, as she tasted this new, sweeter, note.

What could it be? With eyebrows furrowed she looked down into her cup as her tongue pressed the hints of the taste into the roof of her mouth. If she could force the answer she would.

"Dearest," King Francisco spoke, "is everything alright?" He tilted his head toward her.

"Of, course. I'm just wondering what this tastes like." Her lips pursed.

The king's fingers grazed over the rough edge of his mahogany desk. He sat sideways at her, squinting his eyes at the cup. "It's not your usual?"

"If it was, I wouldn't be wondering, now would I?"

He chuckled. "I guess not. Amplio." Then he snapped his fingers. The sound of the snap almost made her flinch. It reverberated through the room.

"What was that for?" Her nose wrinkled.

"I thought, why waste time wondering when we can go right to the source." The queen shifted in her seat as she placed the cup on the little circular table.

The bedroom door opened and Isabella came in smoothing out the crease in her beige apron. She ambled over and stood between the two of them and bowed.

"Your majesty," Isabella said as she looked to the king. She gave the queen a curt nod, but then snapped her attention right back. "Good morning, your majesty. What can I do?"

"Actually, the queen had a question." He motioned to his wife, with his right palm.

Isabella turned toward the queen. "Isabella, I was wondering if you did something different this morning with the tea?"

"Wh-what do you mean, your majesty?" Her head bowed and then slowly rose. Isabella's hands held firm against her apron, but the queen noticed how she was repeatedly rubbing her hand over the other. Queen Evalyn smiled, softly, hoping to relax her— her gaze, however, was focused.

"Heavens, Isabella, I'm not trying to accuse you of anything."

Isabella grinned.

"I was only wondering what you did different. I am certain the flavor profile tastes, well, different. It's delicious but there's this sweetness of sorts."

Isabella beamed. "I'm pleased you like it, your majesty. I did add something."

The queen nodded. "I thought so. What is it?" She leaned forward as if she was sitting on the very edge of the velvet cushion of her chair.

"Why, it's vanilla. I was told it would mix seamlessly with some of the bitters of that herbal mix."

"It does, indeed. Thank you. I'm sorry to have kept you from your work."

Isabella nodded. Bowed. Then she left.

"Well, mystery solved." The king crooned.

Evalyn turned her sights onto her husband. She glowered at him, just a bit. "What is it, exactly, that you have been doing over at your desk? Isn't it a bit early in the day for your letter writing?"

"Someone is quite curious this morning?"

The queen continued to glower. He started to laugh, cleared his throat, and then grabbed some kind of book and walked toward her. He handed it to her and sat in the chair nearest. She hadn't seen it for some time. Evalyn rubbed her hand against the black leather cover. There were gold swirls at the four corners with the family crest at the center. While she gripped the edge of the book she flipped it open. There were so many memories. Some of which was in her handwriting, some from Francisco, and then there were tiny paintings from past events.

With pages opened, she clutched it at her chest. "I can't believe you found this." She felt a tear prick the corner of her left eye.

"You were quite the collector of memories." King Francisco leaned over and pressed his lips to her forehead.

"That's sweet." She went back to scanning the pages of the book.

"We look so, well, young." He hesitated.

"We were," she just shook her head. It was hard to imagine. It felt like a world away. She continued flipping through the pages and then stopped. Her hand held firm to the page as her throat felt dry, like she hadn't just been guzzling down tea.

"Evalyn, what's wrong?" She could hear the concern but shook her head. "Darling, don't tell me that you're alright. I can see that you're not."

Her muscles felt strained by the pressure of how hard she squeezed the edge of the page.

"I-I—" she bit her lip and then finally glanced at her husband. "Do you remember this?"

King Francisco leaned as far as he could, until he saw the page. "Wasn't this one of our many outings?" The queen didn't speak, but merely pointed at a person.

He swallowed. "Wasn't that your friend? I can't remember her name, but she was so secretive and mysterious."

"Jezzabell," her voice cracked. "Her name was Jezzabell."

His eyebrows furrowed. "What do you mean was? Did she change her name or something?"

She grabbed his hand and laced her fingers around his. "Of course not, silly. I just haven't seen or heard from her for a while."

"I'm sure she's fine. How long has it been?" His foot bounced a bit.

He was so patient. So, understanding of it all. She was not a woman who believed in coincidence, but it had been a long time.

She shook her head and focused back on her husband. "It has been about sixteen years."

His eyes bulged. "That's right. The day Aironell was born." He looked away. She followed his gaze down to his foot tapping against the ground.

She cleared her throat. "Francisco. We-we have to tell Aironell."

His gaze darted up as he starred right at her. "Do we? Do you want to put that burden on her shoulders? I-I-I almost forgot about it. I mean we could just —forget."

She tilted her head and gazed at him. *She knew how tired he was of all of it. She knew what they have endured. No, she couldn't do that.*

"Francisco, we can't keep this from her. She would *never* forgive us."

There was a flash of pain mixed with anger in his gaze. He stood up, pacing. He didn't stop. He just kept going back and forth, in that open space. She closed the book and placed it on that little table and strolled over to him. she stopped right in front of him as he turned to pace, again.

"Francisco—"

"Don't." He held his hand up. Her body moved back, instinctively.

"I don't like it but you're right." His hands rubbed at his temples. "She wouldn't trust us if we kept something like that from her."

The queen nodded.

"So, when should we tell her?"

Queen Evalyn placed her hand over his heart, gently. He grabbed her other hand and placed a tender kiss on it.

"Why don't we do it after breakfast."

He nodded.

Alzerion stared out his window. He gazed as the raindrops continued to fall making giant puddles in the dirt. He shook his head as he walked toward the middle of his room, beaming. He pulled on his dark blue jeans and then sat on the edge of his bed as he took care of his boots. He pulled on his undershirt, then stood, as he slipped his arms through his black long sleeve top. Almost done, he thought. He grabbed the black tie and adjusted it until it laid handsomely between his black shirt and undershirt.

He looked himself over, satisfied, he ran his hands through his hair. His hands pressed against his lips. He smirked. Many memories that hoped he'd never forget about. He licked his lips and left his room. He walked across East Wing corridor until he got to Aironell's room. He took a slow, deep breath and then opened her door. He saw her nestled under her blankets. She was so beautiful, even while she slept. He closed the door and walked so quietly he could have been part feline. He grazed his fingers against one of her curls and watched it spring back.

Unsure as to the best course of action, he pulled her blanket down on one side, and slowly crawled into bed beside her. He laid on his side, watching her. He hoped she wouldn't think him a stalker. He loved how peaceful she looked. He took his hand and lightly brushed it against her cheek. Aironell moved her legs, and her shoulder rose. He withdrew his hand and steadied it against his chest. Aironell's long lashes started to flutter. Then her sparkly cerulean blue eyes opened, slowly. She blinked, twice. Alzerion just grinned, wide.

"Morning." He whispered.

Aironell rubbed at her eyes and then squeezed the back of her neck. "Good morning," she said.

"I didn't mean to wake you, honest."

"I know, cutie," Aironell grinned as her fingernails trailed a path from his tie to the middle of his chest. He tried not to focus on her touch.

"Cutie, huh?" He winked. He grabbed that hand that was gliding against his chest and he spotted the bracelet. His eyes fixed on the little trinket.

"I never take it off or the necklace." Aironell laid her other hand against the necklace.

Alzerion gazed into her eyes. "That means more than you know." He touched the metal of her necklace with the tips of his fingers.

Aironell grasped his hand and squeezed. "I love it." Her eyes didn't yield. There was no sign of wavering.

He gulped.

"When you gave it to me, I felt so special. Then, as I got older, I didn't see you again." Her voice cracked.

"Aironell, I-I'm very sorry," he admitted as he squeezed her hand a bit. "That was hard for me. It wasn't safe for me to come around again."

Aironell tilted her head toward him. "I use to worry about what happened to you. On my dark days, I even wondered what kind of person would... lie."

He sat up and looked down at her. Speechless. He felt this tightening in his chest. "Aironell." His voice was so low. He couldn't even begin to explain himself. Alzerion looked away. He felt ashamed. Then there was this warm, soft touch on his lower arm. His eyes darted back at Aironell.

"I'm sorry. I didn't mean to bring back painful memories." Aironell sat up and then bit her bottom lip. Her hands laid on her lap.

He tried to turn off his guilt. It would be easy to do, especially if she kept biting that lip of hers. It was drawing his attention to her perfectly shaped mouth. He took a breath. Lately, he couldn't stop thinking about her in ways that kind of worried him. He was being too free when it came to her. *To heck with it*, he thought. Alzerion grasped her hands, brought them to his mouth, and kissed them, so soft. Then he started to graze her one arm with his mouth.

She giggled. "Alzerion that tickles."

"Oh?" He cocked an eyebrow. He saw the cute display of a faint blush. He loved how her mouth twisted into a smile, loved the way she toyed with words, *ugh*, he even loved that 'come and get me' look. He had to be smart. *Hell, wasn't it a little too late for that?* He felt a trembling in his hands. He pulled at his fingers to try and keep it at bay. It was no use. He knew it deep down, that he either left her room right now or-or—

Aironell slid closer as she blinked at him. *No, it was too late. There was no leaving. No turning back. He didn't just want to be near her, to let her gaze upon him; no, he wanted her.* His left hand cupped the back of her head as it moved her face closer, much, much closer. He gulped. He felt this dryness in his mouth, like he was thirsty. Ravenously thirsty and she was the only thing to quench it. He pressed his head against hers. Eyes lost in the other. He almost jumped when he felt her fingers. They danced along the ripples of his biceps. Thank goodness for his shirt. It helped to mask some of the feeling.

"Alzerion," her voice was so soft. The steam from her breath whacked his nose. *Where should he start?* His hands cascaded down her curls, so light and soft. *She smelled of lavender and honeysuckle. Mmmmm.*

Aironell kept watching—waiting, as she continued to work her magic on his arms. Now was the moment to act. Alzerion gripped the bottom of her chin and gently nudged her up and closer. Aironell had this playful look in her eyes, which helped his nerve. As he was coaxing her closer, Aironell moved from a seated position to being on her knees. Then her hand moved and glided against his face. She started at his cheek and moved up. How odd, he thought. Her arms had wrapped around his neck and her fingers did evil things. The one hand played with his hair while the other, grazed the skin at the base of his neck.

Alzerion couldn't take it. In one swift motion he pressed his lips to hers. It was one quick motion after another. His hands slid down her back, pressing her nearer. He sat on his knees, too, so that he could be even closer. *Closer, ugh,* that was all he wanted. He felt her body against him.

Aironell's hands moved to his shoulders as she, too, pulled him in. This was no dress rehearsal. He didn't waver this time, and neither did she, it seemed. His lips crashed into hers until he felt the quick stroke of her tongue. He wasn't expecting that, not from her. He went with it.

It felt so freeing, like he was coming up for air— she was the air. The only thing he needed to keep breathing. It all felt too good, if that was possible. He controlled Aironell's tongue by slowing down his kisses, then he looked deep into her eyes as he bit her bottom lip and pulled, just a bit. He did it once more, but this time Aironell pulled away and he felt her nose nuzzle the side of his neck. He closed his eyes.

Suddenly, the softness of her nose was replaced with a wetness from her mouth. He bit down on his lip, trying to maintain his composure. It was so hard. She worked her way up his neck until she got to his ear and nibbled. He felt the pressure of her teeth against them. He swore he could see stars. Feel every fiber of his being buzzing about.

In that moment, Aironell slid her hands onto his chest and pushed. He crumpled at her touch, falling flat on his back, on her bed. He used his arms to hold his torso up. She still knelt to the side of him. The look in her eyes was playful, indeed, like she was in a frenzy herself. He licked his bottom lip, slowly. Aironell grabbed two pillows and thrust them behind Alzerion, and he used them to prop his back up. Then he grabbed at her arms that hung above. Bending her closer until he craned his neck to kiss, but she pulled her head back and grinned, letting out a little chuckle.

She was evil. Aironell took her hands and grabbed a hold of his. He watched in wonder as she navigated his hands. They were forced to her knees, sliding her lace nightgown up, just enough that her knees were free. He gulped as he let his hands dance down her calf. Aironell held onto the fabric of her nightgown and placed her right leg on his other side as she scooted forward. His hands roamed back up her calves and grazed her lower back. She swallowed, hard, as she lowered her chest closer to him. Her head bent low as her hands and mouth slid across his chest. He sighed. There were no words, only actions—things he wanted. When Aironell's head popped back up, he took a breath. He needed that reprieve. She still had that devilish grin.

"Wh-what," he panted?

She mumbled something, again, he was unsure. He was certain she said something. Whatever it was he found out as she drew her left hand up into a fist. In an instant his black shirt and undershirt were in her hands. She tossed them to the side. His mouth gaped open—only his tie draped across his bare chest. Still staring, Aironell scooted so close to him that he felt her silky lace nightgown against his skin. Her cerulean-blue eyes gazed down at him as her fingers danced along the creases of his abdomen, slowly dancing up and around his chest. Wow, she mouthed.

He smirked. *He was pleased that she was appreciating every muscle. Countless hours of training over many years, he...* his thoughts trailed off as she placed her soft lips against his jaw. He took his arms from around her and pressed. Aironell crushed into him as she rubbed and kissed along his jawline. He was sure she could feel him gulping. He didn't care. He grabbed her head to steady her. Then he pulled her face closer. He could feel this warmth wash over as he bit her top lip and again their lips crashed right into each other. The way waves crash against the shoreline. The heat intensified as each kiss quickened.

He was drowning—drowning in a sea of pleasure. The warmth spread across his body as he wrapped his arms around her and this time forced her back. She held onto him as he laid on top. He kept quickening as each kiss pressed deeper and deeper. *Ugh— No.* He grasped her fingers that slid against his thigh, and pushed against her. It forced himself to sit off to the side of her. He gulped, trying to steady his breathing.

Her eyes furrowed. "What was that for?" she took a breath. "I-I thought you were enjoying it."

He took another deep breath. "Trust me, I was." He nodded.

"Then why?" Aironell sounded a bit sad. She scratched at her chin. "Did, I do something wrong?"

It killed him that she thought that.

"Aironell," he cleared his throat. He turned to face her more. His back was toward her door and the other side of the room.

"You were perfect," he smirked. He wanted to reassure her. "It was—"

"Don't," she demanded. Her voice was stern. Serious with a bite of hurt. Her hands clenched against the sheet of the bed.

"What?" He asked.

"I don't want to hear the old it's not you but me, speech."

Mouth gaped open he shook his head. He laughed.

"What?"

"Aironell, I wasn't going to say that." He cleared his throat. "Sorry, it was a good laugh."

Her stare was cold as her arms crossed in front of her like a barrier.

He scooted a bit closer and rubbed her arm. "Come on, Aironell, please?"

Her scowl softened as she tilted her head at him. Before he could move she slid even closer and pulled him in for a hug. Normally, he wouldn't mind the hug but not after that. It was too fresh on his mind. His body still yearned for her—craved her. He gulped.

Alzerion pulled away and left a soft kiss on her forehead. *Those mesmerizing eyes of hers, ugh, they could convince someone to do anything.* She was his weakness. He felt like jelly, like he lost control of his, well, control. *Did she really not know what she was doing to him?* Every touch sent him spinning.

He cupped her chin and smirked. He felt so free with her. *What would he feel if Ulbrick had his way? No, he couldn't think about that, not now. Not when—*

Alzerion heard the faintest sound. Quickly, he pulled his hand back, snapped his fingers, and his two shirts were back on. Aironell flinched. He got off the bed, reached over and grabbed her. He picked her up and sat her on the edge of the bed. She blinked. Her mouth opened but then closed.

"Aironell, now is not the time."

Her head tilted.

"Someone is coming and the last thing we need is someone asking questions." He sat down next to her to make it seem like they had been chatting.

Aironell nodded. He sensed that she wanted to talk about them— about a future. He was glad someone was coming. It gave him an out. He had no idea what he would say. There was such uncertainty.

Then there was a knock on the door.

Aironell took a breath and said, "Come in."

As the door opened, Isabella stepped forward holding a small metal tray with an ornate little teapot and a couple cups. Isabella went to speak, but then paused. She looked at Alzerion and then at Aironell. She bowed and then walked to the little tea table. Alzerion saw Isabella's lips curl into a smile as she did, so. She knew or at least suspected, something. He had to get out of the room.

After she placed the tray on the table, Isabella strolled over. "Good morning, princess."

Aironell swallowed and turned her gaze to Isabella. She nodded. "Thank you. I appreciate you still checking on me."

Isabella held her hands against her apron. She looked at Alzerion, again, and back at Aironell. "I didn't mean to interrupt anything."

Alzerion smirked. "Nothing to worry about, Isabella. We were done." He stood up and took a few steps away from the bed. "I, too, came to give a proper morning greeting after our outing the other day." He bowed his head at Aironell, then nodded at Isabella as he strolled to the door.

Aironell laughed. "Sorry," she pressed her hand to her mouth.

Isabella kept her eyes on Aironell, thankfully. Alzerion looked at Aironell, almost like he wanted to scold her.

"I didn't know that was what we were calling it."

Alzerion's jaw tensed as he shook his head, then left.

Aironell bounced up, arms embracing Isabella. Then she dashed to her little tea area. She poured the steaming liquid into two cups. Isabella strolled over and sat down, eyes narrowing. Aironell handed her a cup and sat down. Still, Isabella said nothing. Aironell started to feel uneasy. Her fingers rapped against the side of her cup, trying to fill the void of silence.

"Aironell?" Isabella sipped her tea.

Aironell glanced at her, her face giving nothing away.

Isabella's eyes darted to the bed and then back. "So, how was Alzerion this morning?"

Aironell blushed a bit. "He was good." She took a gulp of her tea and then wiped her lips. "Isabella, what did you want to discuss with me?" Aironell placed her cup down on the table.

"Aironell, is there a reason you don't seem to want to speak about Alzerion?"

Aironell shifted in her seat. Lips pressed together, tight.

"Aironell, you know you can always tell me things."

Isabella knew. Not sure how, but she was sure that Isabella picked up on something between them. She went to say something but no words escaped.

Isabella set her cup down, hands folded neatly. "I want to see you happy."

"I am. Isabella, it means a lot to me—to have you still look in on me."

Isabella nodded and her eyes softened. "I am going to be straight forward, like I always did when we lived in the other realm."

"Please do." Aironell breathed out.

"Alzerion, well, he's a very good man. He is quite caring, protective, and well, handsome."

Aironell felt a bit flushed as she cleared her throat.

"You don't have to try and hide it from me. I can see it plastered across your face."

"I won't deny it. You know me well." Aironell pulled a small piece of hair. She combed her fingers through the curl. "I must seem ridiculous, huh?"

Isabella straightened her back. "Why would you think that?"

This time Aironell kept her gaze down. She focused on the piece of hair that she was working on. "I'm sure I sound foolish. I barely know him, but he-he captivates me."

Isabella grabbed her hand and Aironell squeezed. "You're not ridiculous. Some people form attachments quicker than others." She placed her hand under Aironell's chin and gently nudged her face up. "That doesn't make your feelings any less sincere."

Aironell nodded. Isabella always made her feel lighter. "Thank you, Isabella."

"Of course." Isabella stood up and strolled next to her and clasped Aironell's shoulder. "You are your father's daughter after all."

Then she started to walk away.

"Wait," Aironell called as she stumbled to her feet and crossed in front of Isabella. "What does that mean?"

There was this overwhelming desire to understand. It bubbled to the surface like hot water rising.

Isabella grasped Aironell by the shoulder and escorted the two of them to the edge of the bed. Aironell sat as Isabella shifted.

"Comfortable?" Aironell asked.

Isabella straightened her back as she bounced a bit. Aironell chuckled.

"Sorry," Isabella rocked back and forth. "Now, where were we?"

"How am I my father's daughter?" She hunched forward resting her chin on her hands, with elbows pressing into her thighs.

"Did you know your father was quite the swordsman?"

Aironell's brow furrowed. "My, father? He was a swords scholar?"

Isabella nodded as she stood up and started fixing the pillows of the bed.

Wow. It was hard to picture that. Her father wielding a sword. It was cool but that didn't make her like him.

"Aironell? Are you in there?"

"Sorry. Please continue."

"Your father would enter these tournaments with his buddies and—"

"What kind of tournaments?" Aironell sat up and let her leg hang off the bed.

"Well, there were different kinds, jousting, swordsman challenges and the like. Honestly, any excuse for nobles and the royals to gather and display their prowess. That's what I've been told."

Aironell scratched at her head. "Isabella, we don't still have those, do we?"

"Not really, no. Your parents do social gatherings as a way to mingle." Isabella fluffed the last of the pillows. Aironell never realized how many she had as Isabella rounded to the bottom of the bed and started to smooth out the sheet.

"Isabella, I'm not quite seeing how I'm my father's daughter. I mean what am I missing?"

Isabella smoothed out another crease and laughed. "You mentioned not knowing Alzerion well, yet you have feelings."

Aironell blushed and nodded, slowly. *It was true that Alzerion occupied a big space in her mind.*

"Aironell, your father saw your mother for the first time, at one of those tournaments. As the heir to the throne, he was betrothed to a princess from a neighboring kingdom." Isabella's hands settled on her hips as she continued. "As I understand it, your father saw your mother and was in awe of her beauty and charm. He vowed he had to meet her."

Aironell stood up and paced. She strolled to the archway of her balcony and back as Isabella continued. She didn't know what to make of this information.

"Your mother was of noble blood but not a royal." Isabella went back to smoothing out the bed sheets. She slowly moved to where Aironell had been just moments before. "Queen Evalyn is the daughter from a respected noble family from the ancient House of Sorcerers."

Head still spinning, Aironell kept pacing as her fingers massaged, deep, into her head. It was like her fingers were trying to penetrate her brain. "House of Sorcerers?"

"I'm sure your mother has mentioned that before." That wasn't a question, but a statement. She racked her brain but, yes. *There was a small conversation. Huh. Maybe she should have paid better attention.*

"Well, that's done." Isabella smacked her hands together. Aironell felt a tug at her arm as she was pulled. It was quick and jarring. She thought she would topple over, as Isabella pulled her onto the balcony. Isabella patted the marble bench and she sat down.

The change of scenery was nice. The smell of the sweet flowers wafted up from Gorgeous Garden. The feel of the morning breeze washed over her like waves rolling across your body— fast and no chance to feel cold. *Ahhhh.* Aironell sat with the hardness of the smooth marble beneath her, legs swaying a bit as she glanced over at Isabella. Her mouth twisted to the side as her eyes turned up a bit. She recognized that face. It usually meant trouble for her, at least when she was growing up. It was when Isabella picked up on something.

"Did you know that your mother didn't even know who your father was?"

Aironell's brow furrowed. "What do you mean?" Leaning in, Aironell's feet tapped against the floor as she waited. *What could she mean by that? She was hoping even praying that it wasn't something horrid.*

Isabella leaned against the backing of the bench with arms crossed. Again, she was thinking of her words. Aironell knew this pose, all too well.

Open, close, open, and close once more. Aironell tried not to laugh. It was a challenge, when Isabella reminded her of a fish.

"It is hard to explain. Bachusa, as you see it now, was very different." Isabella uncrossed her arms and tapped her fingers against the bench. "Sorry, I am forcing memories to resurface from some time ago."

"How long? What happened? Why was it so different?" The questions poured out like batter pouring out of a funnel. She studied Isabella's face and her whole demeanor. All she could do was wait for more.

"I was a child, myself, so I know how things looked to me, but I also listened, a lot. I came with my mother often to the palace." Aironell tilted her head and Isabella continued. "My mother was a maid here, when your grandparents ruled. I won't say anything about them, except that they were nothing like your parents. Which is why Bachusa was a very different kingdom."

Isabella paused. Aironell had what felt like a million questions. She bit the end of one of her nails, trying to calm her inner thoughts. Isabella had her eyes closed and then let out a long breath.

"Since I was here, often, and I was a child I heard plenty. Your father is a more benevolent ruler than his parents, rest their souls, but that is the gist of it." Aironell rubbed at her chin as she starred off, just listening, taking it all in.

"They didn't really entertain or listen to the pleas of the people. They didn't go to town often. Your father went into town, as often as he could — under supervision from servants, of course. When he got older he would go alone. One of his first projects was to improve the buildings. It took time and he used some of his magic to help, but he got his father to agree. Your father loved his town. He loved his people and wanted to have a better relationship with them. But since his parents didn't do that, it took time for people to know who he was."

Aironell kept soaking it in like a sponge, nodding as she rocked herself.

Isabella continued, "When your father was older, your mother would see him around, but he didn't wear his crown or anything. He blended well, as if he was just a high-born and not the heir to the throne. My understanding is that she didn't know who he was, not until they met at one of the tournaments. I think your father was seventeen."

Aironell's eyes went wide as she shook her head. Then she blinked. Her mouth gaped open. "He was only a year older than me?" Blinking once more to try to steady her head.

Isabella nodded. "He was already set to marry. It was custom to wed by eighteen."

"You have to love how nobody thought that to be odd. Sorry. I know a different world entirely. Wait." Her left hand rubbed at the side of her face. She was still trying to put the pieces together.

"Isabella, I need to know more. I know you said it was love at first sight, but what happened to the woman he didn't marry?" She gulped and then kept right on. "My grandparents sound, well, unpleasant and controlling; if that was the case then how did my father manage to persuade them to change their plans?"

Isabella's hand pressed against her chest as she laughed. Aironell sat firm—arms crossed with eyes that inspected and with foot tapping, she waited.

Isabella cleared her throat. "I'm sorry. I couldn't help it. Your questions kept rolling, one after another like a tidal wave." She reached over and patted her shoulder. The tension in Aironell's shoulder relaxed, just a bit, but she still watched and waited.

"Your father would meet her for little outings—picnics, strolls, the works." Aironell's gaze softened as she continued to listen.

"I remember my mother talking once to the other maids about how they would spend hours just talking. He loved hearing her opinions and he respected her for it. So, after about a month his heart knew what his head thought the first time he saw her."

"Which was?" Aironell's hands flared about.

"He wanted to marry her. I remember when your father spoke with his parents about it. It was quite the display. Your grandfather's temper flared. He was adamant about the arrangement already made. He wanted him married to a princess." Isabella stood up and stretched.

"Then what happened?" She followed Isabella like a little tail toward the other end of the balcony. She almost smashed into Isabella when she stopped. Aironell stood beside her, gazing out.

"Do you see those fields, there?" Isabella pointed just away from the main town.

Aironell nodded.

"That was where they used to hold those events."

Aironell tried to imagine giant tents with many onlookers seated around. It must have been quite the sight. There was a soft rub at her hand and Aironell looked over at Isabella.

"Aironell, you are as curious as ever," she chuckled. "I have to return to my duties around the palace, soon."

Aironell straightened up and shook her head. Before she could say anything, Isabella spoke again.

"Your father loved your mother, deeply. He made a vow to his father." Isabella leaned closer and Aironell bowed her head in.

"I remember your grandfather's rage. At the time I was young so I didn't really understand the significance." Isabella swallowed.

Aironell felt like Isabella wanted to tell her, yet didn't for some reason.

"They allowed the marriage because your father did something unheard of."

Aironell was just itching to know. She squeezed the rails, tight. "What was it that he did? Please Isabella."

"He told his father that if he could not marry the love of his life, then he would not take the throne."

Aironell's lips parted as her eyes bulged, a bit. She released her grip on the rail and leaned her back against it. Her mind was playing out each part in her mind, until she pressed her fingertips to her temples.

"What's wrong?" Isabella placed a hand on Aironell's shoulder and then withdrew.

"I'm just surprised. If my father loved his kingdom and his people, then how? How could he have been willing to give it all up."

Isabella nodded. "I may be crossing more boundaries and I apologize, but I think you know how. He was in love. Plus, it didn't take long for your grandparents to realize how good of a choice your mother was, what with her being from one of the most prominent noble families." Isabella turned and started toward the opening back to the bedroom.

"Wait." Aironell's arm stretched out and she felt the pull of magic. Isabella couldn't move forward. Aironell strolled over and didn't say anything for a moment.

"I'm sorry about that." She waved her hand and Isabella raised her leg to step. "Sometimes I forget."

"Your magic seems to be growing. Be careful." Isabella's tone was low and her eyebrows raised.

"I will, promise. I-I still want to know one more thing."

"Hmm?"

"What happened to that princess, the one he didn't marry?"

"I'm not sure. The only people who know are your parents. Anyway, you should start getting dressed. Your parents are waiting for you downstairs."

Isabella bowed and moseyed past the little table and stopped just short of the door; then turned.

"There is one more thing I want to tell you, unrelated to all this."

"What is it?" Aironell strolled across the room. She stopped by the closet but looked at Isabella.

Isabella took a breath. "Quairken and I have decided to have a baby."

Aironell's mouth twirled up into a grin.

"I've always wanted children but it wasn't the time."

Aironell reached out her hand and spoke. "Oh, Isabella I'm sorry."

"Don't you dare apologize. Quairken and I both feel blessed to have had the honor of raising you."

Aironell's eyes softened and nodded.

"Now that you're grown and we have all returned, well, I'm expecting."

"Isabella, that is remarkable." She dashed toward Isabella and gave her a hug.

As she pulled back she continued. "You both will be great parents… you were for me."

There was a slight tear in Isabella's eyes, but she continued. "Aironell would you be our child's godmother?

"Oh, yes! I would love that." Isabella nodded and opened the door. Aironell couldn't stop thinking about a little baby around the palace. *Godmother.*

She spun around, "Isabella, one thing."

Isabella was already in the hall but she turned her head.

"Who will be the godfather?"

Isabella's little mouth curled up. "Quairken has decided and will be asking Alzerion. I hope that won't be an issue." Her voice sounded playful. Aironell smiled and nodded. Then Isabella left.

This was shaping up to be a great morning. Isabella's news and well her moment with Alzerion, *ahh.* Now she had to ready herself. With both hands facing out, the closet doors opened. Aironell moved so swiftly that she could have been floating on air. She knew what she wanted to wear. Snap. The nightgown was lying on her bed and the red dress was on her. She moved, quickly, to the mirror. Her hands felt the bumps of the beaded bodice as they smoothed out the creases. Aironell gripped a bit of the material as she turned side-to-side, as the bottom billowed.

The dress fit perfectly and she loved how it hugged all her features, in just the right places. Too bad Alzerion did not get to see her in that. Satisfied she sat at the little plump seat of her vanity and leaned forward. Her hands pinched and pulled at her skin. Aironell grabbed her lotion and applied that to her bare skin and then worked on her hair. She knew she needed to work fast so she snapped her fingers and the brush, make-up, and brushed floated around. Her hair was brushed out and braided. Aironell nodded and the brush went back into place and the butterfly clip soared around and clipped to the bottom of the braid. The make-up finished and she stood up and smiled. Her hair was in one long braid with a couple curly strays at each side of her face.

Aironell left her room and headed down the hall and the stairs to join her parents. As she opened the door the king and queen glanced up. Aironell walked in and sat at the table.

The king wiped away the crumbs of his biscuit. "Good morning, honey."

"I'm glad you were able to join us," the queen said. "We were starting to think you had other plans this morning." Queen Evalyn used the knife to splatter a helping of raspberry jam over her biscuit.

"Your mother is right," the king added. "What kept you?" Aironell grabbed a biscuit. *Mmmm they smelled of banana-nut, her father's favorite.* Then she readied it as she spoke with them. "I'm sorry if I worried you, both. I had some visitors this morning."

"Oh?" the king straightened up and Aironell caught his raised eyebrow.

"Doesn't she look radiant?" the queen motioned to the king.

Aironell took one bite of her biscuit, eyes darting between the two of them.

"Sweetheart, you do look gorgeous. I'm sorry I'm still fixed on the comment about visitors. Who?"

Aironell swallowed. "Well, Alzerion came to say good morning and —"

"Alzerion?" King Francisco's eyebrows drew even closer together. He sat still as he observed her.

What did I get myself into? She looked at her mother but she saw the wheels turning in her eyes. *Great.*

"Father, I'm sure you know that he escorted me into town the other day."

"I do. I'm not sure why he would be visiting you so early in the morning. Surely, he has a number of other things to do?"

"I'm sure he does. He promised to check in on me in the morning."

His face had this scowl and his eyebrows were permanently dipped down.

"Oh, that was nice of him, don't you think, Francisco?"

He didn't face the queen. His stare stayed on Aironell.

"Am I the only one that thinks it ridiculous that he came to visit? I'm sorry maybe that's not the correct word. I-well, ugh." He stood up and started pacing around the table. Aironell sat unsure what to say.

Queen Evalyn gave Aironell a reassuring smile. "Francisco, dear. I think it was meant to be a sweet gesture. Right?"

"It was."

King Francisco had this pinched expression as he walked over and sat beside Aironell. "Darling. I want to be perfectly clear."

Aironell nodded, still unsure what to say. Well, she was pretty sure she just got Alzerion into some sort of trouble. *Oops.*

"I do not want anyone of the male variety in your room, in the early hours of morning. Am I clear?"

She gulped. "I understand." Her arms crossed over her chest. "I don't want to upset you but I'm not sure why. Nothing—happened."

King Francisco placed his hand up and Aironell couldn't hear her voice. He stood up and made his way to sit beside his wife. Once he sat down, he snapped his fingers.

"That was really not necessary." Aironell pouted.

"Well, I did not want any details—none." His hands clenched into fists on the table as he shook his head. "I'm sorry, where is Alzerion this morning, anyway? I think we need to have words."

"Francisco, calm down." Evalyn placed her hand, gently on his shoulder. Then she patted his fist and took a breath. "Let's hear what our daughter would like to say."

Queen Evalyn turned back to Aironell. "Aironell, I think he knows Alzerion meant to be sweet, but it makes your father uncomfortable." Evalyn continued to massage at his fist. Finally, his hands relaxed.

"Oh." She glanced over at her father who was taking slow breaths and rubbing at the back of his neck.

"I don't want to upset you," she focused on the king. "Alzerion was only there this morning and then Isabella visited, too."

He nodded. His expression softening.

"Isabella and I had an interesting conversation."

"Oh?" King Francisco grabbed a cup and poured some tea. "What was it about?"

She had to think carefully, yet quickly. She wanted some answers, but didn't want to step on any other invisible mine fields, again.

"You both know that I do have some feelings for Alzerion, right?" She swallowed as her gaze met her father's. His nostrils flared, a bit, then he nodded. "Your mother told me about the conversation between the two of you." He took a sip of the hot tea. His eyes gazed back above the rim of his cup.

Aironell caught her breath, for a moment. Neither seemed surprised. Whew. She was worried how her father would take it. Thank goodness.

Queen Evalyn's hand stretched across the table, palms up. Her fingers looked like they were dancing as they motioned. Aironell placed her hands in her mother's.

"Aironell, what does Alzerion have to do with Isabella's morning visit?"

She felt the queen's grip around her hands. It was probably meant to be comforting, but for some reason she felt it more like a constricting snake's grip. She had no reason to feel this way, yet she couldn't help it.

"Aironell?" King Francisco probed as he placed his mug down.

Just say it, she told herself. "I want to know who the other princess was." Her foot was tapping feverishly. The queen tilted her head and the king's brows furrowed. "Father, I know you were betrothed to another and I want to know about her. Isabella said I am like you, and well, I just want to fully understand everything."

She saw her father's face was paler than usual and his eyes did not seem angry. *Whew.* No. Instead they looked muddled, with the slightest hint of sadness. Aironell darted her gaze to the queen. Her mother had a hint of a blush. The queen opened her mouth, closed it, and opened it again– nothing. Nothing came out, but her grip loosened and she pulled her hands back toward her chest, clutching the frill of her gown.

Finally, the king leaned forward as he rubbed the queen's shoulder. "Aironell, I will admit that I'm not entirely pleased that Isabella brought that up."

"Father, please don't be upset with her. I-I was persistent." She looked at him more sincerely than she ever had. "I just want to know how I'm like you, father." Her eyes shone bright as she kept firm contact with him. "She told me about how the kingdom was different and you, well, you were Bachusa's biggest champion."

Aironell stood with her weight pressing down her arms full force on her hands. Hands that pressed into the table.

"Oh, sweetie." His tone was soft. There was no rasp or sternness. His face gave nothing away.

She didn't want him to try to back out of giving her an answer. "I promise I can take it, whatever the reason or answer. I, well, I'm not a little kid." Aironell gazed at her mother who still had her mouth gaped open, but her eyes revealed a sense of understanding. Aironell snapped her attention back to her father. "I'm an adult by Bachusa standards, please?" She felt sure, ready.

King Francisco grabbed his wife's hand, pulled it to his lips and kissed her knuckles. Then he held onto her hand. Aironell smiled at the sight. It was hard to imagine him with another woman.

"Aironell," the queen broke her silence. "You are right. You are an adult." Queen Evalyn glanced to her husband and then continued. "We need you to know that this is hard for us."

The king nodded. He looked grave but took a breath. "I'm not proud of what happened. Please don't judge us too harshly."

Aironell nodded and sat down in her chair. Her hands folded beneath her chin.

"Did you break her heart?"

The king swallowed and then shook his head. "Neither of us truly loved the other. No, I'm just ashamed because I single-handedly changed the course of her life."

"I will never condemn you." Her eyes shifted to her mother. "Both of you have been nothing but generous and kind to me."

The queen blew her a kiss.

"That means more than you know," King Francisco said. He placed his hands on the table and sat back, just a bit.

"Father, is this the reason we have a rebellion on our hands? I was told about how you worked hard to improve the kingdom, yet I know there are people that are not pleased with us."

He grimaced as his hands rubbed at his muscled arms. "Aironell, you are quite wise, maybe even to clever."

"We had no way of knowing that our marriage would have such an effect." Queen Evalyn said.

"Your mother is right. Sweetheart, the princess I was to marry was not in love—at least not with me." He lowered his gaze.

Aironell bit at her lower lip but she was alert. Maybe there was a peaceful way to end this rebellion.

"I'm sorry, father."

"Don't be. At one time that fact pained me, but things changed when I met your mother." He took a sip of his tea. Aironell sat soaking in each detail.

"She was in love with a man from her own kingdom."

Aironell frowned as her brows creased together.

"He was not considered a suitable match." The queen added.

"What was wrong with him?" Aironell looked between the both of them. "Was he a bad man?"

The king did not look at her.

"No," Queen Evalyn said. "He was from a family of sorcerers, like me." Aironell tilted her head to the side and continued to frown.

"Her parents expected her to marry someone with…more to offer."

"More to offer? What does that mean?" Aironell could feel this rage storm within her. "Does that mean what I think?"

"They wanted her married to a future king, and well, Bachusa could offer their kingdom an alliance; which they needed."

Aironell looked aghast. "That's ridiculous."

"Sweetie, things tend to work very differently in this realm than the other realm where you grew up," the king said. His gaze met hers. She saw pain.

Aironell took a breath and continued. "What happened?"

"Well, when our engagement ended her family did not take it well and they disowned her. She was left with nothing but the clothes she was wearing." King Francisco said. His voice sounded a bit strained. "She and the man she loved fled, here."

"Wait, you mean they live in Bachusa?"

Queen Evalyn nodded.

"I promised, no I vowed to protect them anyway I could." King Francisco said. He licked his lips and straightened up. He looked to the queen.

Queen Evalyn spoke. "Your father sanctioned their marriage. None of her family attended, but his did."

Aironell fixed her gaze on them. She didn't want to ask any questions. She was still trying to piece together the story, like her life depended on it.

"They gave them some money, but it wasn't what each was used to living with." Queen Evalyn stood and paced around, gown billowing as she strode around.

There was a silence. It felt like a void that neither wanted to speak about.

Aironell went over to her father and touched his shoulder. He looked at her and shook his head. Aironell bit her cheek and then locked eyes with her mother, across the room. She had tears and then turned around.

"Father," she pleaded. "What happened once they married."

King Francisco pulled himself up. He stood like a statue, unmoving as he gazed down at her. He caressed her cheek, "My sweet darling daughter." The king's arms opened as he wrapped them around her and hugged her. Aironell could feel his heart racing, but the comfort of her father was nice. She opened her eyes when she heard the queen's shoes clack against the floor. Her mother joined them. The mingling of lavender and sandalwood was soothing.

"They bought a modest house and within the year had a child." King Francisco's breathed out warm against her head. He pulled back and stared at her. Queen Evalyn circled around and stood next to him. "A child should have been a happy occasion, but I'm afraid to admit that was the decline."

Aironell rubbed at her chin. "I don't under—"

"Over the years, she confided in me that they fought, often. He was not the man she had fallen in love." King Francisco breathed out. "He grew cold and distant and controlling." His voice cracked. He cleared his throat.

"You still speak with her?"

"We do," the queen's lips parted. It was not quite a smile. "I would say we have a unique closeness with her."

Aironell stepped back. "What am I missing? Why would you? If her life took a turn for the worse, why would she even want to be around, either of you?"

She saw them exchange glances. "I don't mean to be cruel. I hope you know that?" Aironell added.

The king rubbed at the back of his neck. "Before you were born she came to me. We met frequently." He reached out a hand to Aironell and she grabbed it. He escorted her back to the table and he sat down right next to her. Then he motioned to the queen who sat on the other side of her.

"Your mother and I felt like we couldn't deny her, when she asked for a favor."

"A favor?" Aironell fiddled with the end of one of her curls. "What kind of favor?"

"She was and is quite selfless." Queen Evalyn spoke. "Her favor could have been for money or anything to better her life."

"Money wasn't what she wanted." King Francisco spoke firmly. "The only thing she cared about was her child. So, she asked us to provide a better future for her child."

"Aironell," Queen Evalyn stared into her eyes with such intensity. "We didn't have any children of our own, yet, and we knew we could help. So, we did just that. Your father and I gave her child a great education."

Aironell felt like her heart stopped. She scanned the look on both of their faces. Both so solid in what they did. Why did their generosity make her feel odd, like there was still a piece she was missing? Wait. They gave her child an education. She went pale. She pressed against the ground, forcing her chair back, so she could see the both of them, at once.

"Who is her child?" Unsure if she wanted to know. She felt this lump in her throat. This chill came over her as she waited. Fingers dug into the wood of her chair.

King Francisco fixed his gaze on her. "Sweetheart, I think you already know. You *are* my daughter and your senses must be screaming that answer.

Aironell felt the lump in her throat worsen. She blinked once, twice, and felt hot tears prick at the corners of her eyes.

"No!" She couldn't stop the words from streaming from her mouth. "It can't be. He would've told me!"

"We know how you must be feeling." Queen Evalyn spoke with a soothing tone as she reached for her hand.

"No. I don't think you do." Her voice boomed as she stood up and darted away from the table. She stared blankly at a portrait on the wall. Hands clenched around her elbows, like she was pulling herself into a hug. Then she spun around. Anger still welling inside. Tears streaming down her face. "H-h-how?" She swiped at her tear-stained face and then her hands gripped her, once more.

"Aironell, please," Queen Evalyn pleaded.

"Then tell us, sweetheart," King Francisco spoke, calmly.

"How could either of you not tell me." She felt the stinging at her eyes once more. How could he…" The pain gripped her heart like it was being squished and twisted into thin pieces. She clutched at the half-heart necklace and then dropped to her knees. Alzerion. He was the child. She knew it down to her core.

The king and queen ran toward her, both knelt down beside her. She felt her mother's delicate hand rubbing her back.

"Oh, Aironell," the king's voice cracked. "We never meant to hurt you. We… didn't know how deep your feelings would be."

"Neither did I," she mumbled. "He should have told me."

The queen took her sleeve and dabbed at Aironell's cheek. "I'm sure it's not something he is proud to admit."

"He could have been your child," she sniffled as she looked at her father.

He pulled her in, tight. "You are my child, my one and only. My heart, darling." He kissed her forehead.

They sat like this until Aironell felt her breaths start to slow down to her normal pace. She pulled back and smiled at them. They were right. The bigger picture was more important. Alzerion is safe and healthy, and that was because of her parents.

"Thank you—both of you." She nodded. "If you hadn't stepped in then I may not have ever met Alzerion."

Queen Evalyn kissed her fingers and then pressed them to Aironell's cheek. "You are as close to perfect as it gets."

Aironell beamed as she let go of her necklace. She knew how she felt and it warmed her. She wanted Alzerion to know that *nothing* could change how she feels about him.

They stood up and the king held out his arm for Aironell to grab. He escorted her back to her chair and they all sat down.

"Do you think you can take any more news? There is something we wanted to tell you?"

They both stared at her, closely.

"As long as you're not about to tell me I have sibling that I never knew about." Aironell laughed. "Sorry, I guess it was a bad joke."

The king chuckled and shook his head. "No. Nothing like that."

"We don't want to alarm you," Queen Evalyn said. "But there is something you should know about from the day of your birth celebration."

"Oh?" Aironell pursed her lips.

"Your father and I were so thrilled when you were born, that we had a feast on your behalf." Queen Evalyn spoke with fluid motion. She appeared relaxed. "Many people came to see you, our bright light."

Aironell didn't know what to say. She felt this warmth dancing inside.

"A special friend of mine even came to lay her eyes on you," the queen cleared her throat. She wasn't smiling but instead bit at her bottom lip.

"What your mother means to say, is that her friend had a unique magical gift."

"That's right."

"What kind of gift?" Aironell rubbed her hands together.

"She has the ability to see glimpses of the future or fragments of possibilities, as she would say."

"Oh! She is a seer?" Aironell's worded bubbled out. "I read about them in a book from the library."

The queen nodded.

"When she held you," King Francisco said, "we knew she saw something."

"I begged her to tell us," Queen Evalyn fiddled with the edge of the table. "Eventually she told us. She said what we made of it was up to us."

Aironell's head flinched back, a bit. That was an odd thing to say. "What did she tell you?"

Queen Evalyn stared at her for a moment. Aironell did not recoil. She wanted to know. No. She felt like she needed to know.

The king cleared his throat. Aironell looked over at him. "Sweetheart, she said that you were the hope for Bachusa, but things were not going to be easy. That you would have to fight for your rightful place on the throne. Which now we know that there is truth in that."

Aironell nodded, slowly. Her life hadn't been harmonious. The queen placed her hand under Aironell's chin and gently lifted. Aironell gazed back at her mother.

"She also told your father and I what seems like a riddle of sorts."

Aironell's forehead creased as she waited. She rubbed her hand around her mouth and then placed her hands in her lap.

"Success is but a mystery. Elusive but not history. Two hearts bound, never to be undone. Protection will be key, but lost from the elusive, one." Queen Evalyn spoke as if she had heard it just yesterday.

Aironell closed her eyes, trying to think.

"Was it too much?" King Francisco patted Aironell's shoulder.

Aironell shook her head. "Sorry, I was just—"

"Trying to get your bearings?" He finished.

Aironell nodded.

"Darling, we wish we could fill in the blanks for you," the queen said. "I could never convince my friend, Jezzabell, to explain or to say more."

"Only time will tell," King Francisco added. "You are our special little girl, no matter how old you get." He smiled.

"We know that success is possible, that much is certain." Queen Evalyn stood, leaned in, and kissed Aironell on the head.

"I appreciate the confidence, but it doesn't make me feel any better." Aironell stood. "The pressure of it all. The kingdom. The rebellion. It all rests on my shoulders."

King Francisco strolled to her side and said, "Don't worry. We are by your side, always."

Aironell took a deep breath and nodded.

"Do you have any plans, today?" Queen Evalyn asked.

"I think I'm going to practice. After this discussion, I feel it couldn't hurt."

"Very good," the king nodded.

"Later today, I will be spending some time with Alzerion. I just want you both to know."

The queen beamed.

"Thank you," King Francisco walked toward his wife and grasped her hand. "We have meetings to attend."

Aironell watched as they left the room.

THE BETRAYAL

Alzerion waited for the soldiers. Training was about to start. He had to get his mind on target. Practice, skills, defensive maneuvers. Ugh, he had to get her out of his mind. He fought the urge to grin. Instead he tried to ground his thoughts. He smelled the leather from the soldier's jerkin. He felt a tap on the shoulder, and he pulled out his sword, swung it around, and stopped short when he saw Quairken.

Quairken stared wide-eyed. "Woah. Someone is on edge."

"I guess. Sorry," Alzerion chuckled. "Lots on my mind."

Other soldiers were coming out from the barracks now. Quairken straightened up and said "Sir, permission to speak?"

"Of course," Alzerion sheathed his sword back into the scabbard at his hip. "What can I do for you?"

Quairken walked away from the others coming out of the barracks moved toward the walls of the palace. Alzerion followed. "It is that kind of conversation, eh?"

"What do you mean?" Quairken tilted his head.

"You don't want the others to hear. Is this serious?" Alzerion scanned Quairken's demeanor. He didn't appear to be troubled by something.

"Oh no. Nothing serious. I just have some personal news to share and the other is more of a concern about you."

"How curious." Alzerion smirked. "What concerns you?"

"You seem distracted, sir."

Alzerion patted Quairken on the back. "You don't need to be formal. We are out of earshot from the others." Alzerion glanced back at the soldiers. They had pulled out the training dummies and were grouping up into training formation.

Quairken swallowed. "Okay. Well I don't want to question you but are you focused?"

"Quairken, we have trained by each other long enough. You know I would never let anything distract me in battle."

"That doesn't answer the question." Quairken took one step back and angled himself.

Alzerion pressed, hard, on his lips as he thought of the best way to explain. He knew there was a wrong way to tread, when it came to what he wanted to say.

"Quairken, I am focused. I allowed myself a brief moment of distraction as I waited for everyone."

Quairken adjusted his scabbard as he leaned in and whispered, "Care to share what was on your mind?"

Alzerion's mouth gaped open. Quairken gave him a sly wink. "I, err, don't know what you mean."

Quairken's posture perked up as he circled around. Alzerion sensed his presence. He had to tell Quairken. He didn't keep things from him, well, most things. Alzerion motioned toward Quairken and they strolled further away from the soldiers practicing their drills. Alzerion stopped where there was nothing around. He nobody would see them from the training grounds, but the sword of the clanking swords was still audible, but barely.

Alzerion took a deep breath and smelled the roses from Gorgeous Garden.

"Alzerion, it seems like you don't want to tell me something." He paced around. *Whew*, Alzerion thought. It helped to not see his face.

Alzerion cleared his throat. "I don't mean to, but I-well-have some-thing or *someone* on my mind of late."

Quairken stopped mid pace and turned, slowly, back to Alzerion. His head was tilted. "Someone?"

Alzerion nodded. He kept eye contact and hoped Quairken would understand.

He grinned wide and then smacked his hands together. "Well, well, well. It has finally happened."

Alzerion stayed quiet and didn't give anything away. He watched and listened. Then Quairken started laughing. It was a loud uncontrollable laugh, where he bent over and touched his knees.

"Are you okay?" There was no response, just the raucous sound. "It's not that funny, seriously." Alzerion folded his arms across his chest. He watched as Quairken squatted and that sat on the ground with his legs out. He moved to more of a low giggle, but it was slowing. When it stopped he kept breathing heavily as he pressed his hand against the sides of his ribs.

Alzerion just stood his ground as he tapped his booted-foot. "That was a bit uncalled for."

"Sorry, honest," he spoke in wheezy breaths. He was still catching his breath from that laughing fit. Quairken closed his eyes and took a few more slow breaths.

Alzerion moved closer. His hands touched and then moved apart, then back together and apart once more. Then he snapped his fingers. Alzerion felt the ground rumble and quake beneath his feet. Quairken looked down as his hands clenched handfuls of the grass.

Alzerion smirked as Quairken head wiped around. Finally, two curved stones started to emerge. Quairken looked down as his body started to rise. "What in the—"

"I thought we could sit on these." Alzerion spotted his near Quairken and sat down as Quairken's hands sprang up as his stone curved upward. Both were a mixture of dark and light greys. They were smooth and curved at the sides to rest your arms on. Quairken touched the stones and even knocked on his.

"What do you think you will fall in?" Alzerion chuckled.

"No." He shot back. "You nearly scared me. I thought the ground was going to break."

Alzerion shook his head as he picked two blades of grass and twisted them about.

Quairken broke the brief silence. "Look I hope I didn't offend you before. It's just, well, I needed a good chuckle. I mean things are pretty tense and I know we are working hard to defeat the rebels, but—"

"But you needed a break." Alzerion looked at Quairken. "I get it." Then he gazed back down and continued twisting his blades of grass. He heard shuffling so he looked back up. "What?"

"Isabella and I both always wondered, you know, if you would meet someone."

"Quairken are we about to *talk* about this?" Quairken turned a shade of light pink. He pivoted his face away. "I know it's not what we do, but maybe this once?" He squinted back at Alzerion.

Alzerion hesitated, but nodded anyway.

"Well, who is the lucky girl?" Quairken reached his arm over and patted Alzerion on the back.

Alzerion used one hand to rub at the back of his neck as his gaze lingered at Quairken's expecting face.

"Come on."

Alzerion swallowed but found that he couldn't find the words. No. He couldn't will himself to say them. He pulled his legs in and wrapped his arms around them, pulling them tighter into his chest.

"Alzerion?"

He had to say something. Quairken was expecting an answer. *Ugh.* His grip tightened so much that he felt the buckle of his boots press against his chest. "Quairken, I need you to understand, it wasn't planned, alright?"

"Wasn't planned? I would assume not." He grinned. "You have had this savior complex for years now. I'm just amazed that you let your guard down at all."

Alzerion bit down on his lip so hard that he had this metal taste. He continued to grip his legs with one hand and the other touched his lip. He drew a little bit of blood. *Great.*

He wiped it away. "I guess I deserve that comment. I have been focused on one goal, but it's my duty."

Quairken nodded. Alzerion knew he understood. Duty was at the core part of being a soldier.

"Quairken," Alzerion exhaled as he stood up. "I didn't know feelings until they were smacking me in the face. I, err... I never expected to think about her in this way, I swear."

Quairken's eyebrows furrowed as he stood. He held his hands up, palms out. "Hold on. You're not talking about my wife, right?"

"Oh, heavens no!" Why would you think that?"

Quairken wiped at his forehead. "Alzerion, it was the way you were talking. Like you were apologizing to me."

"I didn't mean to alarm you." Then Alzerion started the trek back toward the training field. He heard Quairken beside him.

"Then who? Who else would you apologize to me about?" There was a silence.

Alzerion kept walking forward until he felt this grip on his arm that pulled him. Alzerion was pulled in and close to Quairken. He saw Quairken's face scanning him. "Aironell."

"What about her?" Alzerion swallowed.

"It's her, isn't it? There isn't anyone else you would ever feel this guilty about."

He nodded. Quairken let go of his grip. Alzerion stepped forward a few more paces and he could see the soldiers.

"Hey, we aren't done." Quairken sprinted over to him.

"Quairken, maybe—"

"No. I have something to say." He breathed out as he clapped his hand down on Alzerion's shoulder. "You better do right by her. Understood?"

Alzerion nodded.

"I mean it. I'm happy for you, truly, but I helped raise that girl."

Alzerion's eyes darted back at Quairken. "I know. That was why I had such a terrible time telling you. Despite what I feel, I don't know how not to shake off the ick."

"Just don't think about it. Alright? She doesn't need to know. She doesn't need to ever feel like a burden."

"Agreed."

They walked into the barracks, grabbed a couple shields, and hurried to the field. Quairken and Alzerion usually partnered up, unless Alzerion was hoping to work on a specific soldier's skills.

Alzerion tapped at his throat and his voice boomed onto the training grounds. "Men." The last of the clanging ceased as eyes turned to Alzerion. "Good warm-up. Now I want you to work in your pairings and focus on close-quarter combat. Be sure to use the practice swords, we don't need any injuries."

Once he was satisfied with watching the slash, deflect, and parrying he turned his attention back to Quairken. Quairken had this devilish grin as he swung his sword down at him. Alzerion deflected the move as he quickly pivoted to the side.

"I didn't know we were starting."

"Always take your opponent by surprise, you taught us that."

Alzerion smirked as they engaged in two stab and slash thrusts, in quick succession. "Who knew you were paying attention." With that Quairken slashed and their practice swords hit, parry for parry.

Alzerion deflected the last blow and forced the swords in an arch up and over, causing Quairken to stumble. He pushed off the ground and spun around just in time to deflect the blow headed for his thigh. Practice continued blow after blow. Aiming to make each hit count.

"Break," Alzerion panted. Quairken gave a curt nod as he placed the practice sword on the wooden table. Alzerion took a few slow, controlled breaths as he walked past Quairken and observed the soldiers. Again, he adjusted the volume of his voice.

He heard some groans as they turned to him. "How does it feel?" Alzerion asked. Silence. He surveyed them and eyes shifted from one to the other. Finally, one soldier stepped forward.

"It felt like torture, sir."

Alzerion moved toward him and patted him on the back. "I bet, Castro." He exchanged glances and then paced around all his men. "I'm sorry for the lengthy practices. Remember our duty."

"Protect the royal family, at any cost!" Castro called out. Alzerion turned to him and nodded.

"Defeat the rebellion," Quairken said as Alzerion glanced over at him.

"That's what we are here for. That and to protect our families, too. Never lose sight of that." Alzerion's voice didn't waver, even as he wiped the sweat off with the back of his hand.

"Now, wash up and head out."

The men grabbed their practice weapons and dashed to the barracks. "Huh, I thought they were tired?"

"Oh," Quairken laughed. "Ouch." It sounded like a laughing groan. "Sorry. Sharp pain in my side." Alzerion stood next to Quairken and crossed his arms.

"What? You don't believe me? That's why the men left, quick."

"I'll humor you. What do you mean?"

Quairken placed an arm around Alzerion. "They wanted to leave before you changed your mind."

Alzerion smirked as he fixed his gaze on Quairken. "Oh, really. Is that so?"

"Oh, yea." Quairken pulled away and then turned back to Alzerion. "There's something else I had to discuss with you. I almost forgot."

"Is it important or can it wait another time? I'm running a bit behind schedule." Alzerion rubbed the back of his neck.

"I'll be brief." Alzerion looked at Quairken his expression shifted. He was much more serious.

"Of course, let's sit."

They sat on the rickety wooden chairs by the training table. "What is it?" Alzerion sked.

"I'm no good at this so I'm going to get right to it." Alzerion nodded. He was completely fixed on Quairken and nothing else. "Isabella and I are going to have a baby."

"Wait, you guys are pregnant?"

Quairken opened his mouth but there were no words, so he nodded.

Alzerion bolted up. "Quairken, that's amazing. Just great news for the both of you!"

"Thanks." Alzerion ushered them away from the training ground. As they walked Quairken slowed his pace. "Alzerion, I have a favor to ask."

"Oh?" Alzerion stopped and faced him.

"If something were to happen, would you be my child's godfather?"

Alzerion blinked, twice. "You want me to—"

"Yes. I can't think of anyone who would be a better choice."

Alzerion turned around, full circle as he cleared his throat. He felt a little choked up and didn't want Quairken to know. He faced Quairken with sincerity in his eyes as he pulled Quairken in for a quick hug. "I would be honored."

Quairken nodded. He was beaming.

"Why don't you head off to check on Isabella."

Quairken started toward the palace and then turned around. "Maybe you can surprise, Aironell, maybe." He winked and then dashed away.

Alzerion's jaw gaped open and then he shook his head.

Alzerion strolled through the field a bit. He wasn't quite ready to head back to the palace. Instead, he wandered soaking in the beautiful day. He heard a noise in the distance and peered out. He saw a figure standing back against a tree in the woods. He ran to the enclosed area and grabbed the person by the shirt collar and turned them to face him.

"Warren, what are you doing here? This is a bit risky, don't you think?" Alzerion let go of his grip and stepped aside. He made sure to stay hidden by the branches and the large star-shaped leaves.

"I-I had to see you."

Alzerion shifted, moving so his back was to the opening. He scrutinized Warren, briefly. "What's wrong?"

"Nothing." Warren gulped and his gaze darted to the ground.

He knew something was up. Something felt odd about this. They never met this close to the palace.

"Is Ulbrick here somewhere?"

"No." He shifted his weight and Alzerion noticed that he picked at the hem of his black shirt.

"So, plans are still set?" Alzerion's brows narrowed as he continued to inspect Warren.

"Huh? Wait, yea."

Something was definitely off. Warren was normally chattier than this.

Alzerion placed his hands, firmly, on Warren's shoulders. It forced Warren to look at Alzerion. "Tell me. Whatever it is, we can figure it out, together."

Warren swallowed. He shook his head and shoved passed Alzerion. Alzerion meandered around to see his face. There was this heaviness in his stomach, like a reactive volcano just waiting to erupt within.

Warren appeared paler than normal. He hunched a bit with his shifty gaze. Alzerion stared, waiting, back against the bark of the nearest tree.

"I did something. I couldn't help it. You know how *he* gets."

"Whoa," Alzerion stretched out his hands. "What did you do?"

Warren began pacing as he scratched at his neck. "I was stupid, okay. I want, no, I need to tell you something but if I do..."

Alzerion felt that internal pressure tighten in his chest. He tried to pace alongside Warren. "Warren, please stop." Alzerion sat on a large rock as he looked up at Warren, eyebrows squished together.

"You won't get it. You won't, just no. I shouldn't have come." He started to run through the woods.

Alzerion bolted up and dashed after him. He knew where this would come out, so he veered left, jumped over the large set of rocks, ducked under a low hanging branch, and caught his boot on a root of one of the sycamore trees.

"Ventus!" A burst of wind pushed against his body and he kicked off and sped off.

There was a chill against his back, but he didn't care, it helped to increase his speed. It pushed him forward. When he reached the end of the woods he saw Warren approaching. His body hurled across the woods over and under tree branches until he collided with Warren.

He grabbed him and they fell to the ground as Alzerion said, "Absentis."

The wind force was gone and he grabbed Warren and stood up. "What has gotten into you!"

Warren growled as he lunged toward Alzerion. *He has lost his mind,* Alzerion thought, as he pivoted to the side and grabbed Warren by the back of his shirt. In an instant, he grabbed his arms and twisted them in and up into a pretzel behind his back.

"Enough! I won't be so kind or gentle if you keep avoiding me."

Warren bucked against Alzerion's grip, but he was no match for Alzerion in brute strength. Slowly, Alzerion felt Warren's resistance give out. He loosened his grip on Warren's arms as he uncurled his arms and they faced each other.

Warren raised his chin, "I told Ulbrick about you."

"What did you tell him? I haven't done anything, that I can think of."

Warren's gaze was unflinching. He could see that Warren may have regrets, but he also spotted rage. He ran his hand through his hair. "Don't lie!" he spat. "Not to me."

Alzerion stepped closer but Warren stepped back. "Warren—"

"What hurts the most is you- you didn't even tell me about her."

Alzerion felt a dryness in his throat. He focused in on Warren as he continued.

"I saw you kiss her. You said there was nothing going on."

Alzerion felt like someone just gut punched him. "W-Wait," he shook his head.

"It's too late. Ulbrick knows. I-I, couldn't lie to him." Alzerion felt large a boulder was dropped on him, like he was being squashed, repeatedly. His mind was racing yet nothing seemed clear.

"How could you?"

"How could I?" Warren's head pulled back and tilted. "No, how could you?"

"I didn't tell you so you wouldn't have been in this situation." Alzerion moved closer. He looked him right in the eye. "I knew you would never be able to keep it from Ulbrick."

Warren stepped back and turned. "So, you lied to me." He craned his neck around. "I thought we were friends."

Alzerion shook his head. His jaw was set open. He had no words.

"I guess I was wrong," Warren spat.

"We were, but you betrayed me," Alzerion sounded breathy. He took small steps toward Warren. "Ulbrick will want her dead."

Warren was glaring at him. "You were kidding yourself if you ever thought he wanted to let her live."

Alzerion felt this stabbing pain with each of his breaths. His fists clenched as he let those words sink in. *He couldn't believe what he heard. No, he didn't mean it. He was just upset.*

"Warren you know I would never let any harm come to her. I thought I could convince her to leave and never return."

Warren chuckled. "Alzerion, there is no way you thought Ulbrick would agree to that."

Alzerion lowered his head. He always hoped but in the end, he wasn't sure. He thought it would be worth the ask. His fists tightened as he smacked them against his legs. "You're right, Warren." Alzerion's lips pinched together. "We were *never* friends. You used me just like Ulbrick."

"I did what I had to. You, you're the one that let feelings get involved. Ulbrick insists that we need you, but I personally think you can be replaced."

Alzerion heard the harsh tone. He shook his head and took a couple steps back. "You lying, bastard!"

"Relax, Alzerion. Now that the cards are all out there, you may want to calm down when you see Ulbrick"

Alzerion stare was cold. He ripped off the U insignia ring and threw it at Warren. "You are the fool if you think I will help either of you!"

Warren picked up the ring and fiddled with it between his fingers. "Ulbrick always gets what he wants, Alzerion, you know that."

"Not anymore." Alzerion's nostrils flared. "He needed me, not the other way around."

"He will see this as a betrayal, and you know that he doesn't forgive traitors." Warren stood firm, like a statue. Alzerion wanted nothing more than to wreck him. To punch that smug smile off his ridiculous face.

"Neither, do I." He spoke with steely coldness. He felt the veins in his neck pulsing, quicker, with each passing second.

Neither blinked or looked away. Warren broke the silence. "I'm sure you will, bend to Ulbrick. You will have no choice."

"In what twisted world do you think that would *ever* happen?" Alzerion straightened up as he clenched his fists, even tighter, to the point where his big knuckles cracked.

"I guess I hit a nerve," Warren chided. "Alzerion you won't let anyone in your corner."

Alzerion's eyebrows narrowed into slits.

Warren laughed. "Oh, so you haven't thought about the repercussion of your choices?" He folded his arms and lounged against a tree stump.

Alzerion started pacing, moving farther from Warren. He was missing something but wasn't sure what. He tilted his head as he looked back at Warren, who was still just relaxing; as if it were an afternoon sitting in Ulbrick's lounge chair.

Warren's lips curled up and he continued. "Alzerion, when everyone learns the truth… you will be all ours." He chuckled. "You didn't just withhold a small something, no, you lied to *them*." Warren pointed back at the palace. "You deceived them including the princess."

Alzerion couldn't move. His eyes widened. He felt each deception hit him blow after blow, like a tidal wave.

"We have our plans and the numbers to crush you." Warren spoke. Alzerion dropped to his knees and his fists pressed against his temples.

Warren stepped around him. "See you on the battlefield, Alzerion." Alzerion heard his grating laughter as he left the woods and head to town.

He beat his fists into the sides of his head. *How could he have been so foolish?* His downfall can be linked to his part. His own destruction that he helped cause. He, he had to figure out how to right the wrongs. His arms went limp at his side. *The only question was would she forgive him and his stupidity?* The king and queen would be disappointed, but he had faith in them, that they would see what was really in his heart.

THE TRUTH

Alzerion woke up early the next day. He felt physically and emotionally drained from the previous day. He sat up and rubbed the sleep out of his eyes. Hell, he still felt tired. It was to be expected when he didn't sleep soundly. How could he? He had to get over that. Alzerion raced to his closet and threw on his clothes. He had to see, Aironell.

The only thing he could think about as he walked to her room was how he would explain. His heart ached at the thought of upsetting her. Maybe he didn't need to tell her, no. she needed to know. She had to hear it from him. when he reached her room and opened the door she wasn't there. His eyes darted from each side, but no, it was empty.

"What are you doing here?" Alzerion spun around to find Isabella. He studied her blank stare.

"I, um, well, you see—"

"No," Isabella dashed pushed him into Aironell's room. "I mean how are you here right now?"

Alzerion's brows furrowed. "Isabella, it's early. I just woke up and there was something I wanted to discuss with Princess Aironell."

"Alzerion," Isabella's voice lowered as she leaned in. "She told us that you were meeting her in town. She even showed me the note."

"What note?" Alzerion's nostrils flared.

Isabella escorted Alzerion over to Aironell's sitting table and handed it to him.

He scanned it and flipped it over. He crumpled it up. "Isabella, I did not write this."

"Then who—"

"I'm sorry I have to go. I must get to her first." Alzerion whooshed passed her and ran. There was no time to stop or pause. He had to meet Aironell before it was too late. Before Warren or Ulbrick could ruin him.

Aironell couldn't wait to see Alzerion. He had some explaining to do but mostly, she just wanted to get lost in his cinnamon-red eyes. The smells of vanilla and cinnamon filled her nose. She looked around to see the baker bringing out the delightfully smelling goods. She was halfway through town when a little girl ran up to her and handed her a crocus. Aironell bent down to grab the flower. She smiled at the child. The little girl bowed her head and ran off.

Aironell continued to make her way to Alzerion's spot while she twirled the flower in her hands. It was white with a pale-yellow center. *So sweet,* she thought as she entered Majestic Park. Once she saw the roses she looked up. It was just as beautiful as the day Alzerion first brought her here. No Alzerion, yet. She was sure she wasn't late. Aironell sat beneath the tallest weeping willow. The silver-purple blooms still amazed her. She sat down and twirled the crocus as she waited. Every so often she would look up and scan the park. Nobody. Aironell leaned her back against the tree and folded her legs like a pretzel. Then she draped her dress around to be sure her legs were covered. Arms folded around her chest tight as she starred up at the silver-purple blooms. *Where was he?* His letter said it was urgent.

Thoughts of making a head wreath with the beautiful blooms filled her mind. Aironell sat up to try and grab a few but her eyes caught a figure approaching. *Finally*, she thought. When she focused her gaze, it was not Alzerion. She did not recognize the man that was steadily coming closer. Head pulled back and eyes narrowed as she fiddled with the stem of the crocus.

"Hello, Princess." He called as he jogged over. His voice sounded pleasant. He bowed his head once he was near. Aironell nodded as she stood up, still holding the crocus.

"I hope I didn't startle you."

"Don't be silly," Aironell forced a smile. She placed her free hand over her chest as she spoke. "I'm at a disadvantage. You know who I am but I don't know you." Her eyes twinkled as she glanced at him.

She caught a slight blush before his head looked down. He seemed harmless. She felt a little more at ease. Surely if he wished her harm he would have done so by now.

"My name is Warren."

"Pleased to meet you, Warren." Something felt odd. She couldn't figure out why. Instead she held out her hand. His head bent to the side as he grasped her hand and then shook it. After a few seconds he released her hand. Aironell shifted her stance and she waited.

"No offense, your highness, but you're not what I was expecting."

"Oh?" Aironell's nose wrinkled as she spoke with a soft voice. His eyes gave away more than he probably bargained for. Aironell could see that he was conflicted. Then he looked off to the side.

"Warren, what is troubling you? Can I help?"

He opened his mouth and then closed it. He sighed, nodded, and then focused his gaze on her. "I fear that I have some terrible news, your highness."

"Oh. What news?" Aironell motioned for him to follow. He did.

She turned around and sat down on the grass. Warren sat on his knees. He rubbed his hands against his pants back and forth, until he spoke again.

"Someone has not been honest with you. It has put you in danger."

Aironell was no longer smiling. She bit the inside of her cheek. "Who? Who is this imposter you speak of?"

She noticed his gaze pained. He was blinking less and then swallowed. Whoever it was, it clearly was tough for him to say.

"You can tell me. Are they part of the rebellion? If they have threatened you, I swear I will keep you safe." Aironell reached out and patted his hand.

He looked down at her hand and then back at her. "It's complicated." He swallowed again. "We were friends and I wanted to keep his secret but I-I, I just can't. You deserve the truth."

Aironell felt her heart pounding beneath her necklace. "Warren, please." She could hear the pleading in her voice. "I need to know who you are talking about. Who is untrustworthy?"

His face was solid, like stone. "Alzerion."

Aironell felt her body tense. No, it couldn't be true. She sat and shook her head. "That can't be. He, I…it can't be."

"I'm sorry, princess. I'm not lying. I will tell you of his deeds."

Aironell pulled her legs in to her chest. As Warren spoke, she felt like her world was crashing. Crashing into tiny pieces that would blow her away in the wind. Once Warren was done, all that was left was this numbness, which was better than the pain she felt at first. Alzerion was helping the leader of this rebellion. That was just the first blow. What hurt the most was the fact that Alzerion worked against her parents.

Warren stood up and turned to leave but then stopped. He circled back around. "There is one more thing."

Aironell looked up with tears in her eyes. *What more could there be?* "What?" she was able to muster.

"Alzerion has always been covering his tracks. Spinning whatever truth he wanted. There is something I forgot to mention. I doubt he will tell you so I feel it is my duty."

Aironell sniffled as she waited. There were no words to convey the depth of her disappointment and pain.

"He knows that the rebel leader, Ulbrick, wants you dead."

Aironell gasped. Head down as she squeezed her legs. "I-I… thank you." Her head was buzzing with this new information.

. . .

Alzerion ran all the way through town. He dodged stalls and people so he wouldn't knock into anything. Once he was out of town and to the clearing of Majestic Park he saw Aironell sitting in their spot. The glimmer of hope vanished when he saw Warren walking away. *Crap!* He sprinted to meet Warren.

"What did you do?" Alzerion said between breaths.

"Relax, Alzerion," Warren held up his hand. "I merely told her the truth." He chuckled. Warren brushed against him as he left. "Good luck fixing this one."

Alzerion spun around. Fists clenched, he thought about pummeling him. *No. He wasn't worth it.* Alzerion focused on Aironell and walked toward her. When he was within arm's reach, he stepped carefully.

He lowered himself to the ground, in a squatting position. He reached to wipe away a tear but Aironell pushed his hand away. Alzerion flinched. He lowered his head. He took a slow breath. He didn't have time to think about his feelings, no. Aironell, she needed him. He bit his lower lip and then gazed back at her.

She covered her face with her hands. Once more he reached forward. This time he placed his hand on her back and began to rub in slow circles. She straightened up and stared at him. A stare might have been putting it kindly. No, she was glaring at him. If she conjured daggers he knew what his fate would be. She pushed her feet off the ground and slid farther away from him.

"Aironell, please. I don't like seeing you so, upset."

Aironell stood up and took a step closer. Then her foot shoved Alzerion's leg. He fell backward. "Hey!"

He scrambled to his feet as she stormed away from him. "Aironell, stop." He grabbed her arm and spun her around.

"No!"

Her eyes were cold and hard. He pulled her in but she tried pulling away. "Aironell, please don't fight me. I want to help."

He held firm and her face reddened as she looked at him.

"Let…Go." Alzerion didn't budge.

Aironell's hands soared up. "Vitis…laedo." Alzerion heard a whooshing from above. He let go of her as he saw one of the weeping willow branches swing down and knock him over. He rubbed his back from the fall. Then he quickly got up as it smacked down again. It missed him. "Aironell, I'm sorry. Please call it off."

"It's a bit late for, sorry, don't you think?" Even her voice was cold. It cut deep like a sword to his chest. She clapped her hands and the attacking branches, ceased.

He jogged over to her. "Can I explain?"

She turned around to face him. "You can try, but it won't do any good." Then she took a step back.

He sighed. He could feel her stare, cutting at his core. He lowered his gaze. The damage was done, but he had to find a way to fix it, he had too.

"I swear it isn't as bad as it seems."

Aironell exhaled. "So you didn't conspire against my parents, your king and queen?" She folded her arms and tapped her fingers against them as she continued. "You didn't take part in traitorous acts? You didn't send…me…away?"

Alzerion opened his mouth but nothing came out. He shook his head. He moved closer to her. He reached out but hesitated. She didn't push his hands away so he placed them on her shoulders.

"It sounds bad, I know. I never meant to do anything to really hurt you. I-I, ugh, everything I did was for you."

Aironell turned away from him. His one hand cupped around her cheek until she faced him. He felt the dried tear stain on her cheek. She grabbed his hand, grazed her fingers against him, and then pushed his hand into his chest. "I can't trust you. Do you understand?"

He could hear her voice quiver. "You keep everyone at a distance, Alzerion. So much you keep to yourself." Her voice cracked as tears flowed down her face. "All my parents have done for you and this is how you repay them."

Alzerion took a deep breath. He felt the heaviness in his chest. "I'm sorry. Aironell, I-I truly did what I thought I needed to keep you safe. My feelings have always been real."

Aironell wiped her eyes and walked away. "You can explain to my parents." She didn't turn back-just kept walking.

Aironell stayed ahead of Alzerion. He was probably staying back. She knew that he could keep up with her if he wanted. She needed the space anyway. So many thoughts playing out in her mind. It all came back to one thing, can he be trusted? She was open with him, but has he ever really been that open with her? She shook the painful thoughts away as she climbed the stairs to the palace and walked to the Great Hall.

She placed her hands on the doors and glanced over her shoulder to Alzerion. "Stay here." Her voice was firm.

Then she pushed open the doors and strolled to her parents.

"Aironell, what's wrong?" Queen Evalyn asked. Her face softened. King Francisco looked up and stood at once. "Sweetie?" He placed an arm around her.

She told them. Left no detail out. The sat with a hand to her mouth, while the king's eyes blurred a bit. She sensed he was fighting tears. She sighed after she finished. King Francisco, hugged her. "I'm sorry."

She wrapped her arms around her father. The tears streamed down her cheeks once more. The warmth and love of his embrace was comforting. He wiped her tears and kissed her forehead. "Sweetheart, send Alzerion in. Your mother and I must speak with him."

Aironell looked over at her mother. She had a pained expression. She knew they both were in some form of shock. They had to be. She certainly was. Aironell nodded and opened the door.

She held the door open and then held her arm out and pointed to her parents. The king had repositioned himself back on the throne. Alzerion walked in, looked at her but she turned away. He made his way toward her parents.

"Thank you," King Francisco said. "We would like a private word with him."

Aironell nodded and left the room.

Alzerion approached them. He couldn't meet their gaze. The queen looked pale as she covered her mouth. Where the king's face didn't give much away. His lip curled. Neither said a word. It was quiet. Eerie. Alzerion found the courage to look at them. The king's face looked hard, like stone. He gulped.

"Is it true?" the queen looked like there were tiny pools of water in her eyes. Alzerion opened his mouth but no words.

"Think carefully about your answer," King Francisco boomed. "Did you do those things, this *Warren* said?"

Alzerion breathed out. "Not entirely."

"Alzerion, we want a straight answer." Queen Evalyn grasped the arms of her throne.

Alzerion ran his hands through his hair. "I can't give you one." He looked up to see the king glaring and the queen tapping her nails into the arms of her throne.

Alzerion's eyes glistened. His chin dropped to his chest as he spoke. "I never meant for things to go this far and I didn't plan for any of it."

"Then explain," King Francisco demanded. "What happened?" His head tilted to the side as he sat firm, unmoving, like a statue. He never realized how imposing the king could seem.

Alzerion shifted his feet as his arms hung at his side. "It started the night Aironell was kidnapped."

"Wh-what?" the queen's voice wavered. She cleared her throat. "Alzerion that, that—"

"That means this has been going on for some time, then." King Francisco finished. He grabbed the queen's hand and held on to her.

Alzerion didn't say anything. Silence. That was all he could do was be silent, for now. He had to come clean. *All he could do was be open, from now on. Aironell, accused him of not letting them in, well, maybe she was right. Hell, his own mother had been telling him the same thing for years. Could he have avoided all this pain and devastation if he chose differently? No, he couldn't go down that path, not now. His eyes watered at the thought of his actions-every choice.*

"I found the leader of the rebellion, that night. He was behind her kidnappings, both of them." Alzerion swallowed. "Ulbrick was behind it all."

"Ulbrick?" Queen Evalyn bit her lip. She exchanged glances with the king.

"Isn't that—"

"Yes," Alzerion answered, quietly.

"So, you have been dealing with him since?" King Francisco asked.

Alzerion closed his eyes, briefly, then nodded.

The queen's expression softened. "Then what happened?"

Alzerion took another breath and continued. "Well, he threatened me. He said that if I didn't help him, he would harm the princess." He took a breath and rubbed his forehead. "That's why she was with me. Ulbrick used her as leverage. I would never let anything happen to her."

Alzerion swallowed and then looked up at the king, right in the eye. "I still would never let anything happen to her. Her safety has always been my first priority."

"Alzerion," the queen's voice cracked. "You should have told us."

He hung his head down. "I'm sorry."

"The queen is right. Alzerion, we might have been able to help shoulder some of this. Maybe we could have found other solutions."

"Ulbrick is ruthless. You both wouldn't have been able to help." Alzerion starred back at them. "I mean no disrespect. You should know how much you both mean to me, after all these years. But, Ulbrick, he's vindictive, hateful, and would love nothing more than to see the downfall of this family."

Alzerion glanced up at the sound of shoes against the floor. The queen strolled toward him and placed a hand under his chin. All he could do was look at her.

"Alzerion," she spoke firmly. "Do you stand with us or with them? I need a clear answer."

Alzerion smirked as his shoulders drooped a bit. "I am always with you. I have never forgotten the hours, the treatment, or the kindness you both have shown me."

Queen Evalyn wrapped her arms around him and squeezed. "Good. That is what I needed to hear." Then she stepped back. King Francisco was by her side.

"Alzerion, we love you," the king added. "That's why this news hit us so hard."

"I am so sorry," he apologized. "I didn't mean for either of you to lose faith in me." The king patted him on the back. "I fear that I may have angered them." Alzerion felt a pressure in his chest. It was deeper, down in his heart.

King Francisco rubbed his chin. "How so?"

"Warren. I-I, was wrong about him. I thought we were friends, but no. He is another brain-washed fool that seeks only Ulbrick's approval. Warren would have told Ulbrick about my true allegiance by now."

"He is no friend of yours." King Francisco nodded. "From what Aironell told us, he painted you in a very bad light."

"I'm not surprised. He was angry with me. Their hope was in poisoning you all against me."

Queen Evalyn's eyebrows bent in. "Why?"

Alzerion swallowed trying to rid himself of a thickness in his throat. "Then I would be alone. If I was alone, then I might still help them. At least that was what Warren said to me."

Queen Evalyn shook her head.

"These are not good people," the king said.

"No."

"Well, we forgive you, Alzerion," King Francisco's voice was firm. Queen Evalyn smiled.

"Unfortunately, I'm not sure if Aironell will."

Alzerion swallowed. "I know."

"You will still lead the Royal Army," King Francisco stood on one side of him. The queen stood on the other as they all walked toward the door.

"Of course," Alzerion nodded.

"Just one thing." The king stopped. Queen Evalyn half-turned to them. "Aironell's happiness means more to us than anything."

"I know that," Alzerion nodded.

"Alzerion, if she can't forgive you then after we defeat the rebels, you won't be welcome here. I'm, sorry but that's the way it'll have to be."

Alzerion bit his lip and slowly nodded. He had to expect that. "If I may, I'd like to go to my room."

King Francisco moved to the side for him. As he passed the king and queen he focused on Aironell. He left the Great Hall and headed to his room, but he hoped Aironell would forgive him. If she didn't well, he felt like he would, no he couldn't think like that. He needed her to forgive him, even if it took the rest of his life.

FATE

Aironell awoke with a shudder. She felt goosebumps on her arms like she caught some sort of chill. In seconds, she sat up, rubbed her arms, and then scanned her room. Nothing was amiss. *Ugh*, she couldn't shake this ominous feeling. She shook her head to focus on something happier. *Alzerion*. He usually was her safe haven, but not now. *He couldn't.* Instead she felt like her heart was being clawed out.

Should I believe and trust him? Does he even really care for me? So many thoughts flooded her mind.

Aironell got out of bed and sat at her desk. She leafed through her spell book. Despite all that happened, she had to be prepared. Betrayal or no, she had to practice to be prepared. Aironell practiced a few spells that she had been working on. Standing in the middle of the room she practiced the motions needed to cast. She went from memorizing the spells to practicing the motions. Casting them for real, could destroy the whole palace, so she played it safe.

After practicing, Aironell saw the sun break over Bachusa. She saw the beautiful colors painted across the sky. Aironell stood in the opening of her balcony, leaning against the stone arch. There came a knock at her door.

She turned around. "Come in."

Queen Evalyn strolled over to her. "Good morning, darling."

Aironell flung her arms around her. "Is everything alright?" Aironell released her grip and pulled back.

"Why don't we sit down." Aironell followed the queen to the sitting table. Queen Evalyn twirled her hand and there was a teapot and two cups filled with hot tea.

Aironell grabbed one of them, blew on it, and then took a slow sip.

"Aironell, I want you to know how much your father and I love you."

"I do know that." A faint crease curved in her lips.

The queen nodded and then took a sip of tea. Then she sat hers on the table. "I don't want to upset you, but I think we should discuss your feelings on everything."

"I'm not sure how I feel," Aironell looked down into her cup of tea. "I would like to say I am over it but, he—"

"He hurt you, didn't he?"

Aironell felt the burning wetness behind her eyes. She blinked, twice. She placed her cup down. The warmth turned into a feeling of heat that crept from cheek to cheek.

"Darling," Queen Evalyn slid her chair next to Aironell and wrapped her arms around her. The hug oozed warmth. Aironell steadied her breathing as she inhaled scents of lavender from her mother.

Aironell nuzzled her head into the soft fabric that covered the queen's arm. "There, there." Aironell breathed in, then out to the rhythmic movement of her mother running her hands through her hair. It was soothing. It reminded her of how Isabella used to do this when she was a little girl. She shut her eyes, tight. Her pain was there.

"I wish I could explain," Aironell said, softly. "It's a deep pain. Like someone took one of those swords the army uses and ran it into my chest."

"Oh, honey," the queen's voice was a bit shaky. She cleared her throat.

Aironell needed to think of anything, but *him*. Each thought of him still brought her to such lowness. What if he can't be trusted? The heat in her eyes trickled down, one quiet sob at a time.

"Mother," her voice cracked as the tears cascaded down, like a rushing waterfall. "I thought…he cared…for me. Now…I—"

"Shhh," Queen Evalyn rubbed her back with one hand and continued running her hand through Aironell's hair. "Darling, I hate seeing you like this. Alzerion, well he is complicated."

Silence. The only thing heard were Aironell's sobs and sniffles.

"Aironell?" the queen broke the silence.

Aironell sniffled. "Yes, mother."

"Your father and I want to help ease your pain. We could ask Alzerion to leave or we can use one of those spells from the book to erase him from your memory."

Aironell used her nightgown hem to wipe near her nose. Then she pulled away and locked eyes with Queen Evalyn.

"No, please." Aironell's lips quivered. "Magic like that, well there would be a cost."

Queen Evalyn leaned in. "It's not one you're willing to live with it."

Aironell shook her head. "In time I will be fine. I wouldn't want to forget him."

"Maybe you are trying to find a way to forgive him?" Queen Evalyn waved at her cup and it slid closer. She grabbed it and took a sip. Her eyes never looked away from Aironell.

"Honestly, I don't know. I don't like the game he was playing." Aironell pressed her back into her chair. Her fingers clung to the wooden arm rests. One finger at a time, she trailed the etchings, trying to keep herself composed.

The queen shifted in her seat watching. "I promise you there was no game." Aironell's gaze shifted up to her mother. "Alzerion has his faults, but he isn't that kind of person. He would never toy with your emotions, for fun."

Aironell bit down on the inside of her cheek. There had to be some trick. She didn't know much about these kinds of feelings, at least not from personal experience. All she had, were memories of watching Isabella and Quairken.

"It shouldn't be like this," Aironell spoke softly.

"Darling, I want to give you some wisdom, hard-earned, I'm afraid. May I?"

Aironell sat up and nodded.

Queen Evalyn set her cup back down on the table and continued. "People are complex. You won't find two that are the same." She paused. Aironell breathed out but kept listening. "We all are a product of our experiences-the good and the bad. Each encounter shapes us."

"I know."

"When it comes to relationships, whether friends or more," she swallowed. "All that past impacts those choices we make. Alzerion, well, he is a good man."

Aironell's face was still as she blinked.

"Our conversation with him, just reinforced that opinion that I always had." She paused and reached out a hand. Aironell grasped it and felt a light squeeze. "I know it doesn't feel like it, but it all came back to *you*. Your safety. He was racked with such guilt, but—"

"Then why do it?" Aironell stood up and paced around the sitting area. "I hear it was for my safety but why keep it from everyone? Why-why let me feel for him?"

The queen shifted. Aironell kept pacing.

"Darling, trying to understand the matters of the heart, why that's not always easy or possible." She turned toward Aironell. "Sometimes it is all up to faith. So, the big question is, do you still believe in him?"

Aironell's gaze lowered. She opened her mouth but then closed it again. Standing there she pressed her fingers into her forehead as she mumbled to herself.

"Well?"

Aironell gazed at the queen but she struggled to find the words. Aironell strolled over to the balcony and peered out at the town. With her eyes closed, she breathed. There was the shuffling of feet and then she felt the soft hand on her shoulder. Aironell opened her eyes and starred at her mother.

"I need more time. I think I trust him to protect Bachusa." She craned her neck back to the outline of the town in the distance. Then she spun around, back pressing against the rail. "I don't know if I trust him and *me*."

Aironell sighed. "I guess we shall see."

Queen Evalyn nodded. "Let's head back in. There is one other thing I must tell you."

Aironell strolled into her room and then turned around. The queen pursed her lips as she moved closer to Aironell. "We need to be prepared for the rebellion."

"Haven't we been preparing?" Aironell tilted her head.

"Darling, I mean there could be an attack any day now."

"What?" Her face scrunched up.

The queen swallowed. "Alzerion says they have been planning their attack for some time. Since he has sided with us, he wouldn't put it passed them to attack soon."

"So, this is based on Alzerion's assumptions?" Aironell crossed her arms.

"He knows them. He is pretty confident that they will. They want to destroy us and punish him. Please no leaving the palace, and let's just be ready for anything."

Aironell's arms dropped to her side and she nodded. "Well, then we have more important things to worry about than my feelings. Has the army been warned?"

"Of course." Queen Evalyn headed to the door. "Alzerion took care of that. They are his soldiers, after all." Then she turned and grabbed the door handle.

"Mother, wait." She dashed to her side. "Don't let him lead the army." Her voice sounded more pleading than she thought it would.

"Aironell, this is what he has been training most of his life for. We *need* him to lead."

Aironell bit her lip to keep it from trembling. She stared up with a little bit of water in her eyes. "What if he gets hurt?"

"So, you do still care about him?" The queen's lips curved into a small smile.

Aironell didn't say anything, she just looked away. Aironell felt her mother's hand under her chin. Then it was lifted, gently. "Aironell, we will trust that he has those matters in hand. For now, get dressed and come join us downstairs."

With that the queen left the room. Aironell looked around at the space she grew to love. She pulled out the most fitting outfit. Her hair was braided into a ponytail clasped with a heart-shaped clip. Instead of wearing a gown, she put on black fitted pants, pulled on long dark-brown leather boots. Next, she grabbed a purple top. Its sleeves were loose, but went to her wrists. Aironell wrapped a black belt around her waist. The belt had the family crest on the front of the buckle. She gazed at herself in the mirror as she touched the half-heart necklace. Satisfied, she left her room.

Meanwhile, Alzerion put on dark gray fitted slacks and black boots. He grabbed the sturdier materials. This was not a practice session. No, today could very well be the real deal. He put on a tight, dark-colored shirt and added his scabbard around his waist. Alzerion picked up his sword, inspected it, and then sheathed it. He grabbed his half-heart necklace from his desk and placed it on. He tucked it under his shirt. This would do for now. He would find his armor at the barracks.

Aironell was on his mind. She hadn't spoken to him since Warren. Now wasn't the time. He had a job to do. Defend the palace and see the army to victory. Aironell would have to wait, for now. He took one more look around and saw a letter on his desk. He dashed toward it. *Maybe it was from Aironell.* Alzerion tore it open and his face twisted with anger, with each word he read.

Dear Alzerion,

I don't believe you would be so foolish to turn your back on me and the cause. I'll forgive this lapse in judgement if you fight against the Royal Army, and hand me Aironell. You are running out of chances! Don't forget what happens to those who cross me. Come to your senses.

Ulbrick

Alzerion ripped the letter and crumpled it. He tossed it in the trash as he left for the barracks.

Back at the palace, Aironell was helping to secure the palace. She went out the front doors and then spun on her heels to face the palace. Aironell clapped her hands together, rubbed them until she felt a spark form over her hands. Then she placed them over her head and slowly pulled them apart. In front of her, she could see a thin veil of light blue and sparkles. It was transparent as she stretched her arms and twirled around. Once she was sure that it covered the whole palace, she breathed out and brought her arms down. In mere seconds, the shield was up and shimmered around the perimeter of the palace.

That should keep everyone safe, she thought. Nobody would be able to enter and no weapon would pierce through. She went back inside the palace and strolled through the halls. As she walked she ran her hands along the walls. Each of her fingertips trailing against the ornate pattern. With each step she focused on her spells. Which ones might be useful for battle. Aironell swallowed. *Most spells were too risky and could cost them.* She shook her head. *No.* That kind of thinking couldn't happen. Not when all she loved was here. Her eyes narrowed. She knew what she needed to do.

Without hesitation Aironell strolled passed some maids. She turned her head, but nobody was watching. *Good.* She dashed up the stairs and down the hall to Alzerion's room. She went to grab the doorknob. Her hand shook for a moment, but then she twisted it and went in. Aironell grabbed a blank piece of paper from his desk and sat in his chair as she wrote. She read it over, twice. Satisfied. She placed it on his bed. Her lisp curled into a small smile as she smelled his scent. She had never been in here. There were no guarantees of anything for the future.

Clomp, Thud. Aironell darted to Alzerion's window and pulled the curtains aside. She saw so many men ready. They wore metal helmets and what looked like thick leather. It covered their arms and there were extra thick pieces around their knees and shoulders. From her studies, she knew this was not the Royal Army. Aironell gulped. The rebels. A man stepped forward. His face was worn. Aironell felt a chill in the air. The man looked around and raised his arm. Some of his men held tight to their bows. He dropped his arm and they released their arrows. At least a dozen or so raced through the air toward the palace.

Aironell peered up to the balcony at the top of the palace. She saw her parents and Alzerion's mother. There were others, but she couldn't quite make them out. *Please let it work. Please.* Her fingers twisted around the other when she heard a boom from the arrows. Aironell grinned. *Thank goodness.* The protection held. The arrows hit, caught fire, and they exploded in the air. Aironell looked back down at the man. He frowned but his eyes went hollow. Aironell left Alzerion's room and ran through the palace. Down the hall and up some stairs, until she opened the steel door that opened out to the balcony.

The king and queen both turned. "Thank goodness," Queen Evalyn looked up to the sky.

Aironell moved toward them. She saw Isabella was with them, clutching her swelling belly. Isabella snapped her attention when Aironell walked by. She forced a smile at her and then snapped back to the scene of the rebels. The Royal Army marched out and stood in formation. Two men led them. *Alzerion. Quairken. Please be safe.*

At first glance, she could see that the numbers were pretty close.

"They can defeat the rebels," Melinda said. Aironell tried to ignore the voices around her. She focused her vision down at Alzerion.

A twinge in her chest. She clasped her necklace and took a big breath. At least they looked prepared. Slim metal plating lined their arms and shoulders. They even had metal that stretched over the leather and covered their chest and backs. It was thin. She remembered from one of her reading sessions, that the slim design would help with better movements.

"Amplio sonus," Aironell muttered. She didn't want the others to know what she did. But she had to do something. Had to be able to hear what was going on down there. If there was any sign of trouble she knew what to do.

. . .

Alzerion looked at Quairken. "Shall we?"

"I will always follow you, sir." Alzerion led the way as Quairken followed. He held his helmet between his arm and his side as they walked. Defeat was not an option.

He saw Warren's smug face as he took a few steps closer.

"Alzerion, did you get my letter?" Ulbrick with his hoarse, raspy sounding voice.

Alzerion nodded. He didn't want to humor them.

"Well?"

Alzerion could hear the demand in his voice. He didn't waver as he spoke. "Ulbrick, I believe I made my choice."

"No!" He fumed. "You will regret this." Ulbrick clenched his fists so tight that his knuckles cracked.

"Go." Alzerion pushed Quairken as they ran. Alzerion placed his helmet on as he reached his men.

The rebels darted toward the Royal Army as one unit, with swords held high.

"Remember our training men. Let's divide!" Alzerion yelled.

Alzerion led a group away from the other half of the army. They darted toward the rebels. Alzerion ran with his sword out. Someone stabbed at him and he pivoted to the right and caught the swing. The loud clanging of steel on steel as Alzerion deflected blow after blow. He ducked as his attacker fell forward and Alzerion slashed his blade at his thigh.

Alzerion didn't have the time to see how Quairken's group was doing. He saw a large guy behind Castro. Alzerion dashed with blade out like a pointed spear.as he got closer Alzerion dodged other rebels and stabbed at others. The body count was rising but Alzerion had to reach that big guy, before it was too late. He squinted. Trying hard to judge his distance before his next move.

In that moment he saw Quairken take position. Alzerion yelled, "Now!" In mere seconds the majority of the rebel forces were trapped in an oval-shaped barrier. The Royal Army kept forcing their way in. Alzerion took a breath as he took his sword and stabbed it at the ground. Then he used his strength to propel himself forward like he was a human slingshot. Alzerion soared through the air, until he collided with the large guy bombarding Castro.

Alzerion and the guy hit the ground. Alzerion quickly scrambled to get up but the other guy was faster. He swung his sword down at Alzerion, who rolled to the side. Alzerion tried to grab the closest sword, but felt a hard hit to his arm. Alzerion clutched at his wound, as he rolled. He felt a searing pain as he rolled onto his back. This time there wasn't another blow as he saw Castro standing with his arm out. Alzerion grabbed it and stood. "Thanks."

"No, thank you, sir." Castro handed him his sword and then deflected a blow from the side.

Alzerion sprinted to a fallen soldier and with his sword sliced off a piece of leather from his uniform. Alzerion dashed behind a boulder, and wrapped it around his wound, and pulled tight. Teeth clenched as he stood up and joined the frenzy. Alzerion caught a glimpse of Ulbrick and he made his way. He sliced through three rebels and blocked a couple blows from someone off to his side.

He saw this red mass spreading across the land. Alzerion blocked and then parried blow after blow. Ugh, he couldn't get to Ulbrick, not yet. Alzerion thrust his sword and his enemy went limp and then fell over. Alzerion pulled his sword back, and felt the warmth from the blood. His hand felt sticky. There were less people still standing. He had but a moment to scan his surroundings. Something caught his attention. The redness that he saw grew larger like a barrier of some kind. Alzerion sniffed the air.

He went pale. He spun around until he finally caught sight of Ulbrick again. He was waving his hand with the sapphire ring. Magic. Damn it. Ulbrick smiled wide as he kept waving his hand. This time there was a swirl of red that circled his hand as he aimed it at Alzerion. *Crap*. Alzerion lunged to the side and then jumped behind a boulder. It wasn't just a barrier it was hot. Ulbrick was spreading a flaming inferno.

Alzerion's cinnamon red eyes filled with rage. He heard screams from some of his men burning. Alzerion peeked out and saw the man on fire. His screams echoed in his mind.

He saw Quairken was a closer distance. "Do you have this?" Alzerion shouted, unsure if Quairken understood.

Quairken stretched his arms out, tackled the soldier, and then smothered the flame with his body and the dirt from the ground.

The flames kept spreading across the land. Would the protection spells work against fire? He couldn't take that chance. Hell, Ulbrick already broke the rules of warfare. Alzerion climbed on top of the boulder. He felt the sharp edges of the boulder slicing into his palms.

He was a ball of tension. His eyes bulged as he looked up to the sky and shouted, "Pluviam." The sky darkened as dark-grey clouds spread across the sky. Down came a torrent of rain. The raging fire died down and he could see steam from the mixture of water and fire. Then he aimed his hands at where Ulbrick was hiding and blew above his hands at Ulbrick.

Quairken, drenched, called out, "Sir, don't."

It was much too late. The wind picked up like a gale of sorts and headed for Ulbrick. Alzerion watched his smug expression shift. He whispered something to one of his followers. He didn't care. He would end this.

Up on the balcony Aironell grasped the ledge. Her knuckles were white from squeezing so hard. *Alzerion, how could you be so reckless?* He placed himself out in the open. She heard Ulbrick tell that man to attack, Alzerion. *Did he not know?* Alzerion didn't move or run. Aironell started to twist her necklace around in her hands. *Come on Alzerion.*

Aironell heard the queen's voice. "Melinda, what has gotten into him? He knows better than to use magic." Aironell turned to observe them.

"Do you mean Alzerion?" Melinda looked troubled, conflicted.

The queen nodded. "He may cost more lives with this rainstorm."

Melinda starred down at Alzerion. She spoke with a tone. "He doesn't cope well against, Ulbrick. He never has."

Queen Evalyn patted her on the back. "I'm sure he will be fine. Alzerion is tough."

"I'm sure they both will come out of this." King Francisco added.

Aironell shook her head. *What?* She must have heard them wrong. *Why did Melinda care about the well-being of the rebel leader?* He was out there trying to kill her son. Clearly, she was missing something. That didn't matter, not now. She turned back to the men.

Alzerion calmed the raging winds down. She saw some men gathering around Alzerion. *Turn, Alzerion.*

Aironell's hand snapped to her mouth. She had to do something. She slowly stepped back. This had to be timed just right. Finally, she was far enough that nobody could see her.

She closed her eyes and swirled her arms around and his she chanted. Then her eyes burst open as she said, "Nubes de magicae."

King Francisco barely turned to her when she sprinted toward the balcony and jumped.

"Aironell!" She heard the screams but focused on the growing white puff.

No, she couldn't look back. She was falling until she landed on that white puff. She grasped a corner of the cloud as she soared through the air. Overcome by equal parts anger and concern. *He wasn't allowed to die. Not while she was still so angry with him. He was supposed to be protecting her, huh.* A few arrows flew at her but she laid on her belly. That way she wouldn't be as big of a target. Nobody from the palace would follow. They couldn't. She saw to that. They were trapped there, for now. *Safe.* That was all that mattered to her. The men on the field were too busy watching her. Then she disappeared. Gone.

What the hell is she doing? Alzerion's gaze darted forward, back, and to the side. He didn't see her. *What happened to her?* He was distracted when he felt a heavy whack against his head. He fell over. Someone gripped him up.

"Well, you may as well surrender. Poor Alzerion. You allowed yourself to get caught. So weak!" Ulbrick spat.

Alzerion turned his head to the balcony. They were the innocents. Ulbrick was a bully at best. Aironell. He felt the tug at his heart. He breathed out as he turned back to face Ulbrick.

"As I predicted, you have nobody." Ulbrick inched moved closer. "There's nobody who can save you."

"That's not true."

Ulbrick looked around and the minion that held him, spun around. Alzerion couldn't see anyone. The voice. It was hers, but how?

"Who's there? Show yourself at once?" Ulbrick demanded.

"I'm right behind you." Ulbrick and his minion turned once more. Alzerion felt like he was being spun round and round. Aironell's voice dancing in the air.

The next time they turned Alzerion felt his body being thrust to the ground as the guy holding him cried in pain. Alzerion quickly stood up and there she was, by his side. She was a vision of a combat princess.

"Wh-what are you doing?" Alzerion stammered.

"Alzerion, do it. Kill her." Each one of Ulbrick's words had a punch to it. Like venom seeping through to infect.

Alzerion's eyebrows curved in as he took another look at Aironell. She tilted her head at him. Those beautiful eyes staring back at him.

Alzerion turned to Ulbrick. "You know I would *never*, do that."

"Not even to earn my forgiveness?"

"No!" Alzerion stepped in front of Aironell.

"What do you mean, no?" Ulbrick's hoarse voice was more of a yell.

"Ulbrick you disgust me! You are delusional if you ever truly thought I would or could hurt her." Alzerion swallowed and continued. "I would die before I ever let harm come to her."

Ulbrick's eyes were hollow. Like a desolate cold rock. Alzerion gulped. He knew that if Ulbrick could, he would probably melt the flesh off of his face.

Ulbrick inched closer to Alzerion. "I guess I will have to do it myself." He raised his hand.

Alzerion reached out, grabbed Ulbrick's hand and twisted it behind his back. "Over my dead body." Alzerion hissed. Then he shoved him back.

"Such a fool, Alzerion. Such a bitter disappointment to the end."

"Stop!" Aironell stepped forward."

"No. Don't move." Alzerion held his arm out so she wouldn't come closer. "This fight is long overdue."

Ulbrick laughed. "Looks like you still won't learn."

"There is not one thing I would want to learn from you!"

Ulbrick glared and then pushed the sapphire on his ring. Alzerion didn't see anything out of the ordinary. He moved closer to Aironell.

"You should go." He looked over at her but she shook her head. Then she grabbed his hand. He nodded. He circled around her but still couldn't see anything.

"Something's wrong," Aironell spoke softly.

Alzerion moved a bit ahead of her. But didn't detect any issues. "Aironell, I don't—" He stopped himself. He heard a whooshing sound.

"No!" Aironell screamed.

Alzerion turned and saw the arrow coming at him. He didn't have the time to move. His armor was fractured from fighting. He gulped.

A flash of green light emerged from Aironell's half-heart necklace. It was so bright Alzerion couldn't see. *Was he dead?* When the light faded he realized what happened.

"No, no, no, no!" He was somehow behind her and before he could grab her the arrow pierced her chest.

When he reached her he laid her in his arms. "Please be okay. Please save her." Alzerion looked up to the sky and then back down. He heard the shouts from the balcony.

Aironell touched her necklace but her hands were shaky. A thin white light wrapped around them. Alzerion tilted his head. He didn't know what was going on, but he saw people talking but heard nothing.

Ulbrick's mouth twisted into a triumphant smile. Alzerion couldn't deal with him just now. He lowered his gaze to Aironell.

"What did you do?" Alzerion's voice cracked. "Why? Why would you do it?" He felt the heat in his eyes.

Aironell's mouth winced and then formed a small smile. "I would do it again."

"That was foolish." He held her hand to his cheek.

"Maybe." She winced. "I would still make the same choices. Alzerion, I couldn't let…you die."

Her breath was becoming ragged.

"I am so sorry for everything." Alzerion choked on a lump in his throat. "I failed you."

Aironell placed her hand over his mouth. "No. Never say that. Fate had other plans. You couldn't save me from this."

Alzerion shot a death glare at Ulbrick. "I hate him."

"Don't let that fill your heart. Alzerion, why…why does he taunt you so?"

He shook his head. "Curious even at the end."

Aironell's lips wavered.

"There is something else, I never told you." His head bent over her. His expression was pained as he gazed at her. "I believe you know some of it already. My mother wanted better for me so she sent me away, to the king and queen. My father well, he was not very nice." Alzerion gulped. "Ulbrick…is my father."

"I…am sorry. It will be better."

"How are you so …calm?" Alzerion's head hung low. He pressed his forehead to hers. He let out a whimper.

"Don't cry." She swallowed. He felt her soft skin against his cheek. "I've accepted my fate. You were right. I am the future of Bachusa."

"This is all wrong," Alzerion's voice wavered.

"It is as it should be." Aironell reached her shaky hand up. He grabbed it and held onto her. "I did it for you. You are the elusive, *one*."

Alzerion's eyebrows pinched together.

She forced a smile. "I-I... love you."

His cinnamon-red eyes were like pools. He pulled her closer and pressed his nose against her cheek. She was growing weaker, he could feel it. He wanted to do something, anything, but couldn't. He didn't have that kind of power. He felt her hand push, feebly against his chest. He stared into her cerulean-blue eyes.

"Do you love me?" she murmured.

He caught his breath. He felt the wave crash within. *How did she not know how he felt?* He grabbed a loose strand of her hair and tucked it behind her ear.

Leaning in he said, "I love you with all of my heart. I always have. My love is unyielding. All my deeds, my sacrifices, it was always for you."

He took a slow breath and cupped his other hand under her chin. He licked his lips and then placed them on hers. He could feel her softness against him. He closed his eyes and let nothing else in. The nice, slow kiss grew deeper. He pressed his lips against hers as she grabbed at his arm and pulled him closer. He felt the connection between the necklaces as sparks glowed bright. Alzerion's breathing grew faster. He opened his eyes and smiled back at her. Panting. Aironell attempted to return a smile but instead grasped at her wound. "Can I ease your suffering?"

"Please, don't worry."

"Aironell, how—"

"Do...you... trust... me?"

"What does that have to do with anything?"

"Do you?"

"Normally, yes, I do, but—"

"It's either yes or no." Her eyes looked glazed. Like she was fighting to stay with him.

He sighed. "Then yes, I trust you."

"Good, then don't worry. You will always be in my heart, and I will always find you."

He pursed his lips but before he could argue, she pulled him in for one more kiss. It felt bittersweet as he kissed her. He felt the sparks fly and this time he looked up to see them catch on the white light around them. He glanced back down at Aironell but she was fading.

She sparkled in magic light and said, "I love you." Then she disappeared. The white light that surrounded him was gone, too.

Alzerion looked around as he merely sat there. Nobody else moved a muscle. He forced himself to swallow. No, no, no, no.

He shook his head and muttered, "It wasn't supposed to end this way."

He felt this heaviness weigh him down, but he stood anyway. He slowly turned He could see the tear-stained faces on the balcony. He clutched his necklace that lay above his heart. *His heart. It was laughable. It would never be the same.*

Alzerion turned again and saw Ulbrick. He was smiling. So smug. So arrogant. So foul. He had to do something.

Alzerion bared his teeth, "You will pay." He felt this cold steely resolve wash over him. It was just the two of them. Alzerion did not see anyone else standing up to fight him. Alzerion ran full force at Ulbrick.

Ulbrick stepped aside. Alzerion's nostrils flared. Seething with vengeance Alzerion shoved Ulbrick. He got back up and they circled one another like they were actually about to duel. Alzerion flung his hands out and muttered something. Ulbrick was smacked by a gust of air until he was forced against the one of the boulders in the field. Then Alzerion snapped his fingers and a sword flew into his hand as he pointed the blade at Ulbrick's neck.

"You going to kill me, Alzerion?" Ulbrick taunted.

He wanted nothing more than to destroy him. That would make him happy. Something inside of him wouldn't let him make that fatal blow.

"No, I'm not. Death would be too kind. You don't deserve that. No, I think you'll live out your days in a prison in the far Grimlands."

"You can't be serious," Ulbrick's eyes widened.

Alzerion glared at him. "I'm quite serious." Alzerion looked around and saw Quairken. He had some scrapes and a gash on his head, but nothing that looked too serious.

"Quairken, I'm glad to see you." They clasped hands. "Was Castro successful?"

Quairken whistled. Alzerion wanted to know what was going on, but didn't want to accidentally break the enchantment that held Ulbrick. Alzerion waited. He saw the king, queen, his mother and Isabella walking towards them. "What are you doing down here?"

"It was a spell." Queen Evalyn said.

"When Princess Aironell," Isabella paused. "Well we were no longer stuck there."

Alzerion stepped back as he held Ulbrick against the boulder with magic. Before he could say anything, Castro was spotted by another one of his soldiers. He was limping, but he had Warren, bound and gagged.

Alzerion turned back to Ulbrick. "You, Warren, and any rebel who lived will join you."

"I will be honored to escort the prisoners," Quairken bowed his head.

"I will help," Castro added. Alzerion heard murmurs from his other soldiers that were okay to do the task.

Alzerion moved behind Ulbrick, grabbed his wrists and in an instant his wrists were tied together, tight. He grabbed him by the arm and handed him to Quairken.

Quairken and Castro moved the few prisoners when Alzerion ran over. "Wait." He walked up to Ulbrick. "Turns out you were wrong. I did learn something."

Ulbrick raised his eyebrows.

"I'm good. You're evil. I guess I take after my mother." Alzerion turned his back as he started toward his mother and the others. He craned his neck and said, "Good-bye. I hope you rot there…father."

Alzerion saw Castro's jaw drop. Quairken looked at Ulbrick and then back at Alzerion, and then shook his head.

Melinda Pulled Alzerion in for a hug. He knew what she wouldn't say, not here. Still a tear fell from her eyes.

"Mother you alright?"

She cleared her throat. "I am. I'm so proud of you." She placed her

hand on his cheek. "I am finally mourning him. The man he used to be."
He followed her gaze to Ulbrick as he was being escorted away.

Alzerion turned to face the king, queen, his mother and Isabella.

"What?" He broke the silence.

"We just want you to know we are here for you," Melinda said. "All of us. We are so sorry."

Alzerion nodded, "I know. But there is much to do. Maybe for now we don't talk about it."

He headed back to the palace.

A GLOOMY CELEBRATION

It felt like forever. Alzerion strolled through the hall. The maids were carrying trays of goodies. This celebration. It was a joke. He knew they were overdue. It had been three weeks. *Three weeks*, he sighed. He kept busy magically fixing the field in front of the palace and by the barracks.

Alzerion couldn't help but feel frustrated. Especially tonight. This party was to celebrate their triumph. It just didn't feel like much of a triumph. He plastered on a smile when someone spoke to him. *Ugh*, he needed to escape. Alzerion looked around. People were dancing and being merry. He slipped out of the Great Hall and made his way to the balcony. *Ah, fresh air.*

He took a deep breath and walked to the edge, noticing the red roses glistening under the moon. The mere thought put a tear in his eye, so instead he turned his gaze to the night sky. His eyes were shut as he clutched his necklace.

"Alzerion," he turned to face Queen Evalyn in the doorway. "What are you doing way out here?"

"I just needed air and a quiet spot to clear my head," he admitted. He turned back to gazing at the night sky.

"Are you alright?" He heard the clacking of her shoes as she her dress ruffled closer to him.

He shrugged as he looked into her eyes. "No, I'm not doing well. I'm sure you know the feeling."

"I do." Queen Evalyn cleared her throat. "But I sense guilt from you."

He shook his head. "It's my fault." Alzerion starred out at the moon.

"How so?" She placed her hand on his back and patted him. "We never blamed you. You tried to keep her safe. This was all her."

"If she didn't save me, then she would be alive. It was my job to keep her safe, not the other way around." His voice was sharp.

"Alzerion, look at me and listen carefully." He faced the queen. "I love my daughter, but she chose to save you. She loved you. That letter she left you should remind you of that love."

Alzerion reached into his pocket and pulled out her letter.

Dear Alzerion,

If you are reading this then the battle did not go as planned and I had to create an alternative plan. I know this is rather morose but just in case something does happen to me, I want to be prepared. Alzerion, please promise me two things. First, please promise to look after my parents because I do not know how they will handle this. Life has been unfair to us, but with your love and support, I know they will be alright. Second, please promise to rule over my wonderful kingdom. Bachusa truly has grown on me, and I want it to thrive. I could not think of anyone else who would be right for the challenge than you. My parents won't have any fight left in them to propel Bachusa where it needs to be, not to mention that they cannot do this forever. We can see how death can come even at an untimely moment. I pray that my passing does not cause you too much pain. Also, you must know that no matter where I am, you will always be in my heart. Always.

Love,

Aironell

P.S: In case I do not get a chance to say it, to admit it to you just once, then here goes. I love you more than you can know. My love for you is constant and shines bright like the moon and the stars, forever and ever.

He dabbed his eyes and turned to Queen Evalyn. "I think she knew that you and the king had already been through so much."

"You're probably right. She chose you to rule over her kingdom. To care for her people." She took a slow breath. "That means something to us."

Alzerion's eyebrows pinched in.

"I believe you would have been her choice of husband, had she lived."

He smirked. That made him feel a little lighter.

"If it is not too much to ask, Alzerion, I was wondering what you two talked about, right before she passed."

He looked down at the stones and then up at the queen. "She told me she loved me." He smiled as he tried to relive those last moments. "Then she asked if I trusted her."

"Alzerion, do you trust her?"

"Of course, but I don't know what to think now that she's gone. Why do you ask?"

"I can't shake this feeling, that there's more to it." She strolled to the ledge and peered out. "Something about some of the magic I saw seems familiar, somehow."

Queen Evalyn wrinkled her nose.

"What are you thinking?" Alzerion stared at her.

"I'm not sure. I'd love to know what she was thinking. I know she is great with magic. Her father and I even gave her our family's book of spells."

Alzerion looked a bit puzzled and asked, "Where is the book?" Alzerion rubbed his hand against his chin.

"It's probably in her room," she replied. "Why?"

"I'd like to give it a look. If that is alright?"

"Of course," she nodded. "Just know that there are a great many spells. Some are so strong that they could cost you your life. So, tread carefully."

With that, Queen Evalyn patted him on the shoulder and walked back to the palace.

Alzerion took a breath and then starred back out at the sky. As if the universe had some kind of answer for him. The wind started to blow, and some leaves rustled.

Then he heard, *"Alzerion"* whispered in the wind.

He shook his head and peered over the balcony ledge, but he didn't see anybody below. Then he heard it again, *"Alzerion."*

He shook his head once more and said, "I think the stress is finally getting to me. I'm officially losing it. I'm hearing things now."

Then he turned around and walked back into the palace.

The wind picked up and there came a sweet laugh. The face of Aironell appeared in the moon.

THANK YOU

Alyssa Rose hopes you enjoyed reading the book and the world of Bachusa.
If you liked the book and following Alzerion's journey, please consider leaving a review or rating wherever you can. Neither have to be long. Reviews and ratings help indie authors such as myself and are much appreciated.

Please Leave a Review.
Thank you, once more!

ENCHANTED FATE (THE FATES ALIGN DUOLOGY, BOOK 2)

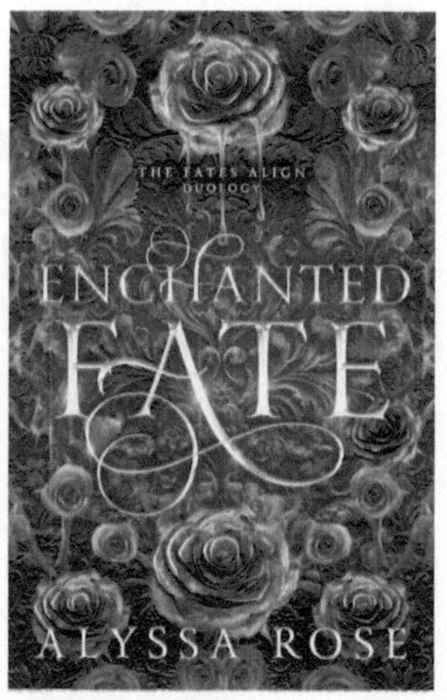

Action packed magical Romantasy with playful banter!

A whisper in the wind…Alzerion travels abroad searching for answers to the hidden messages that plague him of late, but what he finds may change everything. He embarks on a quest to restore what was lost, but along the way, his heart leads him in a new direction. Will Alzerion learn what it means to really love someone? Can he protect Bachusa from the new danger that looms over them? The twists of fate course deeper than any could have expected in the last installment of the Fates Align Duology.

ABOUT THE AUTHOR

Alyssa Rose currently lives in West Virginia with her husband, two children, and fuzzy fur babies. A resident of fantasy worlds since she was a young girl—reading under the comfort of her book light. Now she writes books that convey her love of magic, adventures, and romance in her fantasy novels.

Subscribe at www.alyssarosebooks.com to join my newsletter. Looking for book updates and early access to content—Follow me on Ream.

Follow me on my socials!